Penguin Books
The Return of Reginald Perrin

David Nobbs, author of *The Itinerant Lodger, Ostrich Country* and *A Piece of the Sky is Missing*, is also a highly successful television script writer, whose credits began with *That Was The Week That Was* and have included *The Frost Report, The Two Ronnies* and many more.

The Fall and Rise of Reginald Perrin (1976) has also been published in Penguins.

David Nobbs

The Return of Reginald Perrin

Penguin Books

Penguin Books Ltd, Harmondsworth,
Middlesex, England
Penguin Books, 625 Madison Avenue,
New York, New York 10022, U.S.A.
Penguin Books Australia Ltd, Ringwood,
Victoria, Australia
Penguin Books Canada Ltd, 2801 John Street,
Markham, Ontario, Canada L3R 1B4
Penguin Books (N.Z.) Ltd, 182–190 Wairau Road,
Auckland 10, New Zealand

First published 1977
Published simultaneously by Victor Gollancz Ltd
Copyright © David Nobbs, 1977
All rights reserved

Made and printed in Great Britain by
Cox & Wyman Ltd, London, Reading and Fakenham
Set in Intertype Baskerville

For Mary

Book One

Chapter 1

'You are happy, aren't you, Martin?' said Elizabeth.

'Wonderfully happy,' said Reggie.

It was a Monday morning in March, and the sky was crying gently on to the Poets' Estate.

Elizabeth was reading the paper. Reggie, conveniently for new readers, was reflecting upon the strange events that had led him to this pass – how he had disappeared after life at Sunshine Desserts had become intolerable, how he had left his clothes on a beach in Dorset in imitation of suicide, how he had wandered in many disguises and finally returned to his own memorial service as a fictional old friend called Martin Wellbourne, how as Martin Wellbourne he had re-married his lovely wife Elizabeth and gone back to Sunshine Desserts to run the Reginald Perrin Memorial Foundation.

'Briefcase,' said Elizabeth, handing him his black leather briefcase, engraved with his initials, M.S.W., in gold. How he wished it still said 'R.I.P.'.

'Thanks, my little sweetheart,' he said, because when he was Reggie he would have said: 'Thank you, darling.'

'Umbrella,' said Elizabeth, handing him an object which amply justified her choice of word.

'Thanks, my little sweetheart,' he said.

He didn't adjust his tie in the mirror, because that's what he would have done when he was Reggie.

A telephone engineer was climbing out of a hole in Coleridge Close.

'I hate Martin Wellbourne,' said Reggie suddenly, and the man lurched backwards into the hole.

Reggie walked down Coleridge Close, turned right into Tennyson Avenue, then left into Wordsworth Drive, and down the snicket into Station Road. His legs seemed to resent the measured tread and large steps of his Martin

Wellbourne walk. It was as if they were saying to him: 'Come off it, Reggie. How long is this pantomime going to last?'

How long indeed?

He stood at his usual place on the platform, beside the sand-filled fire bucket, because when he was Reggie he had stood in front of the door marked: 'Isolation Telephone'.

The eight sixteen drew up nine minutes late.

He didn't do the crossword on the train, because that's what Reggie would have done.

He entered the characterless box that housed Sunshine Desserts. The clock, which had been stuck at three forty-six since 1967, had recently been mended. Now it had stuck at nine twenty-seven.

He smiled at the receptionist with the puce fingernails, grimaced at the new sign which proudly announced: 'Sunshine Desserts – one big happy family', and walked up three flights of stairs because the lift was out of order.

He entered his drab little office with its green filing cabinets, and smiled at his secretary Joan, but he didn't throw his umbrella towards the hat-stand, because that was what Reggie would have done.

'Morning, Mr Wellbourne,' said Joan, whose husband had died exactly six months earlier.

'Seventeen minutes late,' he said. 'A defective bogie at Earlsfield.'

On his desk was a pile of questionnaires, in which the staff had expressed their views about life at Sunshine Desserts.

'Dictation time, Mrs Greengross,' he said, because Reggie would have said: 'Take a letter, Joan.'

She crossed her long, slim legs and he felt a shiver of excitement.

He looked away hastily. All that foolishness belonged to Reggie Perrin.

He took another quick peep and felt another shiver of excitement. Briefly, his eyes met Joan's.

'To the Principal, the College of Industrial Psychology, Initiative House, Helions Bumpstead. Dear Sir, thank you for your kind inquiry *re* the Reginald Perrin Memorial

Foundation. The purpose of these legs is to keep the employees happy . . .'

'Legs, Mr Wellbourne?'

Reggie began to sweat.

'Sorry. The purpose of the *foundation* is to keep the employees happy, and therefore efficient. We have regular meetings and policy discussions between the two sides, I have a monthly chat with each employee, we have outings, societies and lunch-time concerts in our new social centre, "The Pudding Club", and . . .'

There was a knock on the door.

'Come in,' he said.

There was another knock.

'Come in,' he yelled.

David Harris-Jones entered for his monthly chat.

'Sorry,' he said. 'I wasn't sure whether I heard you say come in or not. So I thought if you didn't I'd better not, and if you did you'd say it again and I could always come in then.'

'Sit down, David.'

David sat in the chair made warm by Joan. Reggie envied him.

'I'll get you coffee,' said Joan.

'Super,' said David.

When they were alone, Reggie adopted a voice steeped in paternal comfort, as if he were President Roosevelt and David Harris-Jones was America in crisis.

'Well, David, it's good to see you,' he said. 'How are things in the world of ice creams?'

'Super. I'm enjoying working on the new Nut Whirl range immensely.'

'Good. That is splendid news. I see you've joined the Sunshine Singers.'

'Yes, I'm becoming much more . . . well I suppose it's not for me to say . . . maybe I'm not.'

'Much more what?'

'Self-confident. I think I'm much more . . . what can I say? . . . how can I put it?'

'Decisive.'

'Yes.'

'What about the redecoration of your office?' said Reggie, glancing at the pictures of Skegness and Fleetwood which the Office Environment Amelioration Committee had given him to brighten up his dreary box. 'Did you get SCAB?'

'SCAB?'

'The Selection of Colour-scheme Advisory Booklet.'

'Oh. Yes. I can't decide whether to go for red for initiative, green for concentration or blue for loyalty. Which do you think I need more of most – initiative, concentration or loyalty?'

There was another knock.

'Ah, coffee,' said Reggie.

But it wasn't coffee. It was Tony Webster, Reggie's departmental head. He entered the room decisively but not arrogantly.

'Morning, Martin. Morning, David. How's it going?' he said.

'Fine,' said Reggie.

'Super,' said David.

'Great,' said Tony. 'Won't keep you long.' A piece of ash from his large but not ostentatious cigar fell on to the wide but not obtrusive lapel of his modern but not frivolous suit.

'Work force becoming more contented?' he asked. 'Questionnaires proving helpful?'

'I hope so,' said Reggie.

'Great.'

'Super.'

'One little fact bothers me,' said Tony. 'Production is down one point two per cent.'

'I see,' said Reggie.

'Any theories?' said Tony.

'People are too busy filling in questionnaires and wondering what colour to paint their offices and having monthly chats and meeting the other side of industry,' said Reggie.

'Super,' said David.

Tony shot him a withering glance.

12

'Sorry,' said David.

'One other little fact. Absenteeism and sickness are up three point one per cent,' said Tony.

'I see,' said Reggie.

'C.J. has got to be told,' said Tony.

'Yes,' said Reggie.

'The secret of good management is the ability to delegate,' said Tony. 'You tell him, Martin.'

Reggie couldn't tell C.J. that absenteeism and sickness were up, because C.J. was absent sick. Instead he spent the day feeding into the computer the answers which the staff had given to his questionnaires. The results were disturbing.

Elizabeth was on the phone to their daughter Linda when Reggie arrived home. She was sitting in a fluffy white armchair, with her back to the french windows. The fitted carpet was dove grey and there was a faint yellow-green tinge in the patterned wallpaper. On the walls hung pictures of Algarve scenes, painted by Dr Snurd, their dentist. Reggie hadn't liked to refuse them, for fear Dr Snurd would stop giving him injections.

'Here's Reggie,' she said, as she heard the front door.

'Are you ever going to tell him that you know he's Reggie?' said Linda.

'I don't know,' said Elizabeth. 'I just don't know.'

Reggie entered the room rather wearily and Elizabeth said: 'I must go now, love. Here's Martin,' and put the phone down.

'Did you have a good day at the office?' she said.

'Wonderful,' said Reggie, because if he'd been Reggie he'd have said: 'No.'

He poured two dry martinis. He hated dry martini, but Martin Wellbourne liked it, so he had to drink them.

'Are you sure you're happy?' said Elizabeth.

'Deliriously happy,' said Reggie, as he sank into the brown Parker Knoll.

In the spacious garden the trees were bare and puritanical. In the kitchen a mutton casserole simmered, and a plane

13

drowned their conversation as it descended towards Heathrow. It carried, did they but know it, a party from the Icelandic Bar Association, eager to reclothe themselves cheaply at C & A's.

'What did you say?' said Elizabeth.

'I said we're on the flight path again,' said Reggie.

Elizabeth served their supper, and Reggie struggled with his mutton casserole.

'Reggie hated mutton casserole,' she said.

'Did he really?'

'He hated dry martinis too.'

'Did he really? But then I'm not Reggie, am I?'

'No,' she said. 'You aren't, are you?'

'Are you absolutely sure you're happy, Martin?' said Elizabeth as they lay in bed, listening to the Milfords returning noisily after their snifter at the golf club.

'Of course I am,' he said. 'I'm wonderfully happy.'

They made love, but he didn't really enjoy it. He was too busy making sure he didn't do it like Reggie Perrin.

Chapter 2

On the Tuesday morning a watery sun shone fitfully.

'I'm sorry about yesterday,' said Reggie to the GPO engineer, 'but I loathe Martin Wellbourne.'

'That's all right, chief,' said the GPO engineer. 'No bones broken. Who is this Martin Wellbourne anyway?'

'I am,' said Reggie.

The GPO engineer stepped away from Reggie, and fell backwards into his hole.

The eight sixteen reached Waterloo seventeen minutes late, due to track relaying at Queen's Road, and C.J. returned to work.

'Sit down, Martin,' he said.

Reggie pulled up a hard chair and sat on it.

'Don't trust the easy chairs, eh?' said C.J. 'I don't blame you. I didn't get where I am today by trusting the easy chairs.'

'Absolutely not, C.J.,' said Reggie.

C.J.'s office was large, with a thick yellow carpet and two circular red rugs. C.J. sat in a steel swivel chair behind a huge rosewood desk.

'There's something I must tell you, C.J.,' said Reggie.

'Work going well, Martin? Keeping everybody's peckers up?'

'Yes, C.J., I . . .'

'How's the lunch-time folk club going?'

'Very well, C.J. Parker from Flans is singing today.'

'That man could be a second Dylan Thomas,' said C.J.

A tug hooted on the near-by river.

'The thing is, C.J. . . .'

'Participation, that's the name of the game,' said C.J.

'It certainly is, C.J. I . . .'

'I met the firm's ex-doctor on Saturday. Fellow named Morrissey. Sound chap. I sacked him once.'

'Absolutely fascinating, C.J. I . . .'

'I've given him his job back. I realize now how important loyalty and happiness are. Loyalty and happiness, Martin.'

'Exactly, C.J.'

'Now, what is it?' said C.J. 'Spit it out. Proliferation is the thief of time.'

'Production is down one point two per cent and absenteeism is up three point one per cent,' said Reggie.

'I see.'

C.J. strode briskly round the room, examining the pictures on his walls as if for reassurance. The Bratby and the Bacon had been replaced by works more eloquent of happiness – two Lake District scenes, a still life of a lobster and a portrait of Ken Dodd.

'I've had the results of the questionnaires analysed, C.J.'

'And?' barked C.J.

'There are lots of things that lots of people like a lot, C.J.'

'Good. Splendid. Tickety boo.'

'Exactly. As you rightly say, tickety boo. But there are a few little things . . . *little* things . . . that a lot of people dislike rather a lot, C.J.'

'What little things, Martin?'

'Well . . . er . . . just little things. The . . . er . . . the building, C.J. And the . . . er . . . the offices, and the furniture, and . . . er . . .'

'And what?'

'The product, C.J. They just don't like making instant puddings.'

'I see,' said C.J.

He gazed at the Lake District, the lobster and Ken Dodd, and it seemed that he gained new strength.

'Mere bagatelles, Martin,' he said. 'We mustn't let short-term setbacks obscure the long-term view. Neither Mrs C.J. nor I has ever let short-term setbacks obscure the long-term view.'

'I imagine not, C.J.'

C.J. leant forward with sudden vehemence. His eyes sparkled.

16

'The results will come,' he said. 'Carry on the good work. Don't forget, in a sense you are keeping Reggie Perrin alive.'

'I won't forget, C.J.,' said Reggie.

'To the Location of Offices Bureau, South Quay, Tobermory, Mull. Dear Sirs . . .'

He sighed.

'Are you all right, Mr Wellbourne?' said Joan.

'I'm in tip-top form,' said Reggie. 'It's just that this business of making everybody happy is making me miserable.'

'Owen Lewis from Crumbles is coming for his monthly chat in five minutes.'

'Oh. Good,' he said. 'Because I'm going home.'

But Reggie did not go home. Instead he went to visit his lovely daughter Linda, in her lovely detached house in the lovely village of Thames Brightwell.

Linda broached a bottle of Tom's sprout wine and seated herself on the chaise longue. Reggie sat in an armchair and leapt up with a yelp. He picked up a peculiarly shaped knife.

'You've sat on the aubergine-peeler,' said Linda.

'On the what?'

'Tom gave me a set of vegetable knives for Christmas. You get a different tool for each vegetable. An endive-cutter, a courgette-slicer . . .'

'Oh good. No home should be without a courgette-slicer.'

'It's easy for you to mock, dad, but if you want to get on as an estate agent you have to keep up with the Joneses.'

Reggie sat down gingerly.

'You're the only person in the world who knows who I am,' he said.

'Your secret is safe with me,' said Linda.

Reggie sipped his wine and grimaced.

'It's horrible,' he said.

'Nineteen seventy-two was a bad year for sprouts.'

Reggie removed a fluffy wombat from underneath his cushion.

'Your children have very charming toys,' he said.

'Tom refuses to let them have anything violent. He confiscated the working model of the Third Parachute Regiment that Jimmy gave Adam.'

'I thought Tom believed in freedom.'

'Freedom and peace.'

'Principles *are* confusing, aren't they? Oh, Linda, what am I to do?'

'Martin Wellbourne will have to leave all his clothes on the beach and reappear as Reggie Perrin.'

'What, and attend Martin Wellbourne's Memorial Service and marry your mother for the third time? Be serious, Linda.'

'Sorry.'

She kissed her father, flinching from the prickles of his Martin Wellbourne beard.

Reggie looked out over the large lawn, which led down to a Gothic stone folly that Tom had built.

'I was wondering if you could tell your mother the truth,' said Reggie.

'Me? If anyone tells her, it's got to be you.'

'It might not be very easy,' said Reggie. 'She's got used to me as I am. Sometimes I think she prefers me to me.'

'She doesn't prefer you to you,' said Linda. 'She much prefers you.'

'It's going to be an awful shock to her,' said Reggie.

'Maybe not as much as you think,' said Linda. 'Tell her, dad. Tell her tonight.'

'I will,' said Reggie. 'I will. My mind is made up. I'll tell her tonight. Do you really think I ought to tell her?'

'If you want to,' said Linda.

She poured Reggie another glass of the greenish-yellow liquid.

'Dutch courage,' she said.

'More like Belgian courage,' he said.

Adam and Jocasta came running in, closely followed by their father.

'Hello, Tom. How's the bearded wit of the Thames Valley house ads?' said Reggie.

'Hello, Martin. My God, you aren't drinking the sprout wine?'

'Yes.'

'It's undrinkable. My one and only mistake. You can't make wine out of sprouts.'

Tom took the remains of Reggie's drink and poured it down the sink.

Reggie soon left. When he looked back, Adam was slitting the wombat's throat with the aubergine-peeler.

Linda phoned Elizabeth from the telephone box opposite the church. Icy March winds blew through the panes broken by vandals.

'Dad's just been here,' she said. 'He's going to tell you that he's Reggie.'

'Oh.'

A man with a sinister face was hopping from one leg to the other as if the phone box was a lavatory.

'Are you glad?' said Linda.

'I don't know,' said Elizabeth. 'Half the time I've been trying to get him to tell me. Now I feel frightened.'

Linda was sure the man was a breather.

'I thought I'd better prepare you so that you're ready to be surprised,' she said.

The man glanced at his watch. Surely breathers didn't mind at what time they rang?

'I'd better go, mum. There's a man waiting.'

She forced herself to walk right past the man.

'Sorry,' she said.

'No hurry,' said the man in a pleasant, cultured, gently vacuous voice. 'I'm only going in there to do a bit of heavy breathing.'

And he roared with self-satisfied laughter.

Reggie walked slowly up the snicket, up Wordsworth Drive, turned right into Tennyson Avenue, then left into Coleridge Close. It didn't seem fitting that dramatic revelations should be made on this desirable estate, with its pink pavements and mock-Tudor and mock-Georgian houses. For one thing, there were no lace curtains for them to be made behind.

He kissed Elizabeth on the check.

'What's for supper?' he said.

'Boiled silverside.'

Damn! Martin Wellbourne loved boiled silverside, had dreamt of its Anglo-Saxon honesty in the mangrove swamps of Brazil. Reggie loathed it.

He poured their drinks with a shaking hand.

'Prepare yourself for a shock,' he said.

'That sounds ominous,' said Elizabeth.

'Brace yourself for a surprise,' said Reggie.

Elizabeth braced herself.

'I'm not Martin,' said Reggie. 'I'm Reggie.'

He pulled off his false wig, and smiled foolishly.

'My God,' said Elizabeth. 'My God! Reggie! You! ... Reggie! Alive!'

She gave a passable impression of a woman fainting.

When she recovered consciousness Reggie gave her a brandy and she phoned Tom and Linda and her brother Jimmy, asking them to come round. They couldn't phone their son Mark, as he was touring Africa with a theatre group, which was presenting *No Sex Please, We're British* to an audience of bemused Katangans.

'I wish mother was well enough to come,' said Elizabeth.

Reggie closed his eyes, and saw a lonely elderly woman in failing health.

'I don't think of your mother as a hippopotamus any more,' he said.

'Thank you,' said Elizabeth.

They ate their boiled silverside.

'Now I can have meals I like again,' said Reggie.

He believed that all his problems would soon be over, now that he was Reggie Perrin again. He had come home after a long journey in a strange land.

The doorbell rang.

'Oh my God,' he said, and hurried upstairs.

Elizabeth let Tom and Linda in.

'What's all this mystery?' said Tom.

'You'll see,' said Elizabeth.

'I don't like mysteries,' said Tom. 'I'm not a mystery person.'

'That's true,' said Linda.

Darkness had fallen, and the curtains were drawn. They talked of the collapse of property values in the Thames Valley, and the difficulty of finding toys that taught young children about the socio-economic structure of our society.

At a quarter past nine the erstwhile army major drew up in his rusting Ford. He had whisky on his breath and leather patches on his elbows. He was going downhill now that Sheila had left him.

'We were awfully sorry to hear about Sheila,' said Tom.

'Blessing in disguise,' said Jimmy. 'Career in ashes, family life in ruins, new start *de rigueur.*'

'Any idea what you're going to do?' said Tom.

'Yes,' said Jimmy.

'Well,' said Tom. 'What are you going to do?'

'Idle talk costs lives,' said Jimmy.

'Another mystery,' said Tom. 'It's a mystery to me why you all have to have so many mysteries.'

'Tom's not a mystery person,' said Linda.

'Well I'm not,' said Tom. 'What's wrong in saying I'm not a mystery person if I'm not?'

'What's tonight's mystery about?' said Jimmy. 'Like a good mystery.'

Elizabeth stood with her back to Dr Snurd's lurid painting of Albufeira.

'I found something out about Martin tonight,' she said.

'He's not the Monster of the Piccadilly Line?' said Jimmy. 'Sorry. Uncalled for.'

'Martin Wellbourne isn't his real name,' said Elizabeth. 'His real name's Reggie Perrin.'

Tom gawped. Jimmy looked thunderstruck.

'You mean . . . Martin is . . . dad!' said Linda, and she gave a passable imitation of a woman fainting.

When she came round Jimmy gave her a brandy.

'Reggie!' called Elizabeth.

Reggie came downstairs, wigless, and smiled foolishly at them.

'Good God!' said Jimmy.

'Well I must say!' said Tom.

'Must you?' said Reggie.

'Daddy!' said Linda, rushing up to him and hugging him.

'There there,' said Reggie, patting Linda's head. 'Bit of a surprise, eh, old girl?'

'You mean you've been you all the time?' said Jimmy. 'Felt something was wrong. Couldn't put my finger on it.'

Elizabeth went to get a bottle of champagne.

'Why did you do it?' said Tom.

'Does there always have to be an explanation?' said Reggie.

'Yes, I rather think there does,' said Tom.

Elizabeth brought in the champagne and Reggie opened it.

'Not really a champagne wallah,' said Jimmy. 'Cheers.'

'Welcome home, dad,' said Linda.

They toasted Reggie.

'So we had a memorial service for you when you were still alive!' said Tom.

'I was there,' said Reggie.

'I gave 50p,' said Tom.

'Tom!' said Linda.

'It's not the money,' said Tom. 'It's the principle.'

The grandfather clock in the hall struck ten.

'Know the first thing I did when I saw Sheila's note?' said Jimmy. 'Pressed my trousers. Adage of old Colonel Warboys. Nothing looks quite as black when your creases are sharp. Mustard for creases, Warboys. Hated the Free Poles. No creases. Sorry. Talking too much. Hogging limelight. Nerves.'

'Why were you so grumpy today?' said Linda.

They were lying in their orthopaedic bed.

'Life's simple,' said Tom. 'I'm not complicated. I go to work. I bring home money. I love you. It's simple. I can't see why other people can't see it.'

An owl hooted by the river.

'Owls don't leave their clothes on the beach and come back to their own memorial services disguised as pigeons,' said Tom.

'Dad isn't an owl,' said Linda.

They lay at opposite sides of the orthopaedic bed, not touching each other.

'Blast,' said Jimmy.

He had spilt whisky on his pillow.

An owl hooted.

'Shut up,' shouted Jimmy.

'Are you happy, Reggie?' said Elizabeth.

An owl hooted, and the Milfords slammed both doors of their car.

'Wonderfully happy,' said Reggie.

Chapter 3

Wednesday was a typical early spring day of bright sunshine and sudden showers. For the first time since 11 March 1932 no weather records were broken anywhere in Britain.

Reggie stood at the window, watching a blue tit pecking at a ball of fat suspended from the rowan tree to incite just such an ornithological vignette.

'Briefcase,' said Elizabeth, handing him his briefcase, engraved in gold: M.S.W.

'Thank you, darling,' said Reggie.

'Umbrella,' said Elizabeth.

'Thank you, darling,' said Reggie.

'Wig,' said Elizabeth.

'Oh my God.'

Reggie fitted his wig in the downstairs lavatory. Was there never to be an end to this absurdity? Was he to disguise himself every morning as Martin Wellbourne, and take his disguise off every evening?

When the GPO engineer saw Reggie coming, he stepped back into his hole.

'It's all right,' said Reggie. 'I'm not really Martin Wellbourne any more.'

'Good morning, Mrs Greengross,' he said. 'Seventeen minutes late. Flood water seeping through signal cables at Effingham Junction.'

'Good morning, Mr Perrin,' she said.

'Dictation time,' he said, sitting at his desk. You could tell its age from the rings made by many cups of coffee. 'To the Saucy Calendar Company, Buff Road, Orpington. Dear Sirs, could you please quote me for a hundred and fifty saucy calendars to keep our male staff in a constant state of ... You called me Perrin!'

24

'Yes.'

'My name is Wellbourne, Mrs Greengross.'

'Oh Reggie.'

She flung her arms round him and kissed him on the cheek.

'Joan! Please! Joan!'

There was a knock on the door. They leapt apart.

It was C.J.

'Morning, Martin,' said C.J.

'Morning, C.J.'

'I'd like you to have a check up with Doc Morrissey, give the poor old boy something to do on his first morning.'

'Certainly, C.J.' said Reggie.

'Idle hands make heavy work, eh, Joan?'

'They certainly do, C.J.'

'You've got lipstick on your cheek, Martin.'

'Absolutely, C.J. What?'

'Careful, Martin. I didn't get where I am today by having lipstick on my cheek.'

'Absolutely not, C.J. Perish the thought. Sorry, C.J.'

C.J. left the room and Reggie wiped the lipstick off his cheek. Vain exercise! Soon Joan was kissing him once again.

C.J. re-entered the room.

'Martin!' said C.J.

Reggie shot away from Joan's embrace as if catapulted.

'It's an experiment, C.J., he said. 'Part of the scheme to keep the employees happy, keep absenteeism at bay. Everybody kissing each other every morning. Only people of the opposite sex, of course.'

'It's going too far,' said C.J. 'This isn't British Leyland.'

'Sorry, C.J.' said Reggie. 'My enthusiasm got the better of me.'

'You must temper the stew of enthusiasm with the seasoning of moderation,' said C.J. 'I just came back to say: "Be extra friendly to Doc Morrissey." '

'I will,' said Reggie.

C.J. left the room. Joan moved towards him. C.J. opened the door again.

'Neither Mrs C.J. nor I has ever kissed all the employees every morning,' he said.

'Please don't do that again, Joan,' said Reggie when C.J. had finally gone.

'I'm sorry,' said Joan.

'When did you realize?' said Reggie.

'Gradually,' said Joan. 'I just couldn't believe it at first.'

'Memo to all departments,' said Reggie, sitting down again behind his desk and fingering his digital calendar nervously. 'Members of the Pudding Club have been leaving the premises in a condition . . . You aren't taking it down, Joan.'

'I don't feel like it, Mr Perrin.'

'I think, Joan, that you ought to refer to me as Mr Wellbourne.'

Joan went back to her desk and sat down.

'I could tell C.J. that you're Mr Perrin, Mr Wellbourne.' she said.

'You could, yes.'

'I might not, if . . .'

'Is this blackmail, Joan?'

'Not exactly blackmail, Mr Perrin.'

'What then?'

'Well, a sort of blackmail.'

'You might not if what?'

Joan blushed.

'If what, Joan?'

'If you and I . . . together . . . you know.'

'If we had it off together from time to time?'

Joan nodded.

'Joan! What an awful way to put it.'

A cradle with a blond young window-cleaner on it appeared at the window. They pretended to be busy until he had finished.

'I love you,' said Joan, when he had gone.

'This is extremely embarrassing, Joan,' said Reggie, pacing up and down the crowded little office. 'I was attracted to you . . . you were attractive . . . you *are* attractive . . . I *am* attracted. But I'm a married man, I love my wife, and all that was a mistake.'

He leant on Joan's desk and looked into her eyes.

'Tell C.J. if you must,' he said.

'I can't,' she said.

'I know,' said Reggie.

'Oh hell,' said Joan. She blew her nose and said: 'Ready for dictation, Mr Wellbourne.'

The walls of Doc Morrissey's little surgery were decorated with diagrams of the human body. The window was of frosted glass.

'Nice to see you again,' said Reggie.

'You've never seen me before,' said Doc Morrissey.

'I mean it's nice to see you and know that you're here again. Of course I haven't seen you before. Good heavens, no,' said Reggie.

'Take your clothes off,' said Doc Morrissey. 'Put them over there, on top of mine.'

'What?'

'It's a little joke. It puts the patient at his ease.'

'Oh I see. Ha ha.'

'I've been polishing up on psychology while I've been on the dole,' said Doc Morrissey.

Reggie lifted his shirt, and Doc Morrissey pressed a stethoscope to his chest.

'You run this ... say aaaaargh ... this Reginald Perrin Memorial Whatsit, don't you?'

'Yes. Aaaaargh.'

'How's it going ... and again ... going well is it?'

'I don't think people ... aaaaargh ... particularly want to be happy.'

'How many people are you dealing with? Say ninety-nine.'

'About two hundred and thirty-five. Ninety-nine.'

'Thank you. Oh, quite a lot. Of course people don't like to be happy. Happiness is all right for the Latin races. Cough. It doesn't suit the British temperament at all.'

'That's exactly ...' Reggie coughed. '... how I feel.'

'Fine.' Doc Morrissey removed his stethoscope and handed Reggie an empty bottle. 'Go behind that screen.'

Reggie stood behind a little screen, above which only his

head and shoulders were visible. Behind him was a rusty corner cabinet full of bottles of brightly coloured potions.

'It's against nature to be happy at work,' said Doc Morrissey. 'People enjoy being bitchy behind each other's backs, and harbouring grudges, and complaining because the girls in the canteen don't wash their hands after going to the lavatory. It's the British way of life. Like going behind that screen. I know what you're doing. You know what you're doing. You know that I know what you're doing. It's a normal, healthy, natural bodily function, done by everybody, you, me, Denis Compton, the Pope, even Wedgwood-Benn. But we British go behind a screen. Not like those so-called civilized French, standing in rows at their lay-bys. Besides, it's easier behind a screen.'

Reggie emerged and handed Doc Morrissey the empty bottle.

'It's too cold,' he said.

'Still the same old Reggie.'

'Pardon?'

'You're Reggie Perrin. What's all this tomfoolery?' said Doc Morrissey.

'I . . .'

'I shall have to tell C.J. Show him that I'm a force to be reckoned with.'

'In a way it'll be a relief,' said Reggie.

'Sit down, Perrin,' said C.J.

Reggie pulled up a hard chair and sat on that. Doc Morrissey smiled nervously at him from the depths of an easy one.

'I had to do it, Reggie,' he said.

'I always knew you were a good man – unlike you Reggie – this is a disgrace,' said C.J.

'Absolutely, C.J.' said Reggie.

C.J. leant forward and glared at him.

'Pretending to be dead and posing as your long-lost friend from Colombia, how could you think anyone would fall for a thing like that?' he said.

'Absurd,' said Reggie.

'Running your own memorial fund. How could you hope to get away with it?'

'Ridiculous.'

'I didn't get where I am today by posing as my long-lost friend from the Argentine.'

'I realize that, C.J.'

'I could come in here in a dress and pretend to be Kathy Kirby,' said C.J., 'but I don't. That isn't the British way.'

'It certainly isn't,' said Reggie.

'You must have learnt some funny ideas in Peru,' said C.J.

'I wasn't over there,' said Reggie. 'I'm not Martin Wellbourne.'

'I know that,' said C.J. 'I'm not a complete nincompoop. Or am I mistaken, Doc?'

'Oh no,' said Doc Morrissey. 'As a medical man, I'd say you're definitely not a complete nincompoop.'

'There you are,' said C.J. 'Straight from the horse's mouth.'

The ineffectual treble glazing shook as a charter flight from the Belgian Licensed Victuallers' Association flew in en route for Bourne and Hollingsworth's.

'What was that, Doc?' said C.J.

'I said we seem to be on the flight path,' said Doc Morrissey.

'All this nonsense about trying to make the employees happy. It's nonsense,' said C.J. 'Would it surprise you, Reggie, to learn that absenteeism is up three point one per cent?'

'No, C.J. I told you myself.'

'Condemned out of your own mouth. You're sacked.'

'Yes, C.J.'

'You come to me with the idea for this ridiculous foundation.'

'That was your idea, C.J.'

'I practically destroy this firm. I start caring about people. I didn't get where I am today by caring about people. I re-employ this incompetent medic. You're sacked, Morrissey.'

'But C.J....' began Doc Morrissey.

'Doc Morrissey has just revealed to you who I am,' said Reggie.

'Thus proving he's an idiot,' said C.J.

'It seems very unfair to me,' said Doc Morrissey.

'It is unfair,' said C.J. 'Life is unfair. I am unfair. You're both sacked.'

Chapter 4

Reggie became an unemployment statistic on his forty-seventh birthday.

The labour exchange was painted grey and there were notices about the penalties for illegal immigration, the dangers of swine vasicular fever in Shropshire, and the need to check up on vaccination requirements well before your holiday.

'Name?' said the clerk, who had a long nose of the kind from which dewdrops drip, though none dripped now.

'Perrin.'

'Occupation?' said the clerk in his tired voice.

'Middle management.'

'We haven't had ICI on the blower recently,' said the clerk.

'What work do you have?' said Reggie.

'Vacancy at Pelham's Piggery,' said the clerk.

'No, thank you,' said Reggie.

The days of April passed slowly. The weather was mixed.

Every morning Reggie walked with averted eyes down the hostile roads of the Poets' Estate, where people believe that failure is catching. Sometimes people crossed to the other side of the road to avoid speaking to him. Peter Cartwright had started walking to the station down Elizabeth Barrett Browning Crescent.

'I just wouldn't know what to say to him,' he explained to his wife.

Every morning Reggie walked down Climthorpe High Street, where there were seven building societies but no cinema. Sic transit Gloria Swanson.

The aim of his walk was the reference room of the public library, and he was invariably successful in achieving that aim, for his sense of direction had never been in doubt.

In the reference room he sat among students with streaming colds, among emaciated old women searching through obscure back numbers of even more obscure periodicals, among old men with watery eyes waiting for the pubs to open. He worked his way through the newspapers, studying the advertisements for jobs.

There were so many for which he wasn't qualified. He wasn't young, eager or dynamic. He didn't speak nine languages, he didn't have extensive involvement in the whole field of labour relations, he didn't have wide experience of the Persian Gulf or the drilling of bore holes, he didn't have five years of practical midwifery behind him and he didn't have a deep commitment to man-made fibres.

There were some vacancies for which he applied.

One evening, while Angela Rippon read the news with the sound turned down, he discussed the future with Elizabeth.

'I'll go out to work,' she said.

'I've failed you,' he said.

'Oh do stop it,' said Elizabeth. 'Pride is one of the luxuries we can't afford any more.'

Angela Rippon's face went grave. Bad news.

'We'll make economies,' said Reggie.

'We're having four meatless days a week already,' said Elizabeth.

Her face was pale and drawn. Going out in Climthorpe was an ordeal. After she had passed by, people would say: 'It's her I'm sorry for.'

'I'll sell the pictures of the Algarve,' said Reggie.

'What would we do with a whole pound?' said Elizabeth.

'We'd get more than a pound for them,' said Reggie. 'Dr Snurd's got a rising reputation.'

'Who told you that?' said Elizabeth.

'Dr Snurd,' said Reggie. 'His pictures caused quite a stir at the Dental Art Exhibition. He's known as the Picasso of the Molars.'

Elizabeth sighed. Reggie gazed at the two sad and silent women. Elizabeth, burdened by personal anxiety. Angela Rippon, borne down by tragedies on a cosmic scale.

'I've applied for several jobs,' said Reggie. 'One of these days my ship will come in.'

The evenings grew longer, and the weather grew warmer, but Reggie's ship did not come in.

He was granted four interviews. Two he failed outright, the third he failed after being on a short list of six, and the fourth he failed after being on a short list of one.

Every week he went to Climthorpe Labour Exchange. He felt self-conscious among the actors and actresses, Irishmen, chronically bronchitic, West Indians, unfrocked vicars and chronically bronchitic Irish actors. The man in front of him, did he but know it, had played football for England in the forties. He had thirty-two caps and three convictions for shop-lifting.

'Still no word from I C I,' said the clerk.

'Nothing from Unilevers?' said Reggie, forcing himself to join in the fun.

'Not yet,' said the clerk. 'Can't get through, I expect.'

'That'll be it,' said Reggie.

'Vacancy at Pelham's Piggery,' said the clerk.

'No thank you,' said Reggie.

An unseasonal fall of snow caused the tourists to cancel their first net practice at Lords, and there was never any reply to Jimmy's telephone.

They visited Elizabeth's mother in Worthing. Her silence was an eloquent rebuke, a reminder that he was not supporting Elizabeth in the manner to which she had become accustomed.

As they passed through Dorking on the way home, Elizabeth said: 'We can't go on like this. If you don't get a job tomorrow, I'm going out to work.'

'The pigs like you,' said Mr Pelham.

Reggie looked down at the fat pink creatures, slopping greedily at their swill.

'You really think so, guv?' he said.

'I've never known them take to anyone like they have to

33

you, old son,' said Mr Pelham, who was a big, well-built man with a red face.

'Ta ever so,' said Reggie.

It was the end of his first day. Pelham's Piggery was situated in a wedge of sad, neglected countryside that remained by some planning oversight on the western edge of Climthorpe. On one side was the Climthorpe School of Riding. On the other was a used car dump.

'They like older men,' said Mr Pelham. 'They just won't take it from young lads who're still wet behind the ears.'

'I suppose not,' said Reggie.

'You can't blame them,' said Mr Pelham. 'I wouldn't take it from young lads who were still wet behind the ears if I was a pig.'

There were four thousand pigs, housed in long rows. There were twelve pigs in each sty. At the back of the sties there were shelters where the pigs slept. Between the rows of sties there were paths, and on either side of the paths there were ditches, down which the porcine faeces flowed smoothly.

Reggie's legs and back ached and his clothes smelt. Poor pigs. Their love of him was unrequited.

'Grand animals, aren't they?' said Mr Pelham.

'Grand,' said Reggie. 'They're the guv'nors.'

'All those pork chops,' said Mr Pelham. 'All that smoked through-cut.'

Reggie straightened up with difficulty. Mr Pelham had told him that he'd be all right if he mucked in. He had spent most of the day mucking out.

'Think you'll take to it, old son?' said Mr Pelham.

'I hope so,' said Reggie.

The population density was calculated to the last piglet. The pigs got grain in the morning and swill in the afternoon. The rations were worked out to the last ounce. As soon as they were fat enough, they were taken to the slaughterhouse.

'Back to nature,' said Mr Pelham. 'You can't beat it.'

*

The phone call from C.J. was a surprise. So was the invitation to call in his office for drinks. Nobody knew what his middle name was, but it certainly wasn't largesse.

She entered C.J.'s inner sanctum, and battled her way across the thick pile carpet.

A middle-aged woman with a pasty complexion was spraying C.J.'s telephone. She wore a brown uniform emblazoned with the legend: 'Wipe-o-Fone'. She smiled at Elizabeth cheerily.

I'm spoilt, thought Elizabeth. I couldn't smile cheerily at me, if I was wearing a brown uniform emblazoned with the legend: 'Wipe-o-Fone.'

C.J.'s handshake was as firm as steel, as if he were compensating for his lack of a private helicopter.

'I'm sorry I'm late,' she said. 'Chain reaction to a buckled rail at West Byfleet.'

The telephone lady left and Elizabeth sat cautiously in one of the dark brown leather armchairs.

C.J. laughed.

'Reggie's told you about the chairs, I see,' he said. 'These are new. Japanese. Small but silent. It takes our bum-squatting legs-crossed chums to invent a decent chair. Ironic.'

He didn't ask Elizabeth what she wanted to drink. He poured sherry for her and whisky for himself.

The pictures indicative of happiness had been removed and replaced by portraits of famous industrialists.

'We live in a competitive world,' said C.J., proffering the cigar box instinctively and then withdrawing it hastily. 'There's no room for broken reeds, lame ducks or stool pigeons.'

'I imagine not,' said Elizabeth.

'Neither Mrs C.J. nor I has ever had room for broken reeds, lame ducks or stool pigeons.'

'I'm sure you haven't.'

'How *is* Reggie?'

'He's very well.'

'Working?' asked C.J.

'He's swilling out pigs,' said Elizabeth.

'Industry's loss is the porker's gain,' said C.J. 'You mustn't think I don't have a heart.'

'I promise I won't ever think that,' said Elizabeth. 'Nice sherry.'

C.J. glanced at the portrait of Krupp. Krupp hadn't got where he had been yesterday by talking about nice sherry.

'I'm concerned about Reggie,' said C.J. 'Sometimes I wonder if we may have contributed to his troubles.'

He waited for Elizabeth's reply, and seemed put out when none came.

'How will you manage?' he said.

'I can always go out to work.'

'Ah!'

C.J. replenished Elizabeth's glass. He did not replenish his own.

He stood over her, holding out the sherry, looking down into her eyes.

'Do you mind if I ask you a personal question?' he asked.

'Not at all,' laughed Elizabeth.

'Can you type?'

'I'm a bit rusty.'

'It's like riding a bicycle,' said C.J. 'Elephants never forget, as they say.'

And so C.J. offered her the job of Tony Webster's secretary, on a month's trial.

'There is one thing,' said Elizabeth.

'Please!' said C.J., holding up an admonitory hand. 'No thanks.'

'What's the salary?' said Elizabeth.

Perhaps it was just a trick of the light, but she could have sworn that Lord Sieff winked.

'It's the pigs,' said Mr Pelham. 'You don't like the pigs.'

'It's not the pigs,' said Reggie. 'I like the pigs.'

'Pigs are basically very good-natured,' said Mr Pelham. 'They aren't pigs, you know. You'd be surprised. They're very clean beneath all that smell and dirt.'

'It isn't the pigs, honest,' said Reggie.

'Busy time coming up, pigs coming, pigs going, sheds to be repaired, this that the other.'

'It's my back,' said Reggie.

A Boeing 727 flew past, carrying a party from the Würzburg Women's Institute, bound for the outsize department at D. H. Evans.

'Come again,' said Reggie.

'I said we're on the flight path again,' said Mr Pelham. 'I'll miss you, old son. You've got a real gift.'

'I can't risk my back,' said Reggie.

'Backs are buggers,' said Mr Pelham. 'Backs are sods. I had a back once.'

Reggie left the piggery doubled up. He walked, still doubled up, past the Climthorpe School of Riding and the chicken farm that he described to Elizabeth as Stalag Hen 59. He walked doubled up past the rows of low huts where the battery hens were kept in dark, immobile misery. He walked doubled up past the notice board that said: 'Vale Pond Farm – Fresh Farm Eggs – Apply Side Door.'

As soon as he was round the corner he straightened up – because of course it wasn't his back. It was the pigs.

Chapter 5

Late spring merged into early summer. House-martins swooped for mud among the used French letters around the pond beside the cricket ground.

Thud of leather upon willow. Steamy flanks of horses in well-dressed paddocks.

Every morning Reggie cooked breakfast for Elizabeth. Every morning he handed her her umbrella.

'Umbrella,' he said.

'Thank you, darling,' she said, every morning.

Every morning he said: 'Handbag.'

'Thank you, darling,' she said, every morning.

Every morning she walked down Coleridge Close, turned right into Tennyson Avenue, then left into Wordsworth Drive, and down the snicket into Station Road.

Every morning she stood on the platform by the door marked 'Isolation Telephone' and waited for the eight sixteen.

Every morning she was seventeen minutes late.

Every morning Reggie planned the dinner. As soon as Elizabeth had gone, he sat on the lavatory and chose his menu at leisure.

He proved a stickler for culinary exactitude. If the *Oxfam Book of Great Meals* demanded a pinch of basil, Elizabeth would get a pinch of basil.

Every morning, his ablutions completed, Reggie walked to Climthorpe High Street. There were shopping parades of red brick, and a few Georgian buildings, derelict and boarded up.

His shopping was thorough and meticulous. He sniffed out bargains, rejected soft onions, and railed at the price of early Israeli raspberries.

One day, when he bought a cheap cut at the butcher's, he pretended it was for the dog.

He was aware that he was an object of ridicule, his story known equally to Miss E. A. Bigwold at the bank, and the cashier with the perpetual cold at Cash and Carry. He sensed a faint contempt in the manner of L. B. Mayhew, greengrocer and fruiterer, a gleam of amusement in the bloodshot eye of J. F. Walton, family butcher and high-class poulterer.

The daughter of the big couple at Sketchley's giggled whenever he entered.

Sometimes he had a pint at the Bull and Butcher, where drinks were three-quarter price before twelve. Sometimes he did not.

Was the rest of his life to be like this? Was he to be deflated gradually, the slowest puncture in the world, until he ended up, with smoky breath and a sunken chest, in Hove or Eastbourne, having a slow half of Guinness with a few retired cronies in a pub with plastic flowers?

In the afternoons he prepared the food, did a bit of gardening, and watched *Emmerdale Farm*. He'd always been scornful of day-time television, but now he found himself getting interested in the agricultural goings-on.

Every evening Elizabeth arrived home and he kissed her and gave her a drink and she said, 'What's for supper?' and he said, 'risotto', unless it wasn't, in which case he didn't say 'risotto'. For instance, if it was beef casserole he would say 'beef casserole'. There were problems enough without his lying about the food.

But it wasn't often beef casserole. They couldn't afford beef. So quite often it was risotto.

The first time it was risotto Reggie felt that it was not very good. Elizabeth assured him that it was excellent. Emboldened, he provided it with increasing frequency. Elizabeth, whose enthusiasm for even the most excellent risotto was moderate, grew to regret the intemperance of her former enthusiasm and was led to contemplate the difficulties which civilized people bring on themselves as a consequence of their reluctance to hurt the feelings of their fellow beings.

The reader asks: 'Did nothing occur, in the English

39

suburb of Climthorpe, that early summer, except the cooking, eating and discussing of risotto?'

Very little.

Reggie did not relish the reversal of their roles. He felt like
a kept man, an economic eunuch.

Elizabeth invented a fictional employer – the British
Basket Company. She knew that it would make matters
worse if Reggie found out that she was working for Sunshine
Desserts.

'Hello, darling,' he said on the evening of 7 June. 'Good
day at the office?'

'No. What's for supper?'

'Risotto.'

'Lovely. What's on the telly?'

'Nothing much. Just a repeat of that series they repeated
last year. You don't want to watch the telly, do you?'

'You have your *Emmerdale Farm*.'

'Only because I'm bored alone in the house all day. Mind
you, it was quite good today. Joe Sugden had a row with
Kathy Gimbel, and Matt Skilbeck had words with Sam Pear-
son.'

They sat in the garden over their pre-risotto drinks.
Reggie had the sprinklers going.

'You never talk about your work,' he said.

'It's very boring. I type letters about our waste-paper
baskets, most of which no doubt end up in our waste-paper
baskets.'

Ponsonby entered the garden, and a spotted fly-catcher flew
off towards Matthew Arnold Avenue. Ponsonby miaowed
angrily at a malevolent fate.

'What's your boss like?'

'Mr Steele? He's an ex-heavyweight boxer. Scottish-Hungarian. His father came from Budapest and his mother from
Arbroath. He's got a wooden leg and he drinks like a fish.'

'It doesn't sound boring at all,' said Reggie. 'It sounds a lot
more interesting than Sunshine Desserts.'

*

'Hello, darling,' he said on the evening of 13 June. 'Good day at the office?'

'No. What's for supper?'

'Risotto.'

'Oh.'

'Are we having risotto too much?'

'No. Well perhaps slightly too much. It's so nice I don't want to tire of it.'

'It *is* nice, is it?'

'Well perhaps nice isn't exactly the word I'd use for it.'

'What is exactly the word you'd use for it?'

'Unusual.'

'Oh.'

They sat in the garden over their pre-unusual-risotto drinks. Reggie had the sprinklers going.

'There's no mention of the British Basket Company in the phone book,' he said.

'Er . . . no. They've left it out,' she said .'They muddled it up with the other BBC. Mr Steele was furious.'

'Or in the yellow pages.'

'They left it out of there too.'

'They've never heard of it at the Climthorpe Basket Boutique.'

'Well, they wouldn't have done, as it's not in the phone book or the yellow pages. It is only a very small firm. It only makes very small baskets.'

On 17 June Jimmy offered Reggie a job.

He arrived shortly before nine. He looked more military than he had in his army days. Creases were much in evidence. Reggie and Elizabeth were pleased. They had feared that he was letting himself go.

They sat in the garden. Ponsonby was purring on Reggie's lap. An electric saw was going at number fifteen, where they were cutting up the remains of a diseased Dutch elm.

'Whisky, Jimmy?' said Reggie.

'Don't need to give me drinks. On your beam ends. Just a small one.'

They lingered over their whiskies.

'Know things are awkward,' said Jimmy. 'Wouldn't ask normally, but . . .'

'We've got some scrag end of lamb,' said Elizabeth.

'Scrag end, top-hole,' said Jimmy. 'Wouldn't ask normally, only distaff side gone AWOL, yours truly fish out of water in supermarkets, bit of a cock-up on the catering front.'

'Do you want anything else?' said Elizabeth.

'No, no. Mustn't leave cupboard bare. Bit of veg if it's going. Odd sprout. Cheese. Butter. Bacon. Egg. Bit of a greenhorn in the kitchen.'

Elizabeth went to fetch the food. Jimmy moved his chair closer to Reggie.

'Didn't really come for food,' said Jimmy. 'Decoy. Get big sister out of way.'

'Ah! So what's your real purpose?'

'Got a job for you,' said Jimmy. 'Interested?'

'What sort of job?'

'Can't tell you. Hush hush.'

A plane flew in towards Heathrow, carrying a party from the Umbrian Chiropodists' Guild, hell bent for Dickins and Jones.

'I can't take a job unless I know what it is.'

'Put you in picture later,' said Jimmy.

'Do you think the people in that plane are lip-reading through telescopes?'

'Can't be too careful,' said Jimmy. 'Not time or place.'

'When will the time and place be?'

'Next Tuesday.'

'Where?'

'Can't tell you. Classified. D notice on it.'

'That makes it difficult for me to be present.'

'Be told in due course. Well, what's your answer?'

'It's a secret.'

'Fair enough. Good man. And don't breathe a word.'

'There aren't many words that I could breathe,' said Reggie.

42

Elizabeth crossed the lawn with a large carrier bag.

'You needn't take the food if it was only a decoy,' said Reggie.

'Better had,' said Jimmy. 'Don't want her thinking she's gone on an abortive mission.'

Chapter 6

Reggie's instructions were not dramatic. No men wearing pink carnations, no blindfolded drives along twisting country roads to isolated farmhouses. He was merely asked to go to Jimmy's house at eleven o'clock.

Jimmy led him into the living-room. There were cheap armchairs with wooden arms, a threadbare unfitted carpet and framed photographs of Jimmy in major's uniform.

'Sorry, room,' said Jimmy. 'Lost married quarters, better half deserts, chaos.'

'I understand,' said Reggie.

'Coffee?' said Jimmy.

They had coffee.

'Stay to lunch?' said Jimmy. 'Iron rations. Scrag end of lamb, sprouts, cheese.'

'It sounds lovely,' said Reggie.

'Sorry about cloak and dagger methods, Saturday,' said Jimmy. 'Secrecy of the essence.'

'I understand,' said Reggie.

'Someone I wanted you to meet before I spilled beans. Colleague. No offence, Reggie, but wanted to vet you.'

'This is all getting very intriguing, Jimmy. Who is this mysterious colleague?'

'Better you don't know.'

Jimmy walked to the window and stood rigidly to attention, taking the march past of a pair of robins.

'It'd be difficult not to guess who he is when I meet him.'

'Aren't going to.'

Jimmy swung round and looked Reggie straight in the face.

'He's doubtful of you. Wants to remain in background till we're sure.'

Reggie sipped his coffee and returned Jimmy's gaze.

'What are we planning to do – rob a train?'

Jimmy sat down, with his legs straight out in front of him.

'Few questions,' he said. 'Sorry, third degree not my line.'

Reggie fought down his rising annoyance. He was intrigued.

'Are you a right-thinking man?' said Jimmy. 'Are you one of us?'

'Well it rather depends what one of you is.'

Jimmy stood up, sat down and stood up again.

'Come upstairs,' he said.

Their feet clattered on the bare boards.

'Stair carpet ordered. Stuck in siding outside Daventry,' said Jimmy.

They entered a bedroom. It had no carpet or curtains, just a double bed and a cheap chest of drawers. On the chest of drawers there was a silver-plate cup engraved, 'The Haig-Tedder Inter-Services Squash Champion 1956 – Captain J. G. Anderson'.

'Sorry, bedroom,' said Jimmy, waving an apologetic arm. 'Division of trophies. Replacements not yet called up.'

Reggie smiled when he saw that Jimmy had arranged the bedclothes in an army-style bed-pack.

'Habit of lifetime,' said Jimmy. 'Old soldiers die hard.'

'Old habits never die, they only fade away,' said Reggie.

'Exactly. Something I want you to see.'

Jimmy reached under the bed and brought out a dead mouse.

'A dead mouse! Fascinating. I'm glad you called me over,' said Reggie.

'Not that.'

Jimmy held the mouse by its tail and dropped it out of the window.

'Starvation,' he said. 'House all ship-shape. No easy pickings.'

Next he brought out a khaki chamber-pot.

'Amazing,' said Reggie. 'A khaki chamber-pot.'

'Not that either!' said Jimmy with irritation.

He pulled out a tuck box marked J.G.A.

He opened it. It was full of rifles.

'Good God,' said Reggie.

'Know what those are?' said Jimmy.

'Rifles.'

There was a pause.

'What on earth are they for, Jimmy?'

'Secret army,' said Jimmy. 'Setting up vigilante army, watch dog, call it what you will. Yours truly and colleague, man I wanted you to meet, very sound chap.'

'Good God, Jimmy. What sort of secret army?'

'Army equipped to fight for Britain when the balloon goes up.'

Jimmy covered up the rifles, slid the tuck box back under the bed, pushed the khaki chamber-pot in after it, stood up, and inspected his hands for traces of dirt.

'Clean as a whistle,' he said.

'How the hell did you get them?' said Reggie.

'Friends, sympathizers, people who don't like the way the country's going. People who can read between the lines.'

Jimmy led the way down the bare wooden stairs. The ninth one creaked.

'Proper army's a joke,' said Jimmy. 'Pack of cards. Chaps like me, lifetime's experience, piss off. Replaced by acne-ridden louts from labour exchanges. Cutbacks. Obsolete equipment. Joke. Ha ha.'

The living-room seemed like a lush jungle of possessions after the bedroom.

'More coffee?' said Jimmy.

'Please.'

'Fancy whisky with it?'

'Yes, I do.'

'So do I. Wish I had some. Cock-up on the liquid refreshment front.'

He poured two coffees.

'Well, Reggie?'

'Well what?'

'Are you with us?'

46

'Jimmy?' said Reggie. 'Who exactly are you proposing to fight when this balloon of yours goes up?'

Jimmy looked at him in amazement.

'Forces of anarchy,' he said. 'Wreckers of law and order.'

'I see.'

'Communists, maoists, trotskyists, union leaders, communist union leaders.'

'I see.'

'Nihilists, terrorists, students, Dutch elm disease, queers.'

Jimmy's eyes were shining and a vein was pulsing in his forehead.

'Revolutionists, devolutionists, atheists, agnostics, long-haired weirdos, short-haired weirdos, vandals, hooligans, football supporters, namby-pamby probation officers, left-wing social workers, rapists, papists, papist rapists.'

'Oh, Jimmy . . .'

'Foreign surgeons, head-shrinkers who ought to be locked up, Wedgwood Benn, keg bitter, punk rock, alcoholics, glue-sniffers, *Play for Today*, squatters, Clive Jenkins, Roy Jenkins, Up Jenkins, Up everybody's, everybody who's dragging this great country into the mire. Chinese restaurants . . .'

'Jimmy, really.'

'Oh yes. Why do you think Windsor Castle is ringed with Chinese restaurants?'

There was a pause. The vein slowed. The fierce light in Jimmy's eyes faded. He sat down.

'I'd be the last to suggest that everything's perfect in Britain,' said Reggie.

'Good man,' said Jimmy.

'There's a lot wrong with our society.'

'So you're with us?'

It was Reggie's turn to stand up and pace the room.

'Do you realize who you're going to attract?' he said. 'Thugs. Bully-boys. Psychopaths. Sacked policemen. Security guards. Sacked security guards. National Front. National Back. National Back to Front. Racialists. Pakki-bashers. Queer-bashers. Chink-bashers. Anybody-bashers, Basher-bashers.

Rear-admirals. Queer-admirals. Fascists. Neo-fascists. Loonies. Neo-loonies.'

'Really think so?' said Jimmy eagerly. 'Thought support might be difficult.'

Reggie sank back into his chair. Jimmy stood up. It was as if the conversation couldn't continue unless one of them was standing.

'Well, are you with us?' said Jimmy.

'No,' said Reggie.

There was a long pause.

'You won't tell anyone, will you?' said Jimmy.

'No, I won't tell anyone, Jimmy.'

'Not even big sister?'

'Not even big sister.'

'Scouts' honour?'

'Scouts' honour.'

'Are you worried there may not be any money?'

'It isn't the money, Jimmy. 'It's just that I've had the offer of another job that's quite irresistible.'

'They're glad to see you back,' said Mr Pelham.

'The feeling's mutual,' said Reggie.

'I thought we'd seen the last of you with that bloody back of yours.'

'I couldn't keep away.'

It was the hottest day of the summer to date. Whenever Reggie swept a bit of pig shit into the ditch, crowds of flies buzzed angrily at this unwarranted interference with their luncheon.

Some pigs had been slaughtered and replaced. Was it just fancy, or did the new ones treat him more warily than those who had come across him before?

Perhaps these grotesque squealing creatures really did like him. Perhaps he really had found his métier at last.

He shuddered.

Chapter 7

C.J.'s invitation to lunch came as a complete surprise to Elizabeth. They went to the Casa Alicante, a new Spanish restaurant not a melon's throw from Sunshine Desserts.

'It's very private,' said C.J. 'The Sunshine Desserts rabble haven't caught up with it yet.'

David Harris-Jones was seated at a table close to the door, with a plump young lady. She was plainly and inelegantly dressed, in the hope that people would blame the effect of dumpiness upon her clothes rather than her body.

David Harris-Jones blushed, half stood up, half acknowledged them, and sat down again.

'Morning, David,' said C.J. 'Nice place, this.'

'Super.'

C.J. escorted Elizabeth to their alcove table. There were many arches, surmounted by wrought-iron entwined with plastic vines. The wallpaper was of false brick.

While David Harris-Jones was still trying to attract attention, C.J. had ordered aperitifs, food and wine.

'Are you interested in Wimbledon?' he said.

'Very,' said Elizabeth.

'I hear the women are threatening a boycott unless they get equal pay, and the men are threatening a boycott unless they get more than equal pay,' he said.

'So I hear,' said Elizabeth.

'If that's sport, I'm the Duchess of Argyll,' said C.J. 'Tell me, Elizabeth, do you believe in all this women business?'

Be bold. Weakness will not impress C.J.

'I don't believe that women can ever attain real equality,' she said.

'Of course they can't,' said C.J.

'That's why they must never give up the fight for it,' said Elizabeth.

The conversation was interrupted by the arrival of Tony Webster and Joan. They were steered to a table between C.J. and David Harris-Jones. David Harris-Jones half rose, the confusion growing.

'Morning, Tony,' said C.J. 'Nice place, this.'

'Great.'

'You were jolted by my answer, C.J.,' said Elizabeth. 'You didn't get where you are today by having women take the initiative. Especially when you are the boss and I am only a secretary. Why did you employ me, by the way?'

'Perhaps it was conscience,' said C.J.

'Perhaps it wasn't,' said Elizabeth.

Tony Webster was being served. David Harris-Jones was still trying to attract attention. Waiters are as aware of the pecking order as chicken farmers.

'Do you think women are really so unequal?' said C.J.

'Oh yes,' said Elizabeth. 'If Reggie had an affair with Joan, people would say: "Good old Reggie." If I had an affair, they'd be shocked. "Fancy Elizabeth letting herself down like that." '

Their first course arrived, whitebait for C.J., gazpacho for Elizabeth.

'Surely Reggie treats you as an equal?' said C.J.

'Reggie behaves like the main character in a novel,' said Elizabeth. 'It's about time I had a chapter to myself.'

They ate in silence for a few moments. David Harris-Jones was being served at last, and Tony Webster's hand met Joan's beneath the table.

The hands disengaged. Elizabeth caught Joan's eye and smiled. She felt that the smile came out as regal and patronizing. It hid the fear that Joan had had an affair with Reggie.

'I expect I'll be accused of being patronizing,' said C.J. 'But you are a very much more thoughtful person than I had supposed.'

'It's not been required of me,' said Elizabeth. 'I've been an appendage.'

'No longer?'

'Perhaps not. A dramatic development. Little woman fights back. Surrey housewife in Spanish restaurant chat holocaust.'

Tony Webster, the collector of dolly birds, was sexily but not indiscreetly sliding his right hand up Joan's left leg. Had Reggie done that?

At David Harris-Jones's table, the hands remained unengaged.

Their paella arrived, far too succulent a dish to precede an afternoon's work.

Elizabeth met C.J.'s eyes, and it was almost as if they were trying to smile but had forgotten how to do it after all these years, because smiling with the eyes is not like riding a bicycle.

The restaurant was full of the clatter of crockery and conversation. Far away, a loud crash was followed by unshaven Iberian oaths.

'More paella?' said C.J.

'Thank you.'

'You're a beautiful woman, Elizabeth.'

'Thank you.'

'Reggie doesn't appreciate how lucky he is.'

'Thank you.'

C.J. poured more wine. He indicated Tony and Joan with his eyes, then David and his plump young companion. Tony and Joan were talking in an animated if apparently trivial way. At David's table the conversation flowed like glue.

'Hanky-panky,' said C.J. 'I don't like it and I never will. Large lunches, erotic thoughts. The nation can't afford it. The International Monetary Fund would take a dim view. Would you like some trifle?'

'Please.'

C.J. ordered two portions of trifle.

'I didn't get where I am today by indulging in hanky-panky,' he said.

'I'm sure you didn't,' said Elizabeth.

The waiter brought the sweet trolley. They watched as if hypnotized as he gave them their trifle.

'I've got some papers at home that need to be sorted through,' said C.J. 'I wonder if you could come over some time and help me.'

'Certainly,' said Elizabeth.

'How about Saturday?' said C.J.

'Saturday,' said Elizabeth.

Chapter 8

'I don't like your working on a Saturday,' said Reggie.

'Nor do I,' said Elizabeth. 'But what can I do?'

'Especially when I'm working on Sundays,' said Reggie.

He was sitting at the kitchen table, finishing his last cup of coffee. His legs and back ached after a week at the piggery, and the washing machine and spin drier were going full blast, cleaning his pig-infested clothes.

'What time will you be back?' he said.

'I'm not sure,' she said. 'Mr Pardoe said there was a lot to do.'

'I thought your boss was called Steele.'

'What? Oh he is. He's lending me to Mr Pardoe.'

'It makes you sound like a library book.'

The sky was leaden and heavy summer rain drummed against the windows. There was no wind.

'I'll be back sooner if I take the car,' said Elizabeth.

She kissed him and left hurriedly.

Reggie walked to the shops. A lady J P drove through a puddle and splashed him.

'Hooligan,' he shouted.

'Wife away, Mr Perrin?' said J. F. Walton, family butcher and high-class poulterer.

'She's working,' said Reggie.

'Ah!' said L. B. Mayhew, greengrocer and fruiterer. 'Working, eh?'

Was that an innuendo? Reggie wouldn't put anything past a man who raised his tomato prices by 12p a pound at the weekend.

Home again, wet and muggy, Reggie prepared the dinner and listened to the cricket commentators valiantly waffling through the rain. Needless to say, England would have been batting on a perfect pitch before the largest crowd of the season.

The afternoon stretched endlessly before him, bereft of the three E's – Elizabeth, England, and *Emmerdale Farm*. Reggie's mind turned to a weekend a year ago. This was a Saturday, that was a Sunday. This had dawned wet, that had dawned sunny. That time it had been he and Joan. This time it was Elizabeth and . . .'

No! Elizabeth wasn't like that.

But then no more was he, and that hadn't stopped him.

'Oh belt up, Brian Johnston,' he cried, switching off the radio.

Silence, save for the dripping of rain and suspicion.

The Scottish-Hungarian boss, with the wooden leg, who drank like a fish! If his father came from Budapest, and his mother from Arbroath, he'd have a Hungarian name, not Steele.

Steele! Pardoe! False names! Liberal party leaders! An unconscious slip. A Clement Freudian slip.

She was having an affair. And after he had spurned Joan's advances for her sake.

Anger swept over him. He dialled Joan's number savagely, as if it was his telephone that had cuckolded him.

'Three-two-three-six,' said a man, sleepily.

The windscreen wipers hummed their monotonous symphony all the way to Godalming, and on the River Wey sad hirers of leaking cruisers played travel scrabble.

C.J.'s pile was a mock-Tudor edifice, a fantasy of timber, gable and ostentatious thatch, built on the profits founded on the sweat of men like Reggie Perrin. Elizabeth parked beside the privet pheasants, and pulled the Gothic bell-rope.

C.J. opened the door and stood resplendent in a velvet suit.

'Come in, modom. C.J. is expecting you,' he said with ponderous skittishness, leaving her waiting in the living-room with six paintings of ancestors – not C.J.'s ancestors, but presumably somebody's.

C.J. re-entered as himself.

'Elizabeth!' he said. 'Nice to see you.'

54

She sat on the settee, facing the generous fireplace which dominated the mock-Gothic room.

'Well, here we are,' he said.

'Yes, here we are,' she said.

'Champagne?'

'Champagne?'

'Why not?'

He poured champagne and joined her on the settee.

She began to feel uneasy.

'Well, here we are,' he said.

'Yes,' she agreed. 'Here we are. What about these papers that need sorting, C.J.?'

'First things first,' he said. 'More haste less speed.'

Her uneasiness grew. Could it be that he was bent on pleasures naughtier than the grape?

No. It couldn't be.

Not C.J.

'Where's Mrs C.J.?' she asked.

'In Luxembourg,' he said. 'More champagne?'

'No, thank you.'

'Very wise,' he said, pouring her another glass.

'Well, here we are,' he said.

'Yes.'

He *was* bent on pleasures naughtier than the grape. Elizabeth couldn't have been more surprised if she'd been told that Attila the Hun had rented a council allotment which was his pride and joy.

C.J. shifted along the settee towards her. She moved away.

'It's wet, isn't it?' she said.

'The champagne?' said C.J., puzzled.

'No. The weather.'

'Oh. Yes. The champagne's dry and the weather's wet.'

C.J.'s laugh was like the mating call of a repressed corn-crake.

'Nasty for them,' he said.

'For who?'

'I don't know. Them. One says: "It's nasty for them."

55

Meaning, I suppose, for the people for whom it's nasty because it's wet.'

She must know the worst. She must find out if there were any papers to sort.

'I am in a bit of a hurry,' she said. 'Can't we get down to it straightaway?'

The moment she had spoken, she regretted her choice of words.

'We'll get down to it after luncheon,' said C.J.

They dispatched the bottle and C.J. left the room.

He re-entered immediately.

'Luncheon is served, modom,' he said.

They lunched off cold duck, stilton and burgundy. When he had drained the last of his wine, C.J. smiled uneasily at Elizabeth.

'We'll get down to it in a minute,' he said.

They returned to the living-room. C.J./butler served coffee and mints. Elizabeth and C.J./host did justice to them.

'Now we'll get down to it,' he said.

He gave a long deep shuddering sigh, and produced a large pile of papers.

'Anybody in your firm called Thorpe?' said Reggie casually in bed that night.

'Not that I know of. Why?'

'Freud? Grimond?'

'What are you talking about, Reggie?'

The Milfords returned noisily from their snifter at the nineteenth.

'There seem to be a lot of people with the names of liberal MPs. Steele, Pardoe.'

'Oh yes. I hadn't thought of that.'

'No.'

On Monday morning Reggie pretended to oversleep. He was due at the piggery at half past seven, but he was still at home at eight o'clock.

The sun had returned, yet he handed Elizabeth her umbrella.

'Umbrella,' he said.

'Thank you,' she said.

He handed her her handbag.

'Handbag,' he said.

'Thank you,' she said.

'Have a good day at the office,' he said.

'I won't.'

'Give my love to Mr Steele and Mr Pardoe and any other members of the liberal party who may be present,' he said. 'And if any of them drink like fishes and ask you to work on Saturday tell them to stick their wooden legs up their baskets.'

Elizabeth ignored the attack.

'Have a good day at the piggery,' she said.

'I won't,' said Reggie.

Nor did he, because he did not go to the piggery. The moment Elizabeth had gone, he telephoned Mr Pelham.

'Mr Pelham?' he said. 'Reg here, Mr Pelham. It's me muvver. She's been taken ill. I'm all she's got, Mr P. Do you mind if I take the day off, like? . . . Thanks, Mr P. . . . Yeah, well, families are important. Very kind of you, Mr P., very kind . . . What? Without pay. Yeah, I understand. Oh, and Mr P.? . . . Give my love to the pigs.'

Over his piggery outfit he put a filthy old raincoat smeared with creosote stains. On his head he jammed a squashed gardening hat.

Thus disguised, he hurried along Coleridge Close. He caught sight of Elizabeth in Tennyson Avenue, followed her along Wordsworth Drive and down the snicket into Station Road.

He waited by the station bookstall until he heard the eight-sixteen come in. Then he rushed on to the platform and boarded the train.

At Waterloo he followed her down the platform. He was only dimly aware of the loudspeaker announcement, apologizing for the fact that they were seventeen minutes late, and blaming track improvements at Clapham Junction.

He lost her briefly on the concourse but caught sight of her again as she walked down the steps out of the station.

Imagine his speculations as he saw her plunge into the mean streets where the head office of Sunshine Desserts was situated.

Judge of his amazement and anger as he watched her walk towards the grim portals, pass beneath the lifeless clock, and disappear into the ignoble building with nary a glance at the bold letters that proudly flashed to an astonished world their familiar message: UNSHIN DESSERTS. He followed her up three flights of stairs, because the lift was out of order, and saw her enter the office where she worked.

The dreadful truth hit him immediately, and he knew what he had to do.

C.J. was staring grimly at his morning mail. The storm-clouds were gathering over Sunshine Desserts. Only he knew on what shifting sands the edifice was built, to coin a phrase.

His jaw relaxed as he thought of the sweet loveliness of Elizabeth Perrin. Perhaps she would be his confidante. Perhaps Mrs C.J. would be injured in Luxembourg. Nothing serious. Just a few weeks in hospital, followed by six months in a convalescent home.

Marion murmured something about Perrin and he said: 'Send her in.'

His face melted into a gentle smile, which froze when he saw Reggie.

'Morning, C.J.' said Reggie.

'Er . . . good . . . er . . . do . . . er . . . sit down.'

'No,' said Reggie.

'You can sit on the . . . er . . . they're new . . . Japanese.'

'I'd rather stand,' said Reggie.

The lunatic was wearing a filthy old hat and coat, but he didn't appear to have a gun. It didn't occur to C.J. that he had done nothing worthy of guilt. He had thought things worthy of guilt – and that was enough.

'It's about Elizabeth,' said Reggie.

'Let's not be hasty,' said C.J.

'She's working here,' said Reggie.

'I know. I gave her a job.'

'She's having an affair.'

'Let's discuss this like . . .'

'She told me she was working on Saturday,' said Reggie. 'Working my foot. I want you to sack her, C.J. And him.'

C.J. lit a cigar with shaking fingers.

'Him?' said C.J.

'Tony Webster.'

'Ah! Tony Webster.'

'Who did you think?' said Reggie.

'Who indeed?' said C.J. 'I was at a loss.'

'Secretaries always fall in love with their bosses,' said Reggie. 'So I've heard anyway.'

'Your story's pure hearsay,' said C.J. 'Though you know what they say: there's no smoke without the worm turning.'

'I can get proof,' said Reggie. 'I'll follow her next Saturday, if she tries that one on again.'

'Of course I know of Webster's reputation,' said C.J. 'His appetites.'

'Appetites?'

'I didn't get where I am today without knowing of Webster's appetites.'

'What do you mean, appetites?' said Reggie.

'Do sit down, and take that dreadful hat off,' said C.J.

Reggie sat in the little Japanese chair, and took his hat off.

'What appetites, C.J.?'

'Let's say he has a weakness for women of mature years,' said C.J.

'He's always with dolly birds.'

'A front, Reggie. I didn't get where I am today without knowing a front when I see one. And I suppose your wife is still quite an attractive woman.'

'She's a very attractive woman.'

'Yes, I suppose she is,' said C.J.

Reggie stood up.

'Will you sack them, C.J.?' he asked.

'I can't,' said C.J.

'You sacked me.'

'That's different.'

Reggie slammed his hat on his head and stormed towards
the door, the tails of his gardening coat flying in his slip-
stream.

'Careful,' said C.J. 'Look before you . . .'

But Reggie had slammed the door, so we will never know
how C.J. would have finished his sentence.

At five-thirty Reggie was to be seen hanging around the
end of the road, near the Feathers.

The aim of his vigil was to catch Tony and Elizabeth in
flagrante.

Tony came down the road alone. That looked bad.
Clearly the guilty parties were trying to avert suspicion.

Reggie approached him.

'Hello, Reggie,' said Tony.

Reggie punched him in the face. Tony staggered backwards. Reggie punched him again. Tony kicked out and
Reggie stumbled.

Reggie got to his feet. Tony watched him in amazement.
Reggie advanced to hit him again, and Tony punched him
in the face. Reggie butted Tony in the stomach, and Tony
gave him a bang on the back of the head.

Commuters hurried past the two grappling figures towards
the safety of their trains. Tony gave Reggie one more punch
and felled him before going down winded himself.

The two men bent gasping by the wall of the Feathers.
Reggie's squashed gardening hat lay in the gutter.

Joan hurried towards them anxiously.

'Oh my darling!' she said. 'My darling! What has he done
to you?'

'He hit me,' said Reggie and Tony in unison.

Both men held out their arms feebly. Joan embraced
Tony. They went into the Feathers for a drink. If the landlord hadn't known them he would have refused to serve
them.

'What have you been doing to my fiancé?' said Joan.

'Your fiancé?' said Reggie.

'Joan and I got engaged on Saturday,' said Tony.

'But I thought Elizabeth was with you on Saturday,' said Reggie.

'With me!' said Tony.

Reggie explained about Elizabeth's outing and the fictional loan of her from Mr Steele to Mr Pardoe.

Tony and Joan exchanged quick looks and remembered C.J.'s lunch with Elizabeth at the Casa Alicante.

Reggie bought large drinks to celebrate their engagement. Tony bought large drinks to celebrate Elizabeth's innocence. Joan bought large drinks to celebrate Reggie and Tony's buying of large drinks. Reggie and Tony bought large drinks to celebrate Joan's buying large drinks. The landlord bought small drinks to celebrate his profits.

Both men developed black eyes. Reggie's was the left eye, Tony's was the right.

When Tony went to the gents', Reggie said: 'I thought you loved me, Joan! That day in the office!'

'You spurned me,' said Joan.

'I hope you'll be happy,' said Reggie, and he kissed her on the lips. Her tongue slid into his mouth.

'We never quite made it, did we?' she said.

Reggie arrived home at a quarter past twelve, full of renewed happiness and love. He opened his mouth to tell Elizabeth the good news that she hadn't been having an affair, and a stream of incomprehensible noises issued forth. He laughed, lurched forward, tripped over Ponsonby, and fell, cracking his head against the nest of tables.

'Late,' he managed to say. 'Wandsworth failure at points.'

Then he passed out.

Quite soon he came round. She poured water over his face and gave him black coffee, and suddenly he was sober.

His other eye, which had struck the nest of tables, was coming out in another magnificent shiner.

And so, sitting in the kitchen with two black eyes, and a wet flannel pressed to his forehead, at a quarter to two on a humid July morning in the sleeping Poets' Estate, Reggie told Elizabeth of his unworthy suspicions, of his conversation with C.J. and his fight with Tony Webster. She seemed to find parts of the story unaccountably funny.

'Who *were* you with?' said Reggie.

'The firm's Luxembourg representative,' she said. 'He's over here on a training scheme. I did some typing for him in his flat in Godalming.'

She couldn't tell Reggie that she had been with C.J. She felt guilty even by association with his unspoken feelings.

She felt awful about lying, but she had eased her conscience slightly by mentioning Godalming.

In the morning Reggie limped into the yard of Pelham's Piggery thirty-seven minutes late.

Mr Pelham approached him. He was carrying a tin bath full of grain, and he looked at Reggie with amazement.

'You seem to have rubbed your mother up the wrong way, old son,' he said.

'Sorry?'

'She appears to have given you two black eyes.'

'Oh those,' said Reggie. 'It's sad really.'

He thought of his own dear kind gentle mother who had died ten years ago, and silently begged her forgiveness.

'She's going doolally,' he said. 'She's convinced she's Joe Bugner.'

'When did Joe Bugner ever give anybody two black eyes?' said Mr Pelham.

That evening three separate events occurred. Mrs C.J. broke a leg when she was knocked down by an ambulance in Echternach, Jimmy set off for his secret HQ, and in Swinburne Way a middle-aged man exposed himself to a schoolgirl with nine 'O' levels.

Chapter 9

Next morning there was a letter from Mark, and Elizabeth wore an unsuitable dress.

'You aren't going to work in that, are you?' said Reggie.

Elizabeth laughed.

'What's so funny?' said Reggie.

'You, trying to be pompous and self-righteous with two black eyes.'

'Darling, you can't wear that dress to work,' said Reggie, biting a piece of toast angrily.

'What's wrong with it?'

'It's too revealing.'

'Mammary horror shocks jelly workers,' said Elizabeth. 'Now can I finish Mark's letter?'

She finished the letter, handed it to Reggie and kissed him.

'Are you really going to wear it?' he asked.

'You're a stickler for convention all of a sudden,' said Elizabeth. ''Bye bye, darling. Have a good day at the piggery.'

'I won't,' he said.

After two and a half hours of mucking out, Reggie went for his tea break in the little brick hut provided. He had two colleagues, both surly. First one in made the tea in a large tin pot. The conversation consisted largely of four letter words, spiced with the occasional seven letter word.

On this occasion Reggie used neither four nor seven letter words. Instead he read Mark's letter.

'Dear old folks,' wrote Mark. 'I was amazed to hear that Martin Wellbourne was Dad all along. Fantastic news. Nice one. Ace. Wish I could see yer, honest.

'The weather here varies. Sometimes it's hot, but the rest

of the time it's bleeding hot. It can get a bit taters at night, though. The steamy heat of the jungle turns me on but none of the chicks in the company do. I may have more luck with the fellers. Failing that, baboons. Sorry, Mater.

'Houses – or should I say "huts"? (Joke!) – are quite good. Tonight we're doing *A Girl in My Soup* to some tribe or other, so quite likely there is a girl in the soup. Oh well, laugh, eh? No? Well we can't all be Einsteins.

'Last month we played to pygmies. Very small audiences. (Ouch!) We gave them *Move Over, Mrs Markham*, but it was over their heads. (Shoot this man!)

'Seriously, folks and folkesses, I miss yer all. Love to the mad major and the fat sister and the bearded wonder and the little monsters and good old Ponsonby and anyone else wot I forgot. There goes the five minute drum. I'm on in a minute. Cheers.'

'You're late,' said Tony.

'I stopped to feed the ducks,' said Elizabeth.

Tony gave her a look, then he had another look at her dress.

'I'm loaning you to David Harris-Jones today, if you don't mind,' he said. 'He's got a bit of a backlog with his trifles.'

'I'm yours to command,' said Elizabeth.

She went along the corridor to David Harris-Jones's office which was tiny but drab. While it was draughty in winter, it was baking hot in summer.

'Here I am,' she said.

David stared at her dress. His eyes almost popped out of his head.

'Super,' he said.

Tom and Linda called round unexpectedly that evening. Tom brought a bottle of his 1973 quince wine.

'You've got two black eyes, Reggie,' he said.

'I know,' said Reggie.

'He knows that,' said Elizabeth. 'There's no point in telling him that.'

64

Linda sat on the settee. Tom remained standing and cleared his throat.

'I've come round here to offer you a job, Reggie,' he said.

'I don't want charity,' said Reggie.

Linda nudged Tom with her eyes.

'It won't be charity,' said Tom. 'A man of your experience has much to offer.'

He sat down beside Linda and put an arm round her waist.

'I'm not a snob,' he said. 'But I don't like the thought of Linda's father working on a pig farm.'

'Nor does Linda's father,' said Reggie.

'I know you think being an estate agent's a boring job,' said Tom. 'But there are some quite exciting challenges in the world of property.'

'It's not as boring as pig farming,' said Reggie. 'I accept with grateful thanks.'

'Excellent. Well, who's for quince wine?' said Tom.

'Claret for me,' said Elizabeth. 'I expect the quince is as horrible as all your other wines.'

'Darling!' said Reggie. 'Darling!'

'No doubt Tom has many talents, which we just don't happen to have come across, but wine-making is not among them,' said Elizabeth.

'Darling!' said Reggie. 'Tom, I'm awfully sorry. I'm longing to try the quince wine.'

'What's up, mum?' said Linda.

'I think it's about time we told the truth,' said Elizabeth, and she left to fetch the claret.

'I am sorry,' said Reggie.

Tom opened the quince wine with some difficulty.

'How did you get your black eyes, Dad?' said Linda.

'A porker ran amok,' said Reggie.

'I'm not a pig person,' grunted Tom, imitating a hairy question mark as he grappled with the recalcitrant cork.

At last the bottle was open. Tom poured Reggie a glass.

'Aren't you having any, Tom?' said Reggie.

'I like the sound of that claret,' said Tom.

The evenings were drawing in, and already the light was fading.

Elizabeth entered with the claret, and three glasses.

'It's the last bottle,' she said.

Reggie sipped his quince wine cautiously. It was much better than the sprout wine, but revolting.

Elizabeth stood with her back to Dr Snurd's bloodshot representation of sunset at Faro, and read Mark's letter. When she had finished Tom said: 'Absence hasn't made me fonder of Mark's jokes.'

'Listen who's talking,' said Elizabeth. 'You've got about as much humour as the National Grid.'

'Darling, stop being rude to Tom,' said Reggie. 'He's come round out of the goodness of his heart to offer me a wonderful job and share his precious quince wine, which really is surprisingly good, though I don't know why I should say surprisingly, and all you do is insult him. It's a bit much.'

'It's all right,' said Tom. 'I'm under no illusions that either of you like me.'

'That's not true,' said Reggie.

'Yes it is,' said Elizabeth.

'Darling,' said Reggie.

'No,' said Linda. 'If mum feels that way, she may as well get it off her chest.'

'It's utter nonsense,' said Reggie. 'We're very attached to Tom.'

'The only thing that's attached to Tom is his beard,' said Elizabeth.

'Stop it,' hissed Reggie desperately.

'Try calling him a bearded prig like you used to,' said Elizabeth.

'That's true, dad,' said Linda. 'You did.'

'I may have done,' said Reggie. 'It was . . . it was a term of endearment. Good old Tom, the bearded prig.'

'Like pompous twit?' said Elizabeth.

'Yes!' Reggie smiled anxiously at Tom. 'Good old Tom. How is the pompous twit? That sort of thing. The sort of thing you only say to your friends. Shows how much I like you, eh, Tom?' He turned to Elizabeth and whispered: 'Shut up.'

Further conversation was prevented by a plane, carrying, it so happened, a party of Basle bank managers on their way to Aspreys.

'Sorry, what did you say?' said Reggie, shutting the french windows.

'I said we're on the flight path again,' said Tom.

They finished the claret and Tom rose to leave.

'I'm big enough to forget what's happened,' he said. 'Glad to have you aboard, Reggie.'

'Thank you,' said Reggie. 'And I'm sorry about . . .' he glanced at Elizabeth '. . . tonight.'

'It's all right for you to be rude,' said Elizabeth, 'but not me.'

'Well . . . you know . . . I mean at that time I was under pressure.'

'Perhaps mum is,' said Linda.

'It's different for a woman,' said Reggie.

'How?' said Elizabeth and Linda.

'It's unladylike,' said Reggie. 'It's embarrassing.'

'Oh God!' said Elizabeth and Linda.

Tom hastily poured the remains of the quince wine.

'Cheers, everyone,' he said.

'Oh shut up, Tom,' said everyone.

'Why are you doing all this?' said Reggie as they lay in bed in the dark.

'What do you think?' said Elizabeth.

'I don't know what to think,' said Reggie.

Elizabeth switched her bedside light on.

'Nothing can ever be the same again,' she said. 'You've got to understand that, Reggie. You've changed me. You've awakened a sleeping tiger.'

'Ah! Well, that's lovely. Who wants their wife to be . . .'

'Dull and ordinary?'

'No. Well, yes. I'm glad you're a tigress, darling.'

'You're terrified.'

'A bit. I mean can't you find a better way of being a tigress than insulting poor Tom? Can't we both find better ways together?'

'We can try,' said Elizabeth.

She kissed him and switched off her bedside light. Reggie switched his on.

'I'm going to read,' he said. 'No point in trying to sleep till the Milfords come back.'

There was a loud crash of splintering glass. Reggie went cautiously downstairs. A brick lay on the living-room carpet, and a pane of the french windows was shattered.

Attached to the brick was a message. It said, in childish capitals: 'Down with flashers.'

'You're pissing me about, old son,' said Mr Pelham. 'Pigs are conservative creatures. They don't like change.'

'I never knew there was so much to pigs,' said Reggie.

'People don't, Reg,' said Mr Pelham. 'People don't. Pigs are sensitive souls. How can you expect them to produce all that lovely gammon if they don't know whether they're coming or going?'

'I'm sorry,' said Reggie. 'Honest.'

'Goodbye, then, old son,' said Mr Pelham. 'Or is it only au revoir?'

'No it bleeding isn't,' said Reggie. 'It's goodbye.'

July drew towards its close, and the days were sunny with brief heavy showers.

Elizabeth behaved very well at the jelly unveiling, all things considered.

There were some eighty people in the Wilberforce Rooms at the Cosmo Hotel. Among them were C.J., Tony, David, the editor of the *Convenience Foodstuffs Gazette,* the jelly correspondent of the *Daily Telegraph,* three dieticians, one of whom had an ulcer, two photographers, a Bible salesman who was in the wrong room, nine people with a sixth sense for free drinks, six people with a ninth sense for free drinks, and several representatives of the catering distributive trades.

At the far end of the stuffy room there was a table, concealed beneath a large dust-cover.

Four pretty girls with tight bums and hard faces dispensed free drinks. Free drinks are never served, they are always dispensed, perhaps in the hope that the unattractive verb will discourage excessive consumption.

The girls had large shining suns pinned to their starched uniforms. They were the Sunshine Girls, hired by C.J. for three hours. In the evening two of them would become the elastoplast girls and the other two would become the machine-tool girls.

C.J. made a speech, explaining that the actor who was to have unveiled the new slim-line jellies had broken his foot.

Tony Webster spoke next. He opined that the jellies were great, and explained that the female singer hired to replace the actor with the broken foot had gone down with a summer cold.

David Harris-Jones gave it as his considered opinion that the jellies were super. He told a joke about an Englishman, an Irishman and a jelly. People talked during his speech, and he dried up. 'Everyone seems to be talking except me,' he complained to an audience of himself.

Nobody heard him explain that they were lucky indeed to have their unveiling done by that legendary celebrity, the Manager of the Cosmo Hotel.

The manager pulled back a rope, and the dust-cover rolled off, revealing eight large, lurid and faintly surprised jellies wobbling on their dishes.

Elizabeth laughed out loud, but not all that loud, and only for about a minute and a half.

She behaved very well, all things considered, at the jelly unveiling.

Reggie behaved very badly, all things considered, at Norris, Wattenburg and Patterson.

Were there mitigating circumstances? There were indeed, gentle reader.

The previous evening, at supper, an unpleasant incident had occurred.

It was Reggie's turn to cook the meal, and while they were eating their Chinese take-away, a brick sailed through the dining-room window and landed in the sweet and sour prawn balls. Reggie and Elizabeth were covered in glutinous orange-red sauce.

Elizabeth laughed.

'I don't see what's so funny,' said Reggie.

'We look like a scene from a Sam Peckinpah film,' said Elizabeth.

'I don't think it's funny having bricks thrown through our windows,' said Reggie. 'They think I'm the man who flashed at that schoolgirl. I'm going to be blamed for anything unusual that happens on this estate.'

'Never mind, you know you aren't the flasher, that's all that matters,' said Elizabeth. 'I mean you aren't, are you?'

'What a dreadful thing to say,' said Reggie. 'I'm your husband.'

'Husbands have flashed in the past, and no doubt husbands will flash in the future,' said Elizabeth, trying to clean some of the sauce from the tablecloth and chairs.

'But I'm me, darling. I'm not a flasher,' said Reggie. 'You know that.'

'I didn't think you were the sort of man who faked suicide by leaving all his clothes on Chesil Bank,' said Elizabeth.

Reggie grabbed her by the arm.

'I'm not the flasher,' he said.

'All right. You're not the flasher. I'm glad,' said Elizabeth. They cleaned the sauce off themselves in the kitchen.

'We'll have to move,' said Reggie. 'Bricks through windows, ostracised by neighbours who don't even know what the word means, outcasts in our own home.'

The next day Tom took Reggie out with him to show a prospective client a beautiful little cottage, situated in a clearing, surrounded by Chiltern beech woods. Facilities were few, and so the cottage was a snip at only £29,995.

'I'll offer twenty-nine thousand,' said the prospective client.

'Twenty-nine thousand, five hundred,' said Reggie.

'What?' said Tom and the prospective client.

'I'll offer twenty-nine thousand, five hundred,' said Reggie.

The prospective client drove off in a huff and an Audi, and Tom turned on Reggie.

'I offer you a job, out of the goodness of my heart,' he said, 'and the first time you come out with me, you outbid our customer. It's the ethical equivalent of a doctor making love to his patients.'

'I'm sorry,' said Reggie. 'I just couldn't resist it.'

'It's comparable professionally to a vet kidnapping his patients and entering them for Crufts,' said Tom.

'I'm sorry,' said Reggie. 'I suddenly felt that I needed a change.'

'You're going to get one,' said Tom. 'You're sacked.'

'Don't worry, Tom,' said Reggie. 'Much better prospects are opening before me.'

'This time it's got to be for keeps,' said Mr Pelham.

'It will be, chief. Honest,' said Reggie.

They walked out into the yard. It was a windy, cool, clammy day, the first day of the school holidays, and a caravan of schoolgirls was clopping down the lane from the Climthorpe School of Riding. Reggie waved and one of the girls waved back. This earned her a stern rebuke for unhorsewomanly conduct.

They looked down at a particularly enormous porker. The stench of the shit of four thousand pigs filled Reggie's nostrils.

'You can't beat red cabbage with pork,' said Mr Pelham.

'No, and nobody makes red cabbage like my old Dutch,' said Reggie.

Mr Pelham stroked the odoriferous giant affectionately. Reggie followed suit in more cautious vein.

'Crackling,' said Mr Pelham. 'Nice crisp crackling, that's the tops.'

'It's my favourite, is crackling,' said Reggie. 'My old Dutch makes cracking crackling.'

Mr Pelham gave him an affectionate scuff on the shoulder.

'Good to have you back, son,' he said.

On the last day in July, C.J. sat in his office facing David
Harris-Jones and Tony Webster. Between them was an
empty chair.

'We'd better see her now,' said C.J.

'Great,' said Tony Webster.

'Super,' said David Harris-Jones.

'There's nothing great or super about it,' said C.J. 'It's
sad.'

'Sorry, C.J.,' said Tony Webster and David Harris-Jones.

'Send her in, Marion,' barked C.J. into his intercom.

Elizabeth entered and sat in the empty chair. Tony and
David avoided meeting her eye.

'Did you dictate a letter to Elizabeth on the subject of
soggy sponges, David?' said C.J.

'I did,' said David Harris-Jones.

'What did you say?'

'I think – sorry, Elizabeth – ' began David Harris-Jones.

'Nothing to be sorry about,' said C.J.

'Sorry, C.J.' said David Harris-Jones.

'Get on with it,' said C.J.

'Sorry,' said David Harris-Jones. 'I said, as I recall: "Dear
Sir, I am sorry" – sorry, C.J., but I was sorry – "I am sorry to
hear of your complaint about soggy sponge in our frozen
trifle. We have received no previous complaints of similar
items deficient in the manner your describe – viz., sogginess of
the sponge – and I would respectfully suggest that there
must have been some error in the storing or unthawing of
the said article or articles.'

'A good letter, David,' said Tony Webster. 'Your best yet.'

'What did Elizabeth actually type, David?' said C.J.

' "Dear Sir," ' read David Harris-Jones.

He turned to Elizabeth.

'Sorry, Elizabeth,' he said.

He turned to C.J.

'Sorry, C.J.,' he said.

He returned to the offending missive.

' "Dear Sir," ' he read. ' "Thank you for your complaint

about soggy sponges. It makes the eleventh this week. The explanation is simple. Frankly, our sponges are soggy. The fault lies in your customers for buying over-priced, over-sweet, unhealthy, synthetic rubbish." '

'Did you write that, Elizabeth?' said C.J.

'Yes.'

'Did you forge David's signature and send it?'

'Yes.'

'Why?'

'It's the truth.'

'Do you think we'd survive for a week if we told the truth?'

'No.'

'I didn't get where I am today by telling the truth. Tony, David, you may leave.'

Tony Webster and David Harris-Jones stood up.

'You've handled this matter very well, both of you,' said C.J.

'Great,' said Tony Webster.

'Super,' said David Harris-Jones.

C.J. gave them a withering glance.

'Sorry, C.J.,' they said.

When they were left alone together, C.J. gazed questioningly at Elizabeth.

'Sorry, Bunny,' she said.

The previous Saturday Elizabeth had visited C.J. in Godalming once more. There had been more champagne, more cold luncheon, more gentle pantomime in which C.J. had played the dual role of butler and country gentleman.

She had spent the afternoon sorting papers and taking letters, but again she had felt that this was not the real purpose of the visit.

In the middle of the afternoon, C.J./butler had brought Earl Grey tea and scones, had retired briefly, and returned as himself to join in the feast.

'Thank you, C.J.,' she had said.

'My friends call me Bunny,' he had said.

Elizabeth had found it difficult to envisage C.J. having friends, and once she had made this prodigious leap of the imagination, she had found it impossible that they should call him Bunny.

She had taken a deep breath.

'Lovely tea, Bunny,' she had said.

Now, when she looked at C.J. squirming behind his rosewood desk, a man not built for fitting easily into chairs, she found even that distant intimacy incredible.

'I'm afraid I must ask you not to call me Bunny in the office,' he said. 'I didn't get where I am today by being called Bunny in the office.'

'I'm sure you didn't, Bu . . . C.J.'

'What is *de rigueur* in Godalming can be *hors de combat* in Head Office.'

'Quite right, C.J.'

The conversation ground to a halt. C.J. seemed unable to continue. He was a lion in moulting. He gazed at the picture of Krupp, in search of strength.

'I'm sorry, C.J.' she said.

He peered suspiciously at his desk, as if he feared it might be bugged.

'Your visits to Godalming were a pleasure,' he said. 'Just for you to be there, in my house. I gave thanks for the lucky chance that provided all those papers to be sorted. Then, when I heard that Mrs C.J. had broken her leg in Echternach, I felt like crying for joy. That sounds heartless, but it is not a serious fracture, and the scenery of the Upper Moselle is famed far and wide for its variety and beauty. I foresaw a golden summer, sorting papers in Godalming. Then you do this. Why? Why?'

'I couldn't help it,' said Elizabeth.

C.J. stabbed his body forward across his desk, held the offending letter aloft in his left hand, and barked: 'Did Reggie put you up to this? Is this Reggie's revenge? Are you his instrument?'

'Reggie knows nothing of this, C.J.'

C.J. came over and placed his hands on her shoulders.

'You can have a month's notice or the money in lieu,' he said.

74

'I think I'd prefer the money in lieu.'

'Yes. Very wise.'

He returned to his desk and sank awkwardly into his chair, as if he was an inexperienced crane operator and his body was a fragile cargo being lowered into the hold of a Panamanian freighter.

'I have only one more question,' he said.

'Yes, C.J.?'

'I'm afraid to ask it because I fear the answer.'

'Ask it, C.J.'

'Yes. What has to be faced, has to be faced.'

'You're absolutely right, C.J.'

'Never put off till tomorrow what you've already put off since yesterday.'

'Quite right, C.J.'

'Here we go, then.'

'Yes.'

'Off the deep end.'

'Quite.'

'Godalming's over, isn't it?'

'I'm very much afraid it is, Bunny.'

Reggie's back groaned in protest as he poured the swill into the trough. He stood up with difficulty and found himself staring into a stern version of Mr Pelham's face.

'Could I see you in the office a mo, Reg?' said Mr Pelham.

'Righto, guv'nor,' said Reggie.

They walked across the yard together.

'Bit taters for July,' said Reggie.

'It is on the cool side, Reg,' said Mr Pelham.

They entered the office. Mr Pelham sat down behind his cluttered desk. He did not invite Reggie to sit.

'Been hearing a few things about you,' said Mr Pelham. 'Full name, Reginald Iolanthe Perrin. Left your clothes on the beach, came back in disguise and married your wife again.'

'It would be idle to deny it.'

'In my book that makes you a nutter.'

Reggie shrugged.

'You've got nothing to say to that?'

.'That I have behaved in a manner that would not normally be called normal is beyond dispute,' said Reggie. 'But I don't think I'm a nutter.'

'All this taters and guv'nor gubbins you come out with is a load of cobblers.'

'Again, protestation would be to no avail.'

'Smart alick, aren't you?'

'No. Smart alicks don't work in piggeries.'

'Why do you work here?'

'It's the best job I can get at the moment. I think you'll agree I work hard and you've said yourself that the pigs like me.'

'They do, Reg. Pigs that are ailing become healthy at your touch.'

'I'm the Edith Cavell of the trough.'

'Come again.'

'I am the Florence Nightingale of the swill.'

Mr Pelham looked out of the window at his estate of mud and corrugated iron.

'The wife's dead,' he said.

'I'm sorry,' said Reggie.

'She stepped in front of a bus.'

'Oh dear.'

'Seven years ago. She'd only gone into Macfisheries to get some Finnan haddock. We'd just come back from France. I reckon she forgot that we drive on the left.'

'It's easily done,' said Reggie.

'You're not wrong, old son,' said Mr Pelham. 'She'd said to me: "Fancy some mussels like what we had at Dieppe?" Sort of trying to keep the holiday atmosphere going. I said: "I wouldn't say no, Ade." I reckon those mussels were her undoing, worrying if she could cook them. Sit down, old son.'

'Thanks.'

Reggie cleared a pile of final reminders and copies of the *VAT News* off the other chair, and sat down.

'I mean she was a good cook, but no Fanny Cradock.'

'Plain and honest.'

'In a nutshell, Reg. Damn it, you've got me talking like I haven't since it happened. Damn it, Reg, I like you. I don't take to people easily. I'm one of your in the pub for the last half hour three pints and don't say more than hello to anybody merchants.'

'Surely I don't have to leave just because you've found me out?' said Reggie.

'You like my pigs, don't you?'

'I adore your pigs, Mr Pelham. I like all pigs, but I adore yours.'

A tear rolled down Mr Pelham's face and landed on the *Observer Book of Animal Husbandry.*

'You're like me, old son. Torn in two. You like pigs and pork equally.'

'Yes.'

'Story of mankind, Reg.'

'Way of the world, Mr Pelham.'

Mr Pelham fumbled in a crowded drawer and produced a grubby snapshot of a loutish youth.

'That's my Kevin.'

'He looks a nice lad.'

'Do us a favour.'

Mr Pelham snatched the photo back and tore it in two.

'If I had my way he'd be in one of these sties and my pigs would be at Gravel Pit Lane Secondary Modern. Don't give me "looks a nice lad",' he said.

'Sorry.'

Mr Pelham produced from his wallet a snapshot of a pretty schoolgirl with a sensuous mouth.

'My Anthea,' he said. 'I favoured Janina but the wife thought it would sound as though we had ideas.'

'A bit of a handful?' said Reggie.

'You're joking. My Anthea's a girl in a million. Quiet, mind. My Anthea's my pride and joy. That's why I'm giving you your cards.'

'I don't see the connection.'

'It hasn't dropped, has it? Maybe I haven't explained it right.'

Mr Pelham took the photo of his Anthea back and re-placed it in his wallet tenderly.

'One of the things I heard about you wasn't too nice, old son,' he said.

'Good God. You think I'm the flasher of the Poets' Estate.'

'I think you could be, Reg. That's good enough for me. My Anthea comes down here. I'm not having her exposed to the risk. She's all I've got.'

'I understand,' said Reggie. 'I'd probably do the same.'

'Find me the flasher,' said Mr Pelham, 'and you can have your job back any time.'

Reggie walked briskly across the yard towards the lane.

'Say goodbye to the pigs if you like,' Mr Pelham called after him.

'No thanks all the same,' shouted Reggie. 'It might break my heart.'

'Good day at the office?' said Reggie, handing Elizabeth a gin and tonic.

'No. Good day at the piggery?'

'No.'

They sat on the settee. Reggie put an arm round Elizabeth's waist.

'I've been sacked,' he said.

'What?'

'Mr Pelham thinks I'm the flasher. I've been sacked.'

'I was just going to say that.'

'What – I've been sacked?'

'Yes.'

'How on earth did you know?'

'How did I know what, Reggie?'

'That I've been sacked.'

'No, no. I was going to say that I've been sacked.'

'You've been sacked?'

'Yes.'

'You mean we've both been sacked?'

'Yes.'

Reggie laughed. Then he stopped laughing abruptly.

78

'It isn't funny,' he said. 'Why were you sacked?'

Elizabeth told him.

'I just don't know what's got into you lately,' he said. 'You work for Sunshine Desserts, you tell me a pack of lies, you dictate stupid letters, you're extremely rude to Tom. I mean people just don't behave like that.'

'You did.'

'Ah. Yes, well, that was a bit different.'

'Why?'

'Well I mean ...'

'Because you're a man?'

'Well, yes, that. But I mean I was under pressure.'

'Perhaps I've been under pressure, Reggie. I've been through some strange experiences.'

Reggie put his arm round her tenderly. They sat in silence in the pleasant, tasteful, conservative room. Reggie's eyes roved over the brown Parker Knoll armchair, over the piano that nobody played now that Linda had left home, over the fluffy white three piece suite, and the ghastly pictures of the Algarve.

'I'm sorry I suspected you of having an affair on those Saturdays,' he said.

'That's all right,' said Elizabeth. 'I once thought you were having an affair with Joan, that time I was in Worthing.'

'Oh well, that's all right, then,' he said.

'You weren't, were you?'

'Of course I wasn't. How could I, with Jimmy and Mark and Tom and Linda and the Black Dyke Mills Band downstairs.'

'So where was Joan?' Elizabeth asked quietly, withdrawing from Reggie's grasp.

'Well ... er ...'

'Upstairs?'

'Sort of.'

'How sort of? In a bed?'

'Sort of.'

'And why was Joan sort of upstairs in a sort of bed?'

Reggie hesitated.

'Migraine?' he suggested.

Elizabeth shook her head.

'All right,' said Reggie. 'We did intend to, as it were, but I'd just decided that I didn't want to, as it were, when all those people came round and we couldn't, as it were. It's been the only time, darling, and I love you.'

Elizabeth put her arm round him, and gave him her tacit, tactile forgiveness.

'What was his name?' said Reggie.

'Who?'

'The man you worked for on Saturdays, with whom nothing happened. The Luxembourg representative.'

'Oh. Him. Er . . . Michel Dubois.'

'Michael of the Woods. How romantic.'

'Yes.'

'Did he fancy you?'

'I rather think he did,' said Elizabeth, and to her chagrin she blushed.

Reggie kissed her.

'We're together,' he said.

'Yes.'

'Things can't get any worse.'

'No.'

'If we hadn't both been sacked, and we hadn't both suspected the other of an affair, and I hadn't got the remains of two black eyes, and we weren't getting bricks thrown through our windows because I'm being mistaken for the flasher, I'd be happy,' he said.

Elizabeth kissed him.

'I have an amazing feeling that everything is going to go well from now on,' he said.

A brick sailed through the window and struck him a glancing blow on the forehead.

'That was the last turn of the screw,' he said when he came round.

Chapter 10

The day that would have been August Bank Holiday, had the government not changed it, was brilliantly sunny and hot. Some of the newspapers even removed 'Phew, what a scorcher!' from their dust-covers, and the nation was informed, in one of those abstruse parallels so beloved of meteorologists, that it was hotter in Tewkesbury than in Cairo. Well done, Britain. We can still pull them out, when the chips are down.

Reggie and Elizabeth were having dinner in the garden with Linda and Tom, who were setting off for Cornwall on Wednesday with their infants. Tom had brought a 1972 blackberry wine.

'It's the best wine you've ever produced, Tom,' said Reggie.

'I'm glad you like it,' said Tom.

'I wouldn't go that far,' said Reggie.

'I think it's lovely,' said Elizabeth. 'I don't know how you can be so rude, Reggie.'

Linda remained silent. After five years of Tom's wine she had nothing left to say. At first she had thought that it would improve with practice. Then she had kidded herself that it was improving. Now she knew that it hadn't been, and that it never would.

'I think we should stop being rude about Tom's wine,' said Elizabeth.

'A pound fine for the next person who's rude about Tom's wine,' said Reggie. 'And that's more than the wine is worth.'

'One pound, dad,' said Linda.

Reggie handed over a pound note.

Behind them, the french windows were open wide. Three of the panes had been boarded up, following brick attacks.

'Are you still going to move?' said Linda.

'No,' said Reggie. 'We're going to stick it out.'

'So losing your job with me was all for nothing,' said Tom.

'What are you going to do, dad?' said Linda.

Reggie squeezed Elizabeth's hand.

'That's really why we've asked you round tonight,' he said. 'To launch our new future.'

He smiled at Elizabeth. Elizabeth smiled at him.

'Just look at that sunset,' he said.

The sky over Elizabeth Barrett Browning Crescent was an indigo jungle.

Reggie took another sip of wine.

'Come on. Spit it out,' said Tom.

'Too late. I've drunk it,' said Reggie.

'A pound, dad,' said Linda.

Reggie handed over his second pound.

'This family really is infuriating,' said Tom. 'It takes half an hour to get anything out of you.'

'That's because they know how it annoys you,' said Linda.

'Teasing is indicative of childish minds,' said Tom.

'Hatred of teasing is indicative of a lack of humour,' said Linda.

'Children, please!' said Elizabeth. 'We are here to break some happy news to you.'

A container train rattled through Climthorpe Station, and a shrew rustled through the lupins in Reggie's garden.

'Since our talents are limited,' said Reggie, 'and our company is often held to be a liability, Elizabeth and I have decided to form ourselves into a limited liability company. Here is the design for our letterhead.'

He handed Tom a sheet of paper. It was headed: 'Perrin Products Ltd. A member of the REC Group of Companies. Head Office – Vortex House. Managing Directors – R. I. Perrin, E. S. Perrin.'

'What are the REC Group of Companies?' said Tom.

'Reginald and Elizabeth of Climthorpe,' said Reggie. 'I thought it sounded good.'

'Where's Vortex House?'

'Here. Plenty of holes in the window panes.'

'You can't start a business like this,' said Tom.

'I think it's lovely,' said Linda. 'You're being churlish, Tom.'

'You aren't a businessman.'

'You've noticed.'

Ponsonby rushed across the lawn in futile pursuit of a starling.

'What are you going to produce?' said Linda.

'There are a few details still to be worked out,' said Reggie.

'Good God, you can't start a business without knowing what kind of a business it is,' said Tom.

'What we're looking for is a concept,' said Reggie.

'Reggie says when you start a business what you need is a new concept,' said Elizabeth.

'Actually that is absolutely right,' said Tom.

'You see, Tom. Dad knows all about it and it's going to be a tremendous success,' said Linda.

A song thrush added melodious assent from the willow tree.

'I hope you don't mind my asking,' said Tom, 'but how much capital do you have?'

'Less than two hundred thousand pounds,' said Reggie.

Tom whistled.

'As much as that!' he said.

'About a hundred and ninety thousand pounds less than that,' said Reggie.

'That's not much to start a business,' said Tom.

'No,' said Reggie. He sipped his blackberry wine. 'Where did you pick these blackberries?'

'Near Henley.'

'They don't travel.'

'Pound.'

Reggie handed over his third pound. Elizabeth cleared away the dinner things. The last rays of the sunset were extinguished, and crickets rubbed their legs together lethargically in the warm dusk. Tom lit a cigar.

Ponsonby purred, a bat fluttered silently by, and far above them an aeroplane winked. Even before he spoke, everyone sensed that it would be Tom who broke the silence.

'Adam said an amusing thing today,' he said.

There was a pause.

'Well I thought it was amusing anyway,' said Tom. 'At the time.'

There was another pause.

'For his age,' said Tom, extinguishing the last pale cinders of anticipation. 'He was kicking Jocasta. It put me in a ticklish position, because we can't condone violence but we believe that discipline is useless unless it is voluntary. Anyway I said: "Adam, old pricklebonce, do you really think it's a good idea to kick your smaller sister like that?" and he said: "Yes," so I said: "I see. And why are you kicking her?" and he said: "Because I'm an urban gorilla." I didn't want to laugh, in case it seemed as though I was approving of his kicking Jocasta, but I just couldn't help myself. You see, he'd heard the phrase urban *gue*rilla, and he'd thought it was some kind of animal, urban *go*rilla.'

'They're funny at that age,' said Elizabeth.

And the crickets rubbed their legs together.

Reggie and Elizabeth spent long days trying to find the ideal product for Perrin Products to produce. The fine weather gave way to teeming rain which turned the cardboard in the broken panes to a mushy pulp. The papers forbore to mention that it was still hot in Cairo but pissing down in Tewkesbury.

'What we need,' said Elizabeth over their frugal lunch, 'is something that's cheap to make and expensive to sell.'

'That shouldn't be too difficult,' said Reggie. 'Every day people are buying some enamel something from Taiwan that some Chink has sold for virtually nothing so that he can have a bowl of rice every second Thursday, covering it with something nasty and synthetic, calling it something tasteless and repulsive and selling it at extortionate prices at every up-market outlet from Lands End to John O'Groats.'

'The only thing you know is desserts,' said Elizabeth.

'Oh God, not desserts again,' said Reggie. 'I've devoted enough of my life to desserts.'

A fierce gust hurled itself against the windows.

'Poor Linda,' said Elizabeth. 'I hope they're all right in Cornwall.'

'Mind you,' said Reggie. 'I like the idea of producing amazingly successful desserts and driving Sunshine Desserts out of business.'

'What about health food desserts?' said Elizabeth.

Reggie laughed.

'Wheatgerm ices,' he said. 'Seaweed jelly.'

'Sometimes I don't think you're taking all this very seriously,' said Elizabeth.

'I'm trying,' said Reggie.

'It's our joint venture,' said Elizabeth.

'I know,' said Reggie.

The rain eased, and Elizabeth went to the shops.

Reggie sat cosily in the living-room, on that August afternoon, with one bar of the electric fire on. Ponsonby sat on the arm of his chair and stared at him with empty curiosity.

'Hello, Ponsonby,' said Reggie.

Ponsonby miaowed.

'What do you think we should make, Ponsonby?' said Reggie. 'At this moment, while we sit here, some people are busy making extra-wet-strength tissues and scientists are busy designing extra-extra-wet-strength tissues. People who were born into a world full of sunlight and beautiful flowers are sitting in smoky rooms deciding on brand names for sanitary towels. Aren't you sorry for them?'

Ponsonby miaowed.

'The point is, Ponsonby, that I am forty-seven years old and I devoted over twenty years of my life to making instant puddings. I don't want to waste the next twenty years. All I really want to do is cock one last snook, and go down with all guns blazing. Fair enough, Ponsonby?'

Ponsonby's gentle miaow seemed to say that it was indeed fair enough.

'Good man. Now let's watch *Emmerdale Farm* and see if Annie Sugden can stop Amos Brearly poking his nose in everywhere.'

Next day more rain swept in from the West. Linda and

Tom were sitting in the car, watching the sea hurling itself against the rocks. In the back seat, Adam and Jocasta were fighting.

On the other side of the glistening road the low stone frontage of the Fishermen's Arms promised warmth and good cheer.

'I like the grandeur of the elements,' said Tom. 'I don't like lying on the beach in the sun. I'm not a sun person.'

Linda opened the door of the car.

'Where are you going?' said Tom.

'I'm going to the pub,' said Linda. 'Sod the grandeur of the elements.'

'Wait!' said Tom.

Linda waited.

'I don't think that's a very good example to set our children,' said Tom.

'Sorry,' said Linda.

'We'll take them back to the hotel,' said Tom. 'Let the child monitoring service look after them.'

'I don't like doing that,' said Linda.

'Correct me if I'm wrong,' said Tom 'but I thought that was why we are paying twenty-eight pounds a week more than at the other hotel.'

'I didn't know I was going to feel like that,' said Linda. 'And it wasn't just that, anyway. There's the tennis court as well.'

'It's flooded.'

'I didn't know it was going to be flooded, and it was for the food as well. The Norrises said it was marvellous last year.'

'It was probably a different chef last year,' said Tom.

'No. The Norrises have got no palate.'

Adam and Jocasta resumed their fighting with renewed intensity.

'Look, Adam,' said Linda. 'Big wave. It may drown some sea-gulls.'

'Where? Where?'

A huge wave did indeed rise up out of the chaos.

'What did you say that for?' said Tom.

'To stop them fighting,' said Linda.

'By dangling the carrot of drowning sea-gulls? Lindy-plops! That's against everything we stand for.'

'I've stood for enough,' said Linda.

'Sea-gulls didn't drown,' complained Adam.

'Didn't drown,' said Jocasta.

'I'm sure the monitoring service will be very good,' said Tom.

'You know how we despise people who leave their children in the car while they have a drink,' said Linda.

'Sea-gulls didn't drown, mummy.'

'You know how we deplore the British attitude to children,' said Linda. 'That's one of the main reasons why we always holiday in France.'

'Oh, we're in France, are we?' said Tom. 'Oh look, there's a British car. Hey, they're driving on the wrong side of the road.'

'Shut up, Tom. You know what I mean. We've always been to France before.'

'Sea-gulls didn't drown. Sea-gulls didn't drown.'

'Seegles didn't drown.'

'No. Aren't you glad the nice sea-gulls are still alive to enjoy their din-dins,' said Tom.

'No,' said Adam.

'What's nice about sea-gulls?' said Linda. 'You were the one who said we should always tell them the truth about nature.'

The rain grew harder. A group in plastic raincoats rushed across the road into the pub.

'I expect the Smythe-Emberrys are entering a little Breton crêperie at this moment, the whole family together, lovely pancakes, wine . . .'

'Bollocks to the Smythe-Emberrys.'

'Tom! The children! Who's setting a bad example now?'

'Sorry. I don't think they heard,' said Tom. 'It's all my fault. I felt we should holiday in Britain this year as a gesture of economic faith. I didn't know it was going to be the wettest August since the Flood.'

'Bollocks to the Smy-Thinglebies,' said Adam.

'Blocks to Smythinbees,' said Jocasta.

'Adam and Jocasta should not learn to rely on us,' said Tom. 'We must prepare them for the harsh realities of life. They can't always be with us, in the nature of things. They've got to learn to live inside any society they come to, and that includes hotel child monitoring services.'

'Jocasta's wet herself,' said Adam.

'You really think if we left them at the hotel and went for a drink together we'd be doing it for their good?' said Linda.

The waves crashed angrily on the deserted beach. Rows of motorists watched in aspic.

'Wet knickers,' said Adam.

'We aren't just making excuses are we, Tom, because we want a drink. Search your conscience.'

'Wet knickers. Wet knickers.'

'I have searched my conscience,' said Tom.

'Wet knickers.'

'I say, old bungletwerp, do you really think it's a good idea to keep feeling Jocasta's knickers?' said Tom.

'Yes,' said Adam.

'All right then,' said Linda. 'We'll leave them.'

And that, dear reader, is precisely what they did. They went into the Fisherman's Arms and there was real ale and two different kinds of quiche and Tom was so happy that he gave 10p for the lifeboats.

'We won't have the quiche,' announced Tom. 'That belongs to our Home Counties persona. We'll have home-made Cornish pasties.'

The pub had low ceilings, a tiled floor, and a plethora of brass knick-knacks. At the bar there was a group of noisy locals, fighting with their elbows to keep a small reservation for themselves, and there were some bedraggled campers fulminating against the climate and the lavatory facilities on their various sites. And there was also Jimmy.

'Good Lord,' said Linda. 'There's Jimmy. Jimmy!'

Jimmy looked embarrassed to see them.

'Hello, surprise surprise,' he said. 'Big kiss. Hello, Tom. On holiday, are you?'

'Yes. You?'

'Yes. Annual leave, that sort of crack. August, Cornwall, dead loss. Well, well, well, how's my favourite niece?'

'Fine, Uncle Jimmy.'

'Less of the uncle. Makes me feel old.'

A very tall, bronzed lean man in his early fifties came over.

'Clive Anstruther. Crony of mine,' said Jimmy. 'Ex-army. We're *holidaying* together, aren't we, Clive?'

'Oh, yes, yes. Jimmy and I are *holidaying* together, yes. Cornwall, August, dead loss.'

Linda gave Tom a meaningful look which he tried to avoid but couldn't.

'Er . . . would you like a drink, or have you got some?' said Tom.

'Make room for a small pint,' said Jimmy.

'Scotch, please. Large or small. Up to you,' said Clive.

Tom struggled through the damp crowd to the bar.

'August, hate it. Crowds,' said Clive.

'Queues. Queue to park your arse,' said Jimmy.

'Why do you come here in August then?' said Linda.

'Ah! Good question,' said Jimmy.

'Excellent question,' said Clive.

There was a pause.

'Linda's my favourite niece,' said Jimmy, patting Linda on the backside.

'Well done,' said Clive.

'Can somebody help me?' said Tom from the bar.

'Reinforcements on way,' said Jimmy.

Jimmy took the glasses one by one from Tom and passed them over the heads of the campers. The bar smelt of beer, toasted sandwiches and drying clothes.

'Good man. Well done,' said Clive. 'Cheers.'

'Happy holidays.'

'Happy holidays.'

'Are you one of these schoolmasters?' said Clive to Tom.

'No,' said Tom.

'Oh,' said Clive.

There was a pause. The lanky adventurer appeared speechless with astonishment at discovering that Tom wasn't one of these schoolmasters.

'What are you then?' he said at last.

'Estate agent,' said Tom.

'Selling houses, that sort of thing?'

'Yes.'

'Well done.'

Jimmy's eyes met Linda's. They were the eyes of two people who can never forget that they have been to bed together.

'Here long?' he said.

'Two weeks,' said Linda. 'What about you?'

'Depends,' said Jimmy. Then he added in a low voice: 'Friday, here, twenty-thirty hours, poss?'

'We'll try,' said Linda.

Jimmy leant forward very slowly and planted a gentle kiss on Linda's forehead.

'Without Tom,' he whispered.

'What are you two whispering about?' said Tom.

'Family joke,' said Linda.

'Well done,' said Clive.

'Three steak sandwiches, one well done, one medium, one rare,' called out the barman.

'Here,' said a little bald man, trapped in a crowded corner in an orange anorak. He had a damp ordnance survey map spread on the table in front of him.

Clive and Jimmy provided a military escort for the sandwiches throughout their perilous journey from the bar.

'Rare,' said Clive.

'Me,' said the little bald man.

'Rare. Well done.'

'No, I'm well done,' said the wife.

'Well done. Well done,' said Clive.

Linda laughed till the tears ran. Tom couldn't understand what she was laughing at.

'Socialists niggers in woodpile in your caper?' said Clive to Tom.

'I voted socialist last time out,' said Tom.

'Well, duty calls,' said Jimmy, looking at his wrist, for he had sold his watch.

'Duty, on holiday?' said Linda.

'Ah. Yes. Sight-seeing fatigues,' said Jimmy. '14.30 hours. Polperro. Come on, Anstruther. Best foot forward.'

'Nice to meet you,' said Clive. 'Next time, my shout.'

As the two stiff-backed staccato veterans left the bar, the driver of the soft drinks delivery van entered.

'All hell's broken loose up at the hotel,' he announced. 'There's a gang of four year old hooligans charging around yelling: "Bollocks to Trust House Fortes." '

That evening, a man attacked a pretty young dental receptionist as she walked home across Climthorpe Cricket Ground. He chased her and flung himself upon her, in front of the scoreboard.

Unbeknown to him, however, the girl was on her way home from her karate class. She repelled his attack and even dealt him some heavy blows before he ran off defeated.

Memory plays strange tricks in moments of crisis. The girl was able to tell the police that the scoreboard had stood at 45 for 3, last man 17, but of her assailant she remembered nothing except that he was 'a bit odd-looking'.

News of the incident spread through Climthorpe like dysentery through a coach party.

'I wonder if it was the flasher,' said Reggie the next night as they sat in the garden in the dark. 'I didn't think flashers ever did anything. You know what Shaw said: "Those that can, do. Those that can't, flash." '

The storms had passed away. The night was warm, and the leaves were quite still in the faint sodium glow.

'If only you hadn't gone for a walk last night, you'd have had a perfect alibi,' said Elizabeth.

'But I did go for a walk,' said Reggie.

The headlights of a car turning into Coleridge Close lit up Ponsonby's green eyes as he lurked by the bird table.

'You don't think it was me, do you?' said Reggie.

'Of course I don't, darling. I just wish you hadn't gone for a walk.'

He had passed quite close to the cricket ground. What a wild scene it must have been – two dim figures fighting in the rain, the numbers on the scoreboard clanking, the poplars behind the pavilion bending before the gale.

'Why *did* you go for a walk?' said Elizabeth.

'You know why I went for a walk,' said Reggie. 'I went to clear my head. I went to try and get some inspiration about Perrin Products.'

There was a loud crash from the front of the house, as a brick sailed through their bedroom window.

Reggie hurried round the side of the house, crashing into the dustbins as he did so. By the time he had got round to the front the phantom brick-thrower had gone.

Mr Milford leant out of an upstairs window. His chest was bare.

'Can't you keep the noise down?' he shouted. 'Some people are trying to get to sleep.'

Linda sat in an alcove in the Fishermen's Arms, with Jimmy beside her.

'You got your late pass, then?' said Jimmy.

'I told Tom that I thought it was a good idea if we both had one evening out on our own, while the other one minds the children, because the hotel won't be responsible for them any more. He said nothing was of any value in a marriage unless it was shared. I said nothing was worth having unless you were prepared to sacrifice it. It would do him good to give up his quiet evening of marital bliss in the hotel with me and stand here all alone and miserable getting drunk on real ale. He agreed.'

Jimmy put his left hand on Linda's right hand.

'Happy with Tom?' he asked.

'It's hard work sometimes,' said Linda. 'I do love him, but he has to work out the social and economic consequences before he blows his nose.'

Jimmy bought another round.

'Looking very pretty, Linda,' he said.

'Thank you, Jimmy.'

'Nice chap, Clive. Top-drawer.'

'What are you really doing down here, Uncle Jimmy?'

'Holidaying. I told you.'

The barman cleared the empties off their table, and wiped it with a smelly cloth.

'These dead?' he said.

'What does it look like?' said Jimmy. When the barman had gone, Jimmy said: 'Nice lad.'

'You were rather abrupt with him,' said Linda.

'Tactics. Keep locals at arm's length.'

'Jimmy, what are you up to?' said Linda.

'Hush hush,' said Jimmy. 'Classified.'

A man and wife came to share their table without apology. Both were tall, pale, thin and miserable. Each had a dog. They spoke to their dogs but not to each other.

'Subject closed,' said Jimmy. 'Walls have ears.'

Linda bought a round, then Jimmy another. It got warm and crowded and noisy in the little pub. Jimmy's hand slipped on to Linda's thigh.

'Don't worry,' he said. 'No monkey business. All that in past.'

He slapped Linda's thigh twice.

'Don't like skinny young things,' he said. 'Nothing to them.'

The couple started to feed crisps to their dogs. The smelly dachshund favoured salt and vinegar, while smoky bacon proved more to the taste of the asthmatic pug.

The woman caught Linda's eye and said: 'They both like spaghetti.' It was the only remark either of them addressed to a human being all evening.

'Nice material. Smooth,' said Jimmy, running his hand over Linda's breasts.

'Jimmy!' said Linda, removing the hand firmly.

'Don't worry,' said Jimmy. 'Safe with me. Earlier incident forgotten. All records destroyed.'

A group of German aqualung enthusiasts entered the bar.

'Germans,' said Jimmy.

'You have Ruddles beer?' said their spokesman. 'You have please Marstons? You have Fullers ESB? You have Theakston's Old Peculier?'

'Arrogant swine,' said Jimmy. 'What do they know about English beer? It's all the same anyway.'

'They seem quite nice to me,' said Linda.

'Lull the enemy,' said Jimmy. 'Then whoosh. U.K. caput. Oldest trick in book. Lucky some of us aren't asleep.'

'What do you mean, Jimmy?'

'Said too much already. Same again?'

'Haven't we had enough, Jimmy?'

'Nonsense. Only live once.'

Jimmy bought two more drinks. Linda noticed that he was weaving more than somewhat. He couldn't take his drink any more.

'Between you me and gatepost,' he said. 'Glad Sheila's gone. Good riddance to bad rubbish.'

'Jimmy!'

'Rat leaves sinking ship.'

'Jimmy!'

'News for her. Last laugh on me. This ship isn't sinking.'

'Jimmy, what *are* you up to?'

'Said too much already.' Jimmy put his mouth very close to Linda's ear, and whispered: 'Dog-loving friends. Could be journalists.' And then he stuck his tongue in Linda's ear.

'Sorry,' he said. 'Out of bounds. Never happened.'

He smiled at the dog-lovers.

'My favourite niece,' he said.

The last bell went.

'One for the road,' said Jimmy.

'No,' said Linda.

'Insist,' said Jimmy.

'Well I'm getting them,' said Linda.

'Compromise,' said Jimmy. 'You pay, I fetch. Scrum at bar.'

When he returned he was walking even more unsteadily.

'Salt of the earth, Sheila,' he said. 'Not her fault. Army

wife, long hours, mess dinners, other wives, married quarters, foreign parts. Poor cow!'

'Try and forget her,' said Linda.

'Best wife in the world,' said Jimmy. 'She'll be back.'

He put his arm round Linda.

'Want to kiss you all over,' he said.

'Jimmy!'

'Not going to. Discretion better part of valour.'

The couple left with their dogs.

'They didn't look like journalists to me,' said Linda.

'Never do. That's the clever part about it,' said Jimmy.

They crossed the road and stood on the low sea-wall, watching the phosphorescence on the water. There was a full moon, and the breeze was from the south.

Four young people were having a noisy midnight swim, with much splashing.

'You can tell me now,' said Linda.

'Government work,' said Jimmy. 'Ministry of Defence.'

'Doing what?' said Linda.

'Told you too much already,' said Jimmy. 'Totally new form of detection. Radar obsolete.'

He slipped his hand into Linda's and squeezed it.

'Lovely night,' he said. 'Fancy a stroll? All above board. No funny stuff.'

They walked up the cliff path. There were litter-bins every three hundred yards. The wind began to freshen, and a cloud covered the moon.

Linda tried to support Jimmy, because she knew that he was drunk. But her legs wouldn't do what she told them.

They stumbled and fell, in the long dewy coarse grass of the cliff-top. Jimmy kissed her and she didn't resist.

He fumbled with her clothes. Grasses like whipcord pricked her naked thighs.

'It's prickly,' she said.

'Golf course over there,' said Jimmy. She pulled her tights up and they walked on to the close-cropped fairway of the 368 yard eleventh. Both of them were breathing hard.

'Green nice and smooth,' said Jimmy.

And so they lay by the lip of the eleventh green, on the lush well-watered grass, and came together in ecstasy. The green had a slight borrow to the right, but neither of them noticed.

'Oh darling,' said Jimmy. 'Oh my beautiful beautiful darling.'

The clouds cleared once more, and gentle stars twinkled on them. As his frustrated body exploded in meteors of delight Jimmy clenched his hand round something hard that lay to his right.

'All I've got,' he said. 'You're all I've got.'

At the moment of exultant climax his clenched hand moved, the hard object turned, and he switched on the stopcock on the water sprinklers.

The sprinklers began to rotate, there was a gentle hissing sound, and they were drenched in fine spray.

The re-arranged August Bank Holiday was cool and grey. Reggie went for a walk, right to the far end of the Poets' Estate, where the spacious detached houses gave way to a council estate on the right, and the beginnings of a neo-Georgian cock-up on the left. The Show House stood alone, tiny and sad, in a sea of mud and rubble.

He walked fast, loping excitedly along. Nobody spoke to him, for he was an outcast, and this suited him, because he was working out an idea, and nobody wants to be interrupted by cries of 'Hello, Reggie, think we'll win the test match?' when he is working out an idea. Who can say how many of his theorems Euclid would ever have completed if everyone had cried out 'I say, why don't you and Mrs Euclid come and make up a bridge four next Tuesday?' all the time?

He walked along Masefield Grove, Matthew Arnold Avenue, Shelley Lane and Longfellow Crescent (Unadopted), returning via Dryden Drive, Anon Avenue and Swinburne Way. And while he walked he found the concept that he was looking for – an idea so ridiculous that it could not succeed, yet not so absurd that he could not produce

96

arguments in its favour, to persuade Elizabeth and his bank manager and the finance companies that it had a sporting chance of success.

'Trash,' he said to Elizabeth on his return.

'What?' she said.

'Grot,' he said.

'I haven't got the faintest idea what you're talking about,' she said.

'The name of our shop,' he said.

'What shop?' she said.

'My plan is to make and sell rubbish,' he said.

'What on earth do you mean?'

'I plan to make things that are of no value,' he said, 'and sell them in our shop at high prices to people who will find them of no possible use whatsoever.'

'Come on, what are we really going to make?'

'I mean it, Elizabeth.'

Elizabeth gazed into his face and saw that it was so.

'Oh Reggie,' she said. 'I thought all that was over. I thought we were serious about this.'

'I am being serious,' said Reggie. 'What do you want me to do, something utterly conventional? I spent twenty-five years being conventional. Do you think I've been through everything just so that I can be conventional all over again? What would you have me produce – bulldog clips? Perrin's epitaph in a country churchyard: "Here lies Reginald Iolanthe Perrin. He made 196,465,287,696 bulldog clips, and they were all exactly the same."?'

'I don't want you to make bulldog clips,' said Elizabeth. 'There are a lot of other things in life apart from bulldog clips.'

He leant forward and stroked her hair.

'The world is absurd,' he said. 'The more absurd you are, the more chance you have of success.'

'People aren't complete fools,' said Elizabeth. 'They'll find out our stuff's rubbish.'

'They'll know all along,' said Reggie. 'We'll put a notice in the window: "Everything sold in this shop is totally useless."

We can sell Tom's wine, Dr Snurd's paintings, your father's old books. All rubbish.'

He went to the cardboard-speckled windows and looked out over the grey Bank Holiday afternoon. It had begun to rain.

'All over the estate, at this moment,' said Reggie, 'people are listening to the Radio Two road works report: "There's a ten mile tail-back at Gallows Corner." And they'll feel all warm inside, because they're not stuck at Gallows Corner with the masses. "We aren't sheep," they'll all think.'

'Don't change the subject,' said Elizabeth. 'The point is, why on earth should people buy utter rubbish?'

'People like rubbish,' said Reggie. 'Look at Christmas crackers. People would feel they'd been done if the jokes were funny and the little plastic knick-knacks worked. Look at punk rock. And how many times do you hear people say they must rush home because there's the worst film they've ever seen on the telly? They brought out a silent LP in America. It sold well. People who dislike noise played it on juke-boxes.'

He switched on the radio. There were seventeen-mile jams at Tadcaster and Keswick, and two-hour delays at Tadcaster.

'Switch it off, darling,' said Elizabeth.

Reggie switched it off.

'It'll be fun,' he said. 'We'll give them a run for their money.'

'That's just the trouble,' said Elizabeth. 'We'll be giving them a run for our money.'

'Don't worry, darling,' he said. 'We'll make our fortunes.'

He kissed the top of her head.

'You just see if we don't,' he said.

The bank manager was sympathetic. If it was up to him personally, he would lend Reggie money like a shot. Certain things which needn't be mentioned had happened. A certain ruse concerning credit cards had been perpetrated last year, and as a result credit facilities had been withdrawn. This was now forgotten. There had been the matter of the will of the late Reginald Iolanthe Perrin, who had turned out not to be dead after all. Then there had been a Mr Martin Wellbourne who had opened an account, paid cheques in and out, developed a healthy overdraft and generally behaved like a model client. Nevertheless, he did not exist, and this was against bank regulations. The banks are broadminded, they will overlook minor peccadillos both financial and moral, especially moral, but there are limits. They cannot permit their clients not to exist. Where would it end if they did? Anybody who was anybody would protest if anybody who was nobody could open a bank account. But even this could be skated over, if it was up to the bank manager personally.

But the manager was responsible to the bank, and they could not at the present moment in time regard Reggie as a man of impeccable financial probity. No doubt they would if it was up to them. But unfortunately it wasn't up to them. They were responsible to the government. The government were decent chaps at heart, despite what everybody said. If it was up to them, they would turn a blind eye to Reggie's misfortunes. Unfortunately however it wasn't up to the government. The government's hands were tied. They were responsible to the International Monetary Fund, and without actually saying so the manager intimated that the International Monetary Fund was a load of foreign bastards.

The finance companies were no more helpful. When Reggie told them that his plan was to make and sell rubbish, they couldn't get rid of him quick enough.

He found a small shop on an unprepossessing site off the wrong end of the High Street, between a pet shop and an architect's office. The seven building societies refused to give him a mortgage. He went to two friendly societies but they were both extremely unfriendly.

C.J. was alarmed to get Reggie's call. Did it mean that he had found out about Elizabeth?

Reggie's appointment was for eleven-thirty on 2 September, and C.J. fortified himself with a medicinal brandy.

The knock came promptly on the dot.

'Come in,' said C.J. in a masterful voice belied by a slight croak.

Reggie entered. He looked diffident rather than angry, and a wave of relief swept over C.J.

Reggie sat in the Japanese chair.

'I'll come straight to the point,' he said. 'There's no sense in beating about the bush.'

'You're talking my language,' said C.J.

'Yes. I . . . I wondered if you could lend me some money,' said Reggie.

A cold certainty struck C.J. It was blackmail.

Reggie explained what he wanted the money for. C.J. looked at him in amazement.

'So what sort of a sum did you have in mind?' said C.J.

'It's up to you, C.J. I was thinking of . . .' Think big, Reggie. You must think big with C.J. 'Something in the region . . .' Pitch it too high and then bring it down. '. . . of . . . er . . . thirty . . . er . . .'

'Thirty?'

'Thousand pounds.'

'Thirty thousand pounds!!'

'Yes,' rather squeakily.

It was blackmail. Reggie knew all about Godalming, the butler, the bogus papers endlessly sorted by an unsuspecting Elizabeth, the name Bunny. She had told Reggie in all innocence, and he, knowing C.J.'s reputation for ruthlessness and as the ultimate defender of the world against hanky-panky, had recognized the innocent tale for what it was – dynamite.

But he had to be sure.

'Did you find out anything more about the business of Elizabeth and the . . . er . . . Tony Webster?' he said.

'Yes, I did. She wasn't with Tony Webster at all.'

'Ah!'

It was a chap who was in your neck of the woods, C.J.'

'Really? Cigar?'

C.J. pushed the box towards Reggie and Reggie took a fat Havana.

'Godalming,' said Reggie.

'Ah, yes, Godalming,' said C.J. 'Quite.'

'She didn't do anything wrong, of course,' said Reggie. 'Ostensibly she'd gone there to work, and that was all she did. But I think really he needed her as female company. I think he felt lonely with his wife so far away in Luxembourg.'

'Quite.'

C.J. admired the delicacy of Reggie's approach, the way in which he spared C.J.'s feelings by making out that he was talking about a complete stranger. The man was a gentlman as well as a nutcase.

'Thirty thousand pounds, you said?'

'Yes.'

C.J. wrote out a cheque for thirty thousand pounds, and handed it to Reggie. Reggie tried to hide his astonishment as he pocketed it.

'It won't bounce,' said C.J.

'Of course not,' said Reggie.

'No further demands, you understand,' said C.J.

'You make it sound as if I'm blackmailing you,' said Reggie.

Despite her misgivings, Elizabeth helped Reggie prepare for the grand opening of Grot. He spent his days making such alterations as were necessary to the interior of the shop, while she stayed at home, making the things that they would sell.

Dame Fortune, that fickle jade, gave certain indications that she looked kindly upon the venture. Reggie put twenty-five pounds on a horse called 'R.I.P.' in the Sanilav Novices Chase at Haydock Park. He won two hundred and thirty-two pounds and eighty-five pence. Emboldened, he put fifty pounds on a horse called 'Golden Rubbish' in the Sello-tape Handicap Hurdle at Ayr, and won four hundred and sixty-two pounds seventy-seven pence. Further em-boldened, he put a hundred pounds on a horse called 'Reggie's Folly' in the Hoovermatic Challenge Cup at Sand-own Park, and won nine hundred and eighty-one pounds thirty-three pence.

Tom, who had not been told that the shop was dedicated to the sale of rubbish, was flattered when Reggie suggested using it as an outlet for his home-made wines.

Dr Snurd was equally pleased when invited to part with ten paintings of the Algarve.

The grand opening was fixed for November the twelfth. Soon it was September the twenty-fifth. Not quite so soon it was October the third. A bit later still it was October the twelfth.

One month to go. Feverish alterations. Frantic preparations.

There was still time before the opening for two major incidents to occur.

Chapter 11

The first major incident was set in motion by an article in
the *Telegraph* colour supplement, giving details of some of
the private armies that were lying low all over Great Britain,
waiting for the balloon to go up.

Some of these organizations were formed by fanatical
right-wingers, usually in isolated premises on the Celtic
fringe. Others were formed by fanatical left-wingers, usually
in dilapidated premises in decaying inner cities. One, the
Army of Moderation, was run by fanatical middle-of-the-
roaders from a council house in Hinckley.

The only one that interested Elizabeth was the one that
was run by Colonel Clive 'Lofty' Anstruther and Major
James 'Cock-up' Anderson 'somewhere in the West
Country'.

A family conference was planned for nine o'clock that
evening. The venue was the living-room of Reginald and
Elizabeth Perrin's desirable residence in Coleridge Close,
Climthorpe.

Coffee and biscuits were served by the charming hostess.

Reggie freely admitted his prior knowledge of Jimmy's
para-military pretensions.

'He offered me a job in it,' he said.

'You might have told me,' said Elizabeth.

'Darling, he swore me to secrecy.'

'Maybe we could have stopped him.'

'I don't think so.'

'We could have tried.'

Tom stood by the french windows. The curtains were
drawn.

'Reggie's right,' he said. 'Even though Jimmy's army is a
violation of everything we hold most dear, Reggie's right.
In our non-violent fight against it, we must always put indi-

103

vidual morality before the common good. That is the only weapon we have.'

'You have been listening to "Individual Morality and the Estate Agent",' said Reggie. 'Next week's programme in our series, *Morality and the Professions,* is entitled: "Chartered Accountants and the Humanist Quandary." '

'This is serious, Reggie,' said Elizabeth.

'He told me he was working for the Ministry of Defence,' said Linda.

'When?' said Tom.

'That day I went out on my own in Cornwall.'

'You never told me,' said Tom.

'He swore me to secrecy.'

'I do think you might have told me.'

'You said it was right for Reggie not to tell,' said Linda.

'Yes, but I'm your husband.'

'So what? Mum's Dad's wife.'

'I'm sure we're all very grateful for being reminded of these relationships,' said Reggie. 'It could prevent quite a few muddles.'

'Please!' said Elizabeth. 'Please! We're supposed to be talking about my brother, who's made a complete fool of himself. There it is in the paper. James "Cock-up" Anderson. I'm going down there to bring him back.'

'He won't come,' said Reggie.

'I know how to deal with him.'

'You'll have to deal with Clive "Lofty" Anstruther as well.'

'We must go there straightaway,' said Elizabeth.

'I can't go now,' said Reggie. 'The shop's opening in less than a month.'

'Hang the shop,' said Elizabeth. 'He's my brother.'

'Linda's the one to go,' said Reggie. 'I don't know if you know it, Linda, but Jimmy's got a soft spot for you.'

'I know it,' said Linda.

'Where Linda goes, I go,' said Tom, who was still standing by the curtains, as if to emphasize that he wasn't one of the immediate family.

'Reggie and I'll go,' said Elizabeth. 'There's plenty of time to work on the shop later. Do we know where Jimmy's headquarters are?'

'We went for a walk on the golf course,' said Linda.

'Was that when it rained?' said Tom.

'Rained?' said Linda.

'You remember. You got soaked to the skin,' said Tom.

'Oh yes. Yes, it poured.'

'We didn't have a drop at the hotel,' said Tom. 'Of rain, I mean. I wrote to the met office about it. They said it must have been an isolated local shower and thanked me for my vigilance. They said the individual can be part of a worldwide network of observations that include satellites, weather ships and meteorological balloons.'

'Fascinating,' said Reggie. 'How dull my correspondence is by comparison. I must write to Dale Carnegie and take a correspondence course to improve my correspondence.'

'May I continue my story about the golf course?' said Linda.

'Please do,' said Elizabeth.

'Riveting so far,' said Reggie. 'The bit about the sudden shower was the best bit.'

'Come on. Finish your story, Plobblechops,' said Tom from his safe vantage point.

Linda swung round and glared at him. The lights blinked to a distant flash of lightning.

'Are you insinuating that the delays are my fault?' she said.

'I'm not insinuating anything,' said Tom. 'I'm pointing out that you have the floor.'

'I don't. You're still talking,' said Linda.

'I'm only talking to tell you that you have the floor,' said Tom. 'I was just trying to hurry things up.'

'You're slowing things down, Tom.'

'Will you both shut up and then we can hear Linda's story,' said Elizabeth.

'How can we hear her story if they've both shut up?' said Reggie.

'Jimmy and I made love on the eleventh green,' said Linda.

Everyone was silent. Tom gawped. Elizabeth turned pale.

'Not really,' said Linda. 'But I had to get your attention somehow. No, the only thing that happened was that he pointed inland, roughly north-west I should think, and said their place was over there.'

'We'll leave in the morning,' said Reggie.

Reggie and Elizabeth set off for Cornwall early the next morning in unsettled October weather, and pulled up in the spacious car park of the Fishermen's Arms five minutes before lunch-time closing.

Reggie ordered a pint of real ale and a gin and tonic. Only then, having established them as typical pub customers, did he make inquiries about Clive 'Lofty' Anstruther and James 'Cock-up' Anderson.

'Tha what? Oh aye, that'll be them rum buggers live at Trepanning House,' said Danny Arkwright, licensed to sell beers, wines and spirits.

'Keep themselves to themselves,' said Annie Arkwright, licensed to live with Danny Arkwright in marital bliss. 'They never say nowt to nobody.'

'They're not widely liked,' said the landlord. 'Incomers, tha knows. We're right canny folk wi' incomers round here.'

'Excuse me,' said Reggie, 'but aren't you incomers yourselves?'

'Running a pub's different,' said the landlord. 'We're in t'public eye, like. In t'limelight. What's tha want wi' them, any road?'

'I'm Mr Anderson's sister,' said Elizabeth.

'Oh. Sorry if I've said owt I shouldn't have, luv.'

'Not at all.'

'All I know is, they play it right close to t'chest. Even built letter-box by t'road for postman. There's probably nowt to it but I reckon they're playing funny buggers.'

'Where is this Trepanning House?' said Reggie.

'It's off main Truro road. A few miles inland, on t'right.

Typical old farmhouse. It's hidden from t'road in a bit of a dip. You can't miss it.'

Danny Arkwright offered them an after-hours drink.

'We'd better get on,' said Elizabeth.

'Well, just a pint,' said Reggie.

It had been decided that Reggie should go alone to Trepanning House. His aim would be to arrange a meeting between brother and sister at which Colonel Clive 'Lofty' Anstruther was conspicuous by his absence. Now that the time was drawing near he wasn't looking forward to his mission. Another pint was most welcome.

They sat on bar stools in the empty bar full of dead glasses. The landlord and his wife talked of how happy they were. They didn't miss the grime of Rotherham at all. Why should they? Of course the chip shops weren't much good in Cornwall. No scraps. But anyway they were all going Chinese in Rotherham. And of course they missed the fortnightly trip to Millmoor to see United.

'Late fifties, early sixties, by, we had some that could play,' said the landlord, 'Ironside in goal. Lambert, Danny Williams.'

'Keith Kettleborough,' said his comely spouse.

'Oh aye, Keith Kettleborough,' said the landlord.

'But it's much cleaner here,' said the landlady.

'Oh aye, much cleaner,' said the landlord.

'Better for the kids,' said the landlady.

'What? There's no comparison,' said the landlord.

'He was a ninety-minute player, was Kettleborough,' said the landlady.

'Oh aye, I've got to give him that, he was a ninety-minute player all right, was Kettleborough,' said the landlord.

Reggie nodded his agreement. It was nice to sip his pint and agree that Kettleborough was a ninety-minute player. If only he didn't have this business of Jimmy to sort out.

'Well, I'd better be on my way,' he said.

'Oh aye, tha'd best be off,' said the landlord.

'Be careful now,' said the landlady.

*

The light was already fading as Reggie drove cautiously up the track towards Trepanning House. The track was pitted with holes that were filled with muddy water, and half way along it was totally blocked by a fallen tree.

He ploughed on in his Wellington boots. Trepanning House was a bleak and comfortless granite house, square, sturdy, unadorned. No welcoming light came from its windows. No comforting animal sounds came from the tumbledown barns and byres.

The ill-tempered sunset died petulantly. The wind howled. On all sides were the derelict towers of old tin workings and in the distance the hills of china clay stood against the evening sky like miniature snowy Dolomites.

Reggie rang the bell three times, but there was no reply. He knocked and knocked, but Trepanning House was deserted.

He crossed the silent farmyard, his feet squelching in cloying mud. There was a brief lull in the wind. A dog barked on a distant farm.

Cautiously Reggie entered the first of the barns. A beam swung across the doorway and struck him on the back of the head, and a huge cage descended around him.

When he came round he was lying on a camp bed in a bare bedroom with peeling wallpaper and a flaking ceiling, and Jimmy was sitting anxiously at his bedside. A one-bar electric fire was making no impression on the chill, damp air.

'He's come round,' called out Jimmy.

'Well done,' came a distant voice.

'My trap worked a dream then,' said Jimmy.

'Yes,' said Reggie wryly, feeling the bumps on his head gingerly.

'Sorry about that,' said Jimmy. 'Not aimed at you. Aimed at intruders.'

Jimmy helped him downstairs. When he had phoned Elizabeth and was seated in an armchair in front of a wood fire, with a brandy in his hand, he began to feel better.

There was a shabby white carpet, two armchairs, a burst

108

sofa, an occasional table and a heavily scratched oak bureau. Beside the fireplace there was a brass fire-tongs.

'I don't see much sign of your secret army,' said Reggie. 'Are things going badly?'

'Very much the reverse,' said Jimmy. 'Fully operational within the twelve-month. Can't say much. Security. Suffice to say, supporters from many quarters – press, city, a leading non-commercial TV company.'

'Money pouring in,' said Clive. 'Donations large and small.'

'Welcome recruit though,' said Jimmy.

'Oh I haven't come to join you,' said Reggie. 'I couldn't join your crazy outfit.'

If looks could kill, Clive's eyes would have got fifteen years.

'Elizabeth read about you in the paper,' said Reggie. 'We've come down to try and persuade you to change your mind.'

'Not an earthly,' said Jimmy.

'She wants to talk to you,' said Reggie.

'No can do,' said Clive. 'Not on.'

'I must see her, Clive,' said Jimmy. 'She's my sister.'

'Absolutely right,' said Clive. 'Good soldier needs a happy mind.'

'Beam worked a treat,' said Jimmy.

'Why have you set up such an elaborate trap?' said Reggie.

'Don't want people nosing around,' said Jimmy.

'Journalists,' said Clive. 'Place is stiff with journalists.'

'Police,' said Jimmy. 'Anarchists. Do-gooders. Bird-watchers. Nosey-parkers in general.'

'On the surface, absolutely normal household,' said Clive.

'No sign of secret activities,' said Jimmy, dropping a log on to the fire. 'No one would ever guess there's a huge armoury hidden in the Dutch barn.'

'Sssssh!' said Clive.

'Sorry,' said Jimmy.

'Don't you think,' said Reggie 'that the average nosey-parker in general might think there was something to hide here when he found paths blocked by fallen trees and beams and cages trapping him when he ventured into barns?'

There was a pause.

'Point, Clive?' said Jimmy.

'Point, Jimmy,' said Clive.

It was half past eleven before they arrived at the Fishermen's Arms, and the lights in the bar had been dimmed. Despite this more than twenty people were still drinking.

'She's upstairs,' said the landlady. 'You're stopping here. Room three.'

Reggie bought drinks and the offer of ham and eggs was warmly accepted.

And so they ate ham and eggs in a little bedroom with daffodil-yellow wallpaper and a matching bedspread. An extra chair was produced, the electric fire warmed the room more than adequately, and the rain and wind soon seemed far away.

Jimmy was shy and embarrassed in Elizabeth's presence.

'Sorry upset you,' he said. 'Not object of exercise.'

'It was all in the papers,' said Elizabeth. 'They called you James "Cock-up" Anderson.'

'Words,' said Jimmy scornfully.

On the bedside table there was a Bible and a copy of the *Cycling News* for July.

'Be honest, Jimmy,' said Reggie. 'Have you honestly got any remote chance of being effective even if your opportunity ever comes?'

Jimmy glanced round the trim, bright little bedroom as if hoping to flush out a few journalists. Then he lowered his voice until it could barely be heard above the wind.

'Breach of security,' he said. 'Clive would kill me if he knew. Clive and I running one cell. Organization has three other cells. Big man head of whole caboosh.'

'Who is this big man?' said Reggie.

'Secret,' said Jimmy. 'Even I don't know.'

'Who does know?'

'Clive.'

Reggie turned the pages of *Cycling News* idly.

'What's your aim, Jimmy?' he said. 'You can't use private armies to influence democratic politics. Do you want a dictatorship?'

'Mussolini . . .'

'. . . made the trains run on time, and the frequency with which we are reminded of it suggests that he didn't achieve all that much else. Personally I am prepared to suffer British Rail to preserve even the tattered remnants of freedom.'

'Question, Reggie,' said Jimmy. 'You, clothes on beach, Martin Wellbourne, etcetera, etcetera, expression of discontent?'

'Yes.'

'Everything in garden not rosy?'

'By no means.'

'My way, different from yours.'

'Very different.'

Reggie glanced quickly through an article entitled: 'By Tandem to Topkapi.' There was a picture of a plump couple in shorts standing beside their tandem in front of the famous museum, giving the thumbs up.

The landlady came in to clear away the ham and eggs.

'Were they all right?' she asked.

'Lovely,' said Reggie.

'Top-hole nosh,' said Jimmy.

'You can keep your frogs' legs,' declared the landlady.

'You certainly can,' said Reggie.

'He says am I to give you any more to drink?' said the landlady.

'I'll have a pint,' said Reggie.

'Pint wouldn't go amiss,' said Jimmy. 'Scottish wine, help it on its way.'

Reggie ordered pints for himself and Jimmy, a gin and tonic for Elizabeth, a large whisky for Jimmy, and drinks for the landlord and his wife.

'Did you hear that?' said Jimmy when the landlady had gone. 'National pride. Still there.'

'Don't you get a lot of your support from the area where

national pride spills over into out and out racialism?' said Reggie.

Jimmy proved evasive. The conversation flagged. The landlord entered with a tray of drinks.

'That's right,' he said. 'You're as snug as bugs in rugs.'

He handed round the drinks.

'Question?' said Jimmy.

'Aye?' said the craggy licensed victualler cautiously.

'Are you a racialist?'

'Tha what? I bloody am not. I can't be doing with it.'

'Do you think there are many racialists in England?'

'Listen. There's this darkie playing for Rotherham reserves, built like a brick shithouse – sorry, luv.'

'That's quite all right,' said Elizabeth.

'One match, there's a big crowd 'cos they're giving away vouchers for cup-tie. There's this yobbo stood standing in front of me, and he yells out: "You're rubbish. Go back where you came from, you black bastard." Sorry, luv.'

'That's all right,' said Elizabeth.

'Where *did* he come from?' said Reggie.

'Maltby,' said the landlord. 'Any road, couple of minutes later, darkie beats three men and scores. T'game continues and this yobbo shouts out: "You're useless, Chadwick. Give it to the black bastard." Now is this yobbo a racialist? Course he isn't. Otherwise why would he want to give t'ball to t'darkie? He'd want to starve him of t'bloody ball, wouldn't he, if he was a racialist? Course he would.'

'He shouldn't call him a black bastard, though, should he?' said Reggie.

'He was a bloody black bastard,' said Danny Arkwright. 'He was as black as the ace of spades. Now, listen. This is t'way I look at it. Let's take t'case of a white man. We'll call him Arnold Notley, for sake of argument. Now Arnold Notley, he works down Rawmarsh Main. He's got nowt against darkies, Chinks, Ities, the lot. They're all right by him. Now Arnold Notley, he goes down to t'Bridge Hotel, right, for a pint and a game of fives and threes, and he finds it full of darkies and Chinks and Ities and I don't know what yelling and shouting all over the bloody shop like let's face it they do and the stink of garlic and curry and I don't know what else besides. He doesn't like it, does he? Course he doesn't. He says: "fuck me." Sorry, luv.'

'That's all right,' said Elizabeth.

'He says: "Oh dearie me, I think I'll try the Anchor." Now let's take t'other side of bloody coin. Let's take your Sikh. Let's call him Bishen Ram Patel, for sake of argument. Now Bishen Ram Patel, he lives in Madras. And he says to his missus: "Oh dear, Mrs Patel. I am feeling the Indian equivalent of right pissed off. I think I'll go down to the Curry and Sacred Cow for a yoghurt and tonic." Down he goes, he opens t'door and it's full of bloody miners from Greasbrough. And this miner, he says: "Hey up, owd lad, does tha fancy a game of fives and threes, our Bishen?" He wouldn't like it, would he? It's human nature.'

There was a brief silence. Reggie and Elizabeth and Jimmy sipped their drinks.

'Do you think this country's finished?' said Jimmy.

'Course I do,' said the landlord. 'It's forced to be. Finito. Caput. Mind you, I daresay we could mess along for another five hundred years not knowing it. We're second division. Crap. Relegation fodder. The Japs and Germans are light years ahead of us. We just don't rate. We come nowhere. There's only one thing to be said in this country's favour. It's still the greatest bloody country in the world to live in.'

'Do you think it will remain so?' said Jimmy.

'I bloody don't and all. It can't do. We're waiting for North Sea Oil. Well, I look at it this way. T'oil'll give us breathing space to get in a bigger jam even than what we are in now.'

'Chap comes along,' said Jimmy. 'Secret army. Supporters. Money. Right ideas. Before you can say Jack Robinson, Britain great again.'

'I'd support him,' said the landlord. 'I bloody would and all.'

'Supposing that meant the overthrow of democracy?' said Reggie.

'Democracy?' said the landlord. 'Democracy's finished. It's a dead duck. I look at it this way. I was a socialist. Now I run a pub. I'm a conservative. Why? Self-interest. What sort of a bloody system's that? No, I'd abolish democracy tomorrow if it was me.'

'How?' said Reggie.

'Referendum,' said the landlord.

'Enough said,' said Jimmy. 'Downstairs, drinks all round.'

On the residents' stairs Jimmy turned to Elizabeth and said, 'Still a crazy scheme?' and Elizabeth shrugged helplessly.

They drank until half past four in the morning. Jimmy got drunk and talked about Sheila's betrayal and the army's betrayal. Danny and Annie Arkwright got drunk and said that you could stick Cornwall – Cornwall was very nice if you liked scenery, but there was nothing in the whole county to compare with the view of the Don Valley between Sheffield and Rotherham at night, with the furnaces blazing, great sparks of steel lighting up the M.1 viaduct, smoke belching from the chimneys of Steel, Peach and Tozer. Elizabeth got slightly drunk and worried about Mark in Africa, and whether Linda was happy with Tom, and how Reggie would take the inevitable failure of his project, and how Jimmy would take the inevitable failure of his project. And Reggie got drunk and saw somewhere in the recesses of his tired and confused mind an answer to the problems of life. The answer was crystal clear but it was both too simple and too subtle to be put into words, and the nearer he got to expressing his knowledge of it, the further away it went, and it seemed to suggest that he was quite wrong to be opening his shop called Grot, and in the morning he would be able to put it all into words and solve his own and everyone else's problems.

In the morning it wasn't clear at all. In the morning the answer eluded him entirely.

In the morning Mrs Arkwright said: 'I look at the sea and I think, "Why didn't we come to Cornwall in t'first place? Why did we waste all that time in t'grime and filth of Rotherham?"'

In the morning they drove Jimmy to the beginning of the track that led to Trepanning House. He didn't want them to go any further.

'Glad we had a chat,' he said. 'Clear the air, no crossed wires.'

'Take care of yourself, Jimmy,' said Elizabeth.

'Love to Linda. See you all soon,' said Jimmy, and he looked an old man as he trudged up the muddy track in the grey October morning.

The second major incident occurred two days before the opening of Grot. A twenty-two-year-old secretary was found raped and strangled in the little park behind the library, quite close to the High Street.

Reggie was working late that night, putting finishing touches to the shop. He was alone.

Chapter 12

At nine o'clock, on the morning of 12 November, Reggie opened the doors of Grot. No celebrity attended the ceremony. There was no waiting queue outside the door.

He walked across the street, and stood looking at the shop. It was a small Victorian two-storey terrace building, with several broken slates on the roof. Above the door, he had painted the word GROT in rather untidy signwriting.

In the window was a sign saying: 'Every single article sold in this shop is guaranteed useless.'

He sat in the shop with Elizabeth. Outside, the morning mist cleared to reveal a grey sky that was better hidden.

Nobody came in. Hardly anybody even passed by.

'Nobody's coming,' she said.

'It doesn't look like it. You go home, darling, and build up the stock.'

'Oh, Reggie,' she said. 'What have we done?'

There were tears in her eyes. He kissed her and she went home.

What had he done?

He had made a complete fool of himself. He'd thought to cock a snook, show his indifference on a grand scale. What arrogance. He deserved to end up with a dim dusty back street shop that nobody would ever visit.

At ten-seventeen he had his first customer, a middle-aged woman, of dowdy mien.

He longed to tell her that they were closed, and never open up again.

'Good morning, madam,' he said instead. 'Can I help you?'

'I'm just looking,' she said.

'Certainly, madame. Look as much as you like. Feast your eyes.'

He saw the stock through her eyes. It was a pathetic display. Even judged as a collection of rubbish it was rubbish.

There were fifty bottles of Tom's wine, and ten of Dr Snurd's paintings of the Algarve. There were some square hoops made by Elizabeth, some puddings which Elizabeth had cooked and which were advertised as 'completely tasteless', a selection of second-hand books including *Methodist Church Architecture*, *The Artistic History of Rugeley and Environs*, *Memoirs of a Bee-keeping Man*, *The Evolution of East European Office Equipment*, and *Bunions in History*, some old tennis rackets with all the strings removed, some cracked pottery over which Reggie had put the notice, 'These aren't seconds. They are all thirds', and a very complicated board game with a map of a town, a police car, an ambulance, six taxis, eight bollards, two sets of traffic lights, twelve counters, a dice, and no rules.

'It's all rubbish,' said the woman.

'Absolutely,' said Reggie. 'It's complete and utter rubbish.'

'It's stupid.'

'Thank you, madam. I'm glad you appreciate our efforts. This is the first of such shops. In time we will have a chain of them stretching from Inverness to Penzance, not to mention the continent of . . .'

But the woman had fled.

At eleven thirty-eight he made his first sale, the only one of the morning.

A balding man in his early fifties, with a little head and stick-out ears, the sort of man who drives at twenty-five miles an hour in the middle of the road, read Reggie's message three times as if he couldn't believe it. Then he entered the shop rather timidly.

'Everything in this shop is rubbish, is it?' he said.

'It's crap,' said Reggie.

'I see. What's the point of that then?'

'There's so much rubbish sold under false pretences,' said Reggie. 'I decided to be honest about it.'

'You've got a point there,' said the man with the stick-out ears. 'There you have got a point. This wine's useless, is it?'

'Repulsive.'

'Only I'm looking for something for the wife's sister.'

'And you don't like her?'

'I can't stand the sight of her.'

'Does she like wine?'

'Oh yes. She fancies herself something rotten with the old vino. Château this, Riesling that, morning, noon and night.'

'In that case,' said Reggie, 'I think she'll hate any of these.'

'Which do you think she'd dislike the most?'

'I think she'll find the blackberry wine at one pound ten mildly unpleasant, if you can run to something worse the turnip is pretty nauseous, that comes at one pound thirty, but if you can afford it, the sprout wine is really horrific.'

'How much is that?'

'One pound seventy-five, but it is disgusting.'

'So the worse a thing is, the more it costs?'

'Exactly.'

The man with the stick-out ears examined the bottle of yellow-green liquid. He seemed irresolute.

'And this is really revolting, is it?'

'Have you ever tasted weasel's piss strained through a mouldy balaclava helmet?'

'I can't say I have, no. It tastes like that, does it?'

'Worse.'

'I'll have it.'

The man with the stick-out ears handed Reggie two pounds. He rang up the till flamboyantly. His first sale.

'I can guarantee dissatisfaction,' he said, handing his customer the bottle wrapped in tissue paper. 'But if she should by any chance like it, I'll refund your money.'

'Thank you.'

At the door the customer turned.

'Odd shop isn't it?' he said.

'Extremely,' said Reggie with a pleasant smile.

'It fills a gap,' said the customer.

At lunch-time, before eating his ham sandwiches in the

empty shop, Reggie put another notice in the window. It said: 'Hundreds of ideal gifts for people you hate.'

At a quarter past three he made his second sale. An over-dressed, rather fat woman with peroxide hair and thick lips entered the shop. On first impression she appeared to be wearing several small dogs.

'This is a new shop isn't it?' she said.

'Yes, madam,' said Reggie. 'We can offer you over-priced rubbish in every range.'

'I love those paintings,' she said. 'That's Marbella, isn't it?'

'The Algarve.'

'I knew it was somewhere in Spain. Who painted them?'

'Dr Eustace Snurd, FRDA.'

'FRDA. What does that mean?'

'Fellow of the Royal Dental Association.'

'Oh. How much are they?'

'They range from six pounds to twelve pounds fifty.'

'I'll have that one there.'

She pointed to a lurid representation of the beach at Faro.

'It's lovely,' she said.

'You mean you actually like it,' said Reggie.

'I love it.'

'It's horrible.'

'Are you trying to teach me about art?' she said. 'I'm a painter myself, and I like it. Wrap it for me, please.'

'But madam,' said Reggie, 'That isn't the point. I am setting out to sell rubbish.'

'Are you refusing to sell it?' said the woman.

'No, of course not.'

'Wrap it, then.'

'Certainly, madam.'

Reggie put a cheque for eight pounds in the till, and almost immediately he made his third sale.

'What is the idea of those square hoops?' said a soberly-dressed lady of some seventy years, whom Reggie adjudged to be a spinster.

'They're impossible to roll along,' said Reggie. 'Quite useless.'

'Is it an Irish idea?' said the woman.

'No, it's my own,' said Reggie.

'I'll have one for my grand-nephew's birthday.'

Suddenly Reggie didn't want to sell the useless hoop. He had a picture of the neatly wrapped parcel – for if this woman wasn't a neat wrapper of a parcel, Reggie was the 'boots' in a crumbling Hungarian health hydro – of the boy's pathetic attempts to roll the hoop, the childish tears, the bitter disappointment.

'I really can't recommend them,' he said.

'Nonsense,' said the woman. 'They've all got everything, but he'll be the only boy in the school with a square hoop. That's what counts at his age.'

Three sales. Total takings – eleven pounds twenty-five pence. Reggie did the books and went home.

A brick had been hurled through the frosted glass of the front door. Attached to it was the message, in childish capitals: 'The killers will be killed.'

He told Elizabeth about his first day at Grot, and she was surprised that he had even made three sales.

When he went to kiss her, she shrank away.

'What's the matter, darling?' he said.

'Last night when you were putting the finishing touches to your shop, did you go for a walk?'

'I did go for a little walk,' he said.

'Why?'

'I had a headache. I went out to clear my head. I didn't rape and strangle a secretary, if that's what you mean. Good God, do you think I'm the Fiend of Climthorpe?'

'I don't know what to think,' said Elizabeth. Her hands were shaking. 'I know that you've done a lot of very odd things.'

'Oh darling, how could you?'

'I'm not trying to suggest that you're evil,' said Elizabeth. 'But you said those hippopotamuses and things just came to you. Do you think . . .'

'Do I think I flashed at a girl, with nine 'O' levels, attempted to rape a dental receptionist, and strangled a secretary without remembering any of those things?'

'It's possible,' she whispered.

'It's not the kind of thing that usually slips one's mind,' said Reggie. 'I don't usually . . . wait a minute, though. I've just remembered. I did rob a bank yesterday. I completely forgot.'

'Oh, Reggie, don't be sarcastic. Please don't be sarcastic.'

After supper he went for a walk round the dark, dimly-lit streets of the Poets' Estate. As he walked he went back, step by step, over the various walks that he had taken on the nights of the crimes.

No, there were no gaps. He could account for every second.

But would he be able to detect the gaps? Could he possibly be sure?

When he got home, he looked at his watch to see if it had gone forward any more than it should have done.

Did this mean that he was beginning to believe that he had black-outs when he wasn't responsible for his actions?

They lay in separate rooms that night. Neither slept much. Towards dawn Reggie nodded off into a nightmare world of dead raped girls with their heads stuck in square hoops, and crude pictures of the Algarve in which, even as he stood watching them, he himself committed dreadful acts of sexual sickness.

He awoke drenched in sweat, had a bath, breakfasted alone, and walked to the shop.

He dreaded that the day would produce fresh evidence of ghastly crimes, dead girls in his garden or in the little yard at the back of the shop.

All it brought was two broken windows. He boarded them up, and closed the shop. Its brief career was over.

A panda car pulled up, with a screech of unnecessary drama. Two policemen walked towards him.

'Broken windows, sir?'

'Yes.'

They asked him, as he had known they would, to accompany them to the station.

They took him into a bare interview room. He expected to be kicked and punched, but they were quite polite, questioned him in detail about his movements on the nights in question, questioned him about his life-history, questioned him about his shop.

He could imagine the comments on the news. A man is helping the police with their inquiries. An arrest is expected shortly.

They took him through his movements again. And again. And again. He lost all sense of time. Cups of coffee came and went. Lunch came and went, or was it supper – lamb and two veg from the canteen.

'You raped and killed her, didn't you?'

'No.'

'Where exactly were you at the time she was killed?'

'I don't know when she was killed.'

Traps a schoolboy could have seen through.

'You've got no evidence,' said Reggie. 'You can't keep me.'

'How do you know we've got no evidence?'

'Because I didn't do it.'

It was tempting to admit it all and end this ordeal.

He mustn't.

It was tempting to admit that he might have been the murderer, that he didn't know, and that if he was so uncertain of himself that he didn't know, then there wasn't any point in not being.

He mustn't.

'Let's go through the movements again, shall we?'

Naked light. Sweat. Smell of socks. Faces moulded into unpleasantness by their job – the search for a sexual maniac.

I am not a sexual maniac. I am not a sexual maniac. I am not a sexual maniac. Say it to yourself like doing lines at school. I. I am. I am not. I am not a. I am not a sexual. I am not a sexual maniac.

Fingerprints. Samples of clothing. They wouldn't find anything.

'Let's just go through your walk by the cricket ground once again, shall we?'

At last they took him home. They searched his house. He didn't object.

It was what he should have expected from the very first moment when he had started to behave in an eccentric fashion, a year and a half ago.

It was all he would ever be able to expect.

They left. They warned him that the house would be watched. He didn't mind.

The neighbours knew. Everybody knew.

Tom and Linda came round, pretending too carefully that it was a chance visit, making it obvious that Elizabeth had asked them to call.

'Have you taken a doctor's advice about all this, Reggie?' said Tom.

'You think dad is the Fiend of Climthorpe,' said Linda. 'You're disgusting. I never want to see you again.'

She burst into tears and rushed out into the night.

She ran down Coleridge Close and up the path that led between the prosperous gardens of the Poets' Estate to the edge of the cricket ground. The poplars behind the pavilion were the wind's playthings, and the hair of the man who blocked her path streamed out behind him.

She recognized him immediately. It was the man who had told her he was going to do the heavy breathing at Thames Brightwell.

She turned to run, and he knocked her to the ground.

They fought, kicked, punched. Desperation gave them both strength. She managed one scream before his hand was clamped firmly across her mouth.

Then there were other people there, pulling the man off her. One of their blows struck her and set her reeling.

She turned in time to see Tom, clear in the light of the nascent moon, punch the man in the face. The man crumpled up in a heap on the ground. Tom examined his fist with a mixture of surprise, horror and respect, and Reggie held Linda in his arms.

123

She looked down at the pleasant, vacuous face of the un-conscious man.

'I don't expect his daughter thinks he's the Fiend of Clim-thorpe,' she said.

Chapter 13

The news of the arrest of the Fiend of Climthorpe was in all the papers. Many people told Reggie that they had never doubted him for a moment. A local glazier offered to repair Grot's windows free of charge.

Quite a few people came to the shop on the day of its re-opening. Some of them merely wandered around, pretending to look at the stock, but in reality taking furtive peeps at Reggie. He responded with bright frank smiles which sent their eyes fleeing from the encounter in embarrassment.

Barely an hour had passed before he sold another of Dr Snurd's paintings of the Algarve.

The vendee was an elderly man, with white hair, sagging skin and a quiet manner suggestive of excellent taste. He was accompanied by a well-dressed lady whom Reggie assumed to be his wife – nor did anything occur in the subsequent dialogue to modify that view.

'Look at those pictures,' said the man.

His wife shuddered.

'Don't you think they'd be perfect for the Webbers?'

'Absolutely.'

Reggie approached them discreetly.

'Can I help you?' he said.

'We'd like one of these pictures,' said the man.

'You like them?'

'Well, no, I don't.'

'They're awful, aren't they?' said Reggie.

'Terrible. Just the thing for our friends.'

'You don't like your friends?'

'Oh yes, they're delightful people. No taste at all, poor souls.'

'I don't know why you say poor souls,' said the wife. 'They're perfectly happy.'

'Which would you say they'd like the best?' said the man.

'Whichever we like the least, darling,' said the woman.

'Awkward, isn't it?' said Reggie. 'Embarrassment of poverty.'

'Which do you like the least?' said the man.

'I think the sunset over Albufeira is pretty awful,' said Reggie. 'I always feel it looks like the bloodshot eye of a drunken Turkish wrestler with cataracts.'

'You and your sales talk,' said the man.

'Or there's this one,' said Reggie, taking down a large canvas of the Praia Da Rocha. 'It's the biggest, so I suppose on that score alone it might be the nastiest.'

'It is rather nasty, isn't it?' said the man.

'Take it outside and have a look in the natural light,' said Reggie.' You aren't seeing it at its worst in here.'

When they had seen the picture in the natural light, they bought it for twelve pounds.

Reggie put a third notice in the window: 'Lots of gifts for people with no taste.'

During the day he sold a few more bottles of Tom's wine, and three square hoops to small boys. He felt badly about this, pointing out the disadvantages inherent in the shape if unencumbered motion was the aim. But it seemed that unencumbered motion was not the aim. Very much the reverse. There was a craze of pretending to be Irish at the school. Timmy Mitchison had a square hoop for his birthday, and this had given him an instant lead in Irishness. They were going to have square hoops whatever the cost, and thought them a snip at one pound fifty.

He also sold some of the tasteless puddings for the first time.

'Are those puddings really tasteless?' said a rather harassed woman in her late thirties.

'Absolutely, madam. I defy the most sensitive palate in Britain to respond to them in any way.'

'I'll have two dozen,' she said.

'You like tasteless puddings?' Reggie asked.

'I don't,' she said. 'It's for my children. Some dislike one taste, some another. Their reactions are always based on what they dislike, not what they like.'

'You are cursed with a malignant brood,' said Reggie.

'Exactly,' said the woman.

'Well, there's nothing for any of them to dislike in these,' said Reggie.

'Exactly,' said the woman.

It was gone seven o'clock when Reggie let himself into the house that night.

'You're late,' said Elizabeth.

'I was doing the books,' said Reggie.

'I wouldn't have thought it would take that long to do the books.'

'We took sixty-three pounds twenty pence.'

'What?'

'We took sixty-three pounds twenty pence.'

'I can't believe it,' said Elizabeth.

'Oh you of little faith,' said Reggie.

'Do you mean we're actually going to make a go of this?'

'Did you ever doubt it?' said Reggie.

Elizabeth began to cry. She wept copious tears. Reggie sat beside her on the settee, ineffectually attempting to offer solace.

He poured them two extra large drinks, and raised his glass. Behind him was a square clean patch on the wallpaper, where a picture of the Algarve had so recently stood.

'To Grot,' he said.

'To Grot,' said Elizabeth.

The next day Reggie sold out of square hoops and he also sold a dozen more bottles of Tom's wine to the man with the stick-out ears and the hateful sister-in-law.

'She really loathed it,' said the man, rubbing his hands. 'Of course I had to drink a glass myself, but it was worth it to see her face. She wouldn't admit she didn't like it, pretended she loved it, so I said I'd get her a dozen.'

'Splendid,' said Reggie. 'Excellent. I'm afraid I've only

got eight bottles of sprout left, though. Will you make up the numbers with quince?'

'Are they as bad?' said the man.

'Almost,' said Reggie. 'If you don't think they're bad enough, keep them. They deteriorate with age.'

'I'm telling all my friends about your shop,' said the man.

Reggie also sold two more of Dr Snurd's paintings to people who thought they were wonderful. This led him to doubt whether works of art, however bad, could ever really be regarded as useless. For the moment, however, the question was academic. Such issues of principle were matters that the infant and sickly business could ill afford to consider.

He also sold the game with no rules, but the cracked pottery and second-hand books didn't sell, and Reggie decided that these were not suitable lines. In fact he grew very attached to some of the books with their statements like, 'The advent of fauvism had no immediate effect on Rugeley' and, 'In the early sixteenth century we find no references to bunions in Spain or Portugal. None of the rulers of the great Italian art cities appear to have suffered from them, or, if they did, the fact has not been recorded.'

That evening, Reggie and Elizabeth were invited to Tom and Linda's for dinner.

On the way Reggie called on his doctor, and offered to sell his paintings in his shop. Painting was Dr Underwood's hobby. His favourite subjects were Mrs Underwood and the Tuscan hill towns. If the abstract and the representative were not Dr Underwood's strongest suits, then oils and water-colours were not his natural materials, and his undeniable shortcomings in imagination and composition were shown up most nakedly when he attempted portraits or landscapes. His paintings would sit very well alongside those of Dr Snurd.

When they arrived at Tom and Linda's lovely house in the delightful village of Thames Brightwell, they were met with the mingled scents of garlic and human excrement.

'Jocasta's shit herself,' explained Adam gleefully.

'They'll go to bed soon,' said Tom, 'but we don't like to

stop them watching *Tomorrow's World*. It's educational.'

When Adam and Jocasta had been persuaded, demo-cratically, in return for certain concessions, to go to bed, the grown-ups sat at the oval dining table in the open-plan living-room, and tucked into their starters.

To Reggie's astonishment, the wine was an excellent white Burgundy.

'Whatever happened to the Château Blackberry?' he in-quired.

Tom's geniality froze.

'You don't like my wines,' he said. 'I went past your shop today, Reggie.'

'Oh yes?'

'Yes. I saw the notice in your window: "Every single item sold in this shop is guaranteed useless." '

'Yes.'

'My wine is sold in your shop.'

'Yes.'

'That's an offence against the Trade Discrimination Act.'

'I'd like to see you prove it,' said Reggie.

'These haddock smokies make delicious starters,' said Elizabeth.

'I want you to withdraw all my wine tomorrow,' said Tom.

'I've sold nineteen bottles already,' said Reggie. 'I owe you twenty-one pounds.'

'Twenty-one pounds?' said Tom. 'In less than a week?'

'Yes.'

'Good God.'

'Yes.'

Linda removed the starter dishes, and produced the mullet niçoise.

'Floppysquirts?' inquired Tom.

There was a pause.

'Sorry, are you speaking to me?' said Linda.

'Well of course I am,' said Tom.

'My name is not Floppysquirts,' said Linda. 'My name is Linda.'

'Sorry, Lindyscoops,' said Tom.

'This mullet is lovely,' said Elizabeth. 'It's the nicest mullet I've ever tasted.'

'It's the only mullet I've ever tasted,' said Reggie.

'We had mullet in Midhurst,' said Elizabeth.

'I've never even been to Midhurst,' said Reggie. 'Lct alone had mullet there.'

'Linda?' said Tom.

'Yes?' said Linda.

'Do you honestly like my home-made wines?'

'I do,' said Linda. 'But I do enjoy having proper wine as well sometimes.'

'What do you mean, proper wine?'

'I mean commercial wine,' said Linda. 'We can afford it.'

'You can sell all the wine you like in your shop, Reggie,' said Tom.

'I'm sorry, Tom,' said Linda.

Tom stood up and raised his hand for silence.

'Thank you,' he said. 'Linda and I thought we'd like to give this little dinner to celebrate the ... er ... the fact that you, Reggie, er ...'

'That I'm not the Fiend of Climthorpe.'

'Well, yes. And also to mark the opening of your shop and wish it success. I was a bit surprised when I saw what kind of a shop it was, but ... er ... I won't make any hasty judgements on it. I'm not a hasty judgement person. So Linda and I would like to ... er ... to drink to the ... er ... the future of ... er ... Grot.'

They raised their glasses.

'To Grot,' said Tom and Linda.

As they drove home, full of hope and mullet, Reggie and Elizabeth allowed themselves to think that they might really be on the verge of a happier future.

The phone was ringing as they entered the house. It was the police informing them that Mark and the whole of the cast of his theatre company had been kidnapped by guerillas while presenting *The Reluctant Debutante* to an audience of Angolan mercenaries.

Book Two

Chapter 14

'I can't help worrying about him,' said Elizabeth.

'I know,' said Reggie.

He held her close and pressed her body softly against him.

It was exactly two years since Mark had been kidnapped. There had been a long silence, then a letter in which he stated that he was free and happy, but he wouldn't be coming home, as there was important work to be done. The letter had been in Mark's handwriting, but it had lacked puns, brackets, exclamation marks, spelling mistakes or any other signs of his personality.

That was eleven months ago. Since then they had heard nothing.

'We'll hear from him soon,' said Reggie. 'I feel it in my bones.'

It was a bright morning in late November, and the garden was laced with the first frost of winter.

'Briefcase,' said Elizabeth, handing him his black leather briefcase, engraved with his initials 'R.I.P.' in gold.

'Thank you, darling,' he said.

'Umbrella,' she said, handing him a smart new article which answered perfectly to her description.

'Thank you, darling,' he said.

She watched him as he set off down the garden path, between the rose bushes which he had pruned so ruthlessly that autumn.

Mr Milford was just getting into the Ford Granada provided by his firm.

'Morning, Reggie,' he sang out, and his breath produced clouds of steam in the sharp air. 'Can you and Elizabeth come to dinner on Saturday and meet the Shorthouses?'

'Awfully sorry, Dennis,' said Reggie. 'It sounds tempting,

we'd love to meet the Shorthouses, but I've got a prior engagement.'

'I understand. It was short notice,' said Mr Milford.

The prior engagement consisted of having a bath and watching *Match of the Day* in his dressing-gown.

He walked down Coleridge Close, turned right into Tennyson Avenue, then left into Wordsworth Drive, and down the snicket into Station Road. There were white gates across the roads on all the entrances to the Poets' Estate, to bar all vulgar and unnecessary traffic.

He stood at his usual place on the platform, in front of the door marked 'Isolation Telephone'.

Several people greeted him warmly.

A hoarding on the down platform bore simple but effective witness to his success.

'GROT,' it said. 'Branches throughout North and South London.'

The eight forty-six reached Waterloo twenty-two minutes late. The loudspeaker announcement blamed black ice at Norbiton.

Reggie set off southwards along the Waterloo Road. A brisk ten-minute walk through grey, inelegant streets brought him to Head Office.

He walked towards the characterless glass and concrete box. Above the main entrance large letters proudly announced: ' ERRIN PRODUCTS.'

He made as if to open the doors, forgetting as always that they slid noiselessly open at his approach.

He smiled in answer to the cheery and respectful 'Morning, Mr Perrin' from the receptionist, and took the lift up to the second floor.

His secretary was already there, in his outer office. Her name was Miss Erith and she was neither pretty nor ugly. She had a figure that was perfect without being attractive, and she was neither young nor old.

Reggie hadn't the enthusiasm to say to her: 'Twenty-two minutes late. Black ice at Norbiton.' There was nothing in her personality to encourage such intimacy.

He entered his inner sanctum and hurled his umbrella at the hat-stand. It missed by a foot and a half.

On his desk there were three telephones, and outside the window there was a window-box, which throughout the summer months had been a riot of colour.

He lifted the red phone.

'Get me Mr Bulstrode, please, Miss Erith,' he said.

He put the phone down and looked at his diary.

Ten thirty. David Harris-Jones.

Eleven thirty. Planning meeting – conference room B.

He smiled. On the surface life was quite similar to the old days at Sunshine Desserts, not much more than a mile away. But there was one enormous difference. He was the boss now. All this was his.

The green phone buzzed.

'Mr Bulstrode on green,' said Miss Erith.

He knew Mr Bulstrode was on green. He had just picked up the green phone, hadn't he?

If only Joan were his secretary.

'Hello, Bulstrode,' he said. 'Listen, there's a "P" missing over the main entrance.'

'Don't worry,' said Mr Bulstrode. 'I'll have a "P" up there within the hour.'

Reggie laughed. The staff were quite used to his laughing from time to time, and took no notice of it.

In Reggie's office there were two awful paintings of the Algarve by Dr Snurd, two abysmal paintings of Siena by Dr Underwood – Reggie called them burnt Siena and unburnt Siena – and two horrendous paintings of Ramsey, Isle of Man, by Dr Wren, his osteopath.

The yellow telephone rang.

'David Harris-Jones on yellow,' said Miss Erith.

'Hello, Reggie,' said David. 'I just rang to say I may be a minute or two late.'

'Good,' said Reggie. 'Better ring off now or you may be three or four minutes late.'

Reggie asked Miss Erith to provide a bottle of champagne on ice. She looked disapproving.

Promptly at ten thirty-one-and-a-half David Harris-Jones arrived. He stuttered across the thick pile carpet, clutching a sheaf of papers. Reggie realized that it was David's lot in life to stutter across thick pile carpets towards large men behind big desks, and say: 'I've got those figures you asked for.'

'I've got those figures you asked for,' said David.

'Champagne, David?' he said.

'Champagne? What's this in aid of?'

'Because I could think of no possible reason for having it.' Reggie handed him a glass of the bubbling liquid.

'Super,' he said.

Reggie summoned Miss Erith.

'Get yourself a glass,' he said.

'Oh no, thank you,' she said.

'Come on. Let your hair down,' he said.

'Thank you, no. I'm on a diet,' said Miss Erith, and she closed the door behind her with the optimum firmness commensurate with quietude.

'Why are women with perfect figures always on diets, and why are female dieticians always sixteen stone?' said Reggie.

'I don't know,' said David.

'Because the world is absurd,' said Reggie. 'Cheers.'

'Cheers.'

'Not sorry you came to work for me?' said Reggie.

'I'll say not,' said David. 'When C.J. made me redundant like that, just before my wedding and everything, it took away all my self-confidence. Did I ever tell you what happened then?'

'Yes,' said Reggie.

'I read about your success, I thought: "Why don't I write?"'

'I know.'

'Eighteen times I drafted letters.'

'I know.'

'Eighteen times I tore them up.'

'I know. Finally Prue made you write. She's a wonderful girl.'

'Oh. You know.'

'Yes. Let's see those figures then.'

'We're up in twenty-five shops, down in ten, and virtually level-pegging in the other nine.'

Reggie studied the detailed figures briefly.

'Not too bad, I suppose,' he said.

'Climthorpe's down rather badly. There's evidence of mismanagement there.'

'Maybe I'd better put a new man in. Top you up?'

'Super.'

Reggie filled David Harris-Jones's glass to the brim.

'Thank you, C.J.,' said David, and blushed in deep confusion, as if calling a man C.J. was the worst insult you could give him. 'Sorry, Reggie.'

Reggie laughed.

'I hope I'm not getting like C.J.'

'No. Perish the thought.'

'Do you think when they made you redundant it was for economy reasons or were they dissatisfied with your work?'

'I'm nothing special, Reggie. No, don't deny it. Oh God, you weren't going to. No, I'm nothing special, but I like to think I'm adequate. I like to think it was purely for economy reasons.'

Reggie stood at the window and looked out over another office building similar to his own. All the lights were on, despite the bright winter sunshine.

He raised his glass to the other office building.

'Cheers, Amalgamated Asbestos,' he said.

He turned to face David.

'So,' he said. 'Sunshine Desserts may be in trouble.'

'I think it's possible,' said David.

'Interesting,' said Reggie.

When David Harris-Jones had left, Reggie telephoned C.J. and asked him out to lunch the following day.

Present at the planning meeting were Reggie, David Harris-Jones, Morris Coates from the advertising agency, and Esther Pigeon from Market Research.

David related the details of the profits of the various shops. Reggie nodded sagely.

Esther Pigeon began to read her findings. She talked in a mechanical voice as if she were an answering machine.

Forty-three per cent thought that the silent LP, *Laryngitis in Thirty Lands*, had been good and would be prepared to buy a sequel. Several pub landlords regularly used it as background silence and found it very popular.

Reggie nodded sagely.

The empty book *Blankety Blank*, which contained 246 blank pages, had sold well in categories B, C, and D, but less well in categories A, AB, DE and E.

Reggie interpolated at this point.

'I'm planning two sequels,' he said. '*It Shouldn't Happen to a Blankety Blank* and *Let Sleeping Blankety Blanks Lie.*'

'Good thinking,' said Morris Coates. 'Like it.'

'Super,' said David Harris-Jones.

'Ridiculous,' said Reggie.

'Pardon?' said Morris Coates.

'Nothing,' said Reggie.

'With you,' said Morris Coates.

'Super,' said David Harris-Jones.

In front of each person there was a blotter, and a glass of water. David Harris-Jones was drawing childish little steam-engines all over his blotter.

'We analysed reaction to the idea of the harmless pill that has no effect whatsoever,' said Esther Pigeon. '32 per cent in the Wirral and 2·1 per cent in the Gorbals found the idea interesting, 17 per cent and 1·6 per cent respectively found it worth consideration, and 21·4 per cent and 66·7 per cent found it difficult to swallow. 26·9 per cent of replies from the Gorbals were rejected by the computer, which suffered two fuses and a blow-out.'

'Why should people buy a pill that they know doesn't do them any good?' said David, looking up momentarily from his engines.

'For many reasons,' said Reggie. 'For comfort, because they're allergic to medicine, because it's safe, because since it has no effects it can have no side effects either, because Catholics can use it, and because you don't have to keep it out of reach of children. It's wonderful.'

Miss Erith brought them sour looks and coffee.

'Thank you, Miss Erith,' said Reggie, passing the cups round the oblong table. 'Any thoughts on advertising, Morris?'

'What about – off the top of the head, toss it in the seed tray, see if the budgie bites – what about "Perrin's Pills – they don't look good – they don't taste good – and they don't do you any good?" ' said Morris Coates.

'Not bad,' said Reggie. 'Not bad at all.'

If looks could speak, Morris Coates's would have said: 'Well, don't sound so surprised!'

'OK,' said Reggie. 'We go for the harmless pills and powders. Perrin's Powders has a ring about it – and how about Perrin's Insoluble Suppositories as well?'

'Like it,' said Morris Coates.

'You thought Perrin's Pills were bad,' said Reggie. 'Now try Perrin's Insoluble Suppositories, and hit rock-bottom.'

'Like it,' said Morris Coates.

'Get those designed, David,' said Reggie. 'Very serious and medical looking – lots of instructions – take three times daily after meals etcetera. Powders in two colours, suppositories in three, pills in four.'

'Super,' said David Harris-Jones.

'Get those adverts rolling, all media,' said Reggie.

'Will do,' said Morris Coates.

They considered several other ideas, deciding in favour of a range of useless pottery including cruet sets with no holes in them, egg-cups so large the eggs couldn't be eaten, and ceramic fruit that was going rotten.

They rejected a nest of tables, built so that the two smaller tables wouldn't come out from beneath the largest. While it was useless as a nest of tables, it could prove useful as a single table, albeit an expensive one.

'I think it falls between two stools,' said Reggie.

Everyone agreed that it fell between two stools.

'And we mustn't lose our integrity.'

Everyone agreed that they mustn't lose their integrity.

But then everyone agreed with everything that Reggie said.

'I believe you did a survey on the attitude of the public to our prices, Miss Pigeon,' said Reggie.

'We did, Mr Perrin,' said Esther Pigeon.

'Would you kindly favour us with the findings of your survey, Miss Pigeon?' asked Reggie.

'Certainly, Mr Perrin,' said Esther Pigeon. 'While 24 per cent of the 43 per cent of people under twenty-five in Staines who used Grot shops felt that prices were "about right", 68 per cent of the 82 per cent of over-sixty-fives in Nottingham who had never been to a Grot shop thought the prices were too high.'

'Could you kindly sum up your findings for us, Miss Pigeon?' said Reggie, when Esther Pigeon had at last finished and silence had fallen around the half-finished coffee-cups in the smoky conference room.

'Certainly, Mr Perrin,' said Esther Pigeon. '78 per cent of the public think your prices are excessive.'

'Thank you, Miss Pigeon,' said Reggie. 'It's clear that we have to establish a greater aura of exclusivity for Grot. Our imprint should be redesigned in gilt letters, and we'll put all our prices up 50 per cent.'

It was already beginning to freeze as Reggie walked home through the Poets' Estate.

The elder Warbleton boy waved cheerily as he sped past in his filthy white MG. It was his seventh car in two years. Some one had written 'Disgusting' with his fingers on the muddy boot.

Reggie smiled. It had been a good day.

He kissed Elizabeth and she gave him a gin and tonic.

'Nice day?' he said.

'Highly exciting. I shopped this morning, did a bit of designing for Grot, had the remains of the lamb, did some more designing. I watched *Emmerdale Farm* – Henry Wilks has met an old flame. Hardly what I expected when we described ourselves as a partnership. Sitting at home and getting fobbed off with the odd designing job.'

'Fobbed off? You're our think-tank. Those four games with no rules that you designed are brilliant. In hundreds of thousands of homes, families are having endless fun working out how to play them.'

Elizabeth sighed.

'Oh, and these came,' she said.

There were invitations to dinner in Swinburne Way and Anon Avenue, and to talk about careers in industry to the Queen Charlotte School for Girls.

'The burdens of success,' said Reggie.

Chapter 15

Reggie and C.J. met for lunch at one o'clock in the Euripides Greek Restaurant. It boasted green flock wallpaper and gold light fittings.

'I always knew you'd do well in the end, Reggie,' said C.J., as they munched olives in the tiny bar. 'The early bird catches the worm, eh?'

'Every time, C.J.,' said Reggie.

'Sooner or later,' said C.J.

'Exactly,' said Reggie.

'Mrs C.J. and I are absolutely delighted. I said to her only yesterday, "I am absolutely delighted with Reggie Perrin's success," and she said, "So am I, C.J. I am absolutely delighted with Reggie Perrin's success." So you see, Reggie, we are both absolutely delighted with your success.'

'Thank you, C.J.'

'I'm embarrassing you, Reggie.'

'Not at all, C.J.'

'Good morning, gentlemen, we have lovely sucking pig,' said the swarthy restaurateur.

'No thank you,' said Reggie, feeling an affection for Mr Pelham's porkers in retrospect which had not been possible at the time.

'Something to drink, gentlemen? Some ouzo, perhaps?'

'Dry sherry,' said C.J.

When they had their dry sherries, C.J. toasted Reggie's success.

'To you and your lovely wife,' he said.

'Thank you,' said Reggie.

'Margaret, isn't it?' said C.J.

'Elizabeth,' said Reggie.

'Sorry,' said C.J. 'I'm rotten with names.'

Reggie smiled. He knew that Elizabeth would laugh when he told her that C.J. had forgotten her name.

'How's Mrs C.J.?' he asked, waking belatedly to his social responsibilities.

C.J. sighed deeply.

'Extremely well,' he said. 'We were playing your latest game with no rules last evening. We've worked out some rather ingenious rules, although they do utilize the lighthouse and the nuclear power station rather more effectively than the llamas.'

'A lot of people have had that trouble,' said Reggie.

The glass-topped tables were very low and their chairs reclined backwards, giving unusual prominence to C.J.'s knees. Reggie had never noticed before how large they were.

'How are things at Sunshine Desserts?' he said.

'We've entered upon a slight wobble,' said C.J. 'I didn't get where I am today without knowing a slight wobble when I'm entering it.'

'I imagine not, C.J.'

'But it is purely temporary. Next week we're launching our new fruit blancmanges. I'm prepared to stick my neck out and state categorically that they will take the nation by storm.'

'That's good news, C.J.,' said Reggie.

Their table was ready. C.J. emerged from his chair with difficulty and they made their way into the restaurant.

'I was surprised when you paid me the loan back,' said C.J. over their kebabs.

'Why should you be surprised?' said Reggie. 'I always pay loans back.'

'Yes, but this wasn't exactly a loan, was it?'

'I'm sorry, C.J. What exactly was it, then?'

'Let's not beat about the bush,' said C.J. 'We weren't born yesterday.'

Reggie waved an admonitory gobbet of lamb at C.J.

'Please tell me exactly what you're talking about,' he said.

'I'm a gentleman, Reggie,' said C.J. 'I regard it as bad form to pay a blackmail ransom back, especially with eight and a half per cent interest. I know you're doing well. You don't have to humiliate me to prove it.'

'Blackmail?' said Reggie. 'Blackmail?'

'It was blackmail, wasn't it?' said C.J.

'It most certainly was not. I've never blackmailed anyone in my life. Good God. I see now why you gave it so readily.'

Reggie roared with laughter. Everyone in the restaurant looked at them. The head-waiter hurried up and poured more wine.

'What was I supposed to be blackmailing you about?' said Reggie.

'The . . . er . . . my . . . er . . . my little peccadillo with . . . er . . . the Dalmatian princess,' said C.J.

'Dalmatian princess?' said Reggie.

'The one I met in Godalming.'

'I had no idea,' said Reggie, between laughs.

'I was led on,' said C.J. 'You know what these Dalmatian princesses are.'

'No,' said Reggie. 'Actually I don't. What are these Dalmatian princesses?'

After lunch Reggie went back to Sunshine Desserts with C.J., and called on Tony Webster. It gave him an excuse to see Joan.

Tony was delighted to see him. He had quite a plush office, with three abstract paintings and a cocktail cabinet.

'You're doing amazingly well, Reggie,' he said, indicating with his arm that Reggie sit in a huge armchair provided for just such an eventuality.

'I can't grumble.'

'Great. Everyone here knew what you were made of.'

'Thank you, Tony.'

'Brandy?'

'Thank you. I can see that you're doing well, too.'

'Amazing. Fantastic. I'm really into the executive bit nowadays. I'm a changed man, Reggie. I'm into security and responsibility and all that crap.'

'I'm happy for you. How are things at Sunshine Desserts?'

'Going from strength to strength. This is success city.'

'Good. Marvellous.'

Tony handed Reggie an excessively large brandy.

'Where's Joan?' said Reggie.

Tony made no reply.

'Where's Joan?' repeated Reggie.

'She's left,' said Tony.

'Oh. Happy event?'

'No.'

'Oh.'

Tony sat side-saddle on his desk.

'We got married,' he said. 'Honeymooned on the Italian Riviera. I thought it would be traditional without being clichéd.'

'How was it?'

'Sewage city. The hotel had a private beach next to the outlet pipe. Joan and I were great. Fantabulous. Honestly, Reggie, it was like there had never been anybody else, know what I mean?'

'Yes, Tony, I know what you mean.'

'Then I went off with this Finnish chick. Joan found out. Exit one marriage. End of story.'

'I see. I . . . er . . . I see.'

There was a pause. Reggie sipped his brandy and waited for Tony to speak.

'Joan's left here,' he said at last. 'We thought it was best.'

'I see. And what about . . . er . . .?'

'The Helsinki raver? I imagine it's raving its little arse off in Helsinki. The whole thing's changed me, I can tell you. It's made me grow up. You know what it was like with me, Reggie. Trendsville, U.S.A. Not any more. That's dull city.'

Reggie refused the offer of some more brandy, but Tony had some.

'So is there no possibility of a reconciliation between you and Joan?'

'No way. But no way. We were both on the rebound anyway. You remember my dolly bird with no tits?'

'I remember a rather lovely blonde. I didn't particularly remark the absence of mammaries.'

'Well anyway I was on the rebound from her, and Joan was on the rebound from . . . Joan was on the rebound as well. How's David Harris-Jones settling in?'

'Very well.'

'Great. Still saying "super" all the time, is he?'

'Yes.'

'Great.'

Reggie stood up. It was time to go.

'Where is Joan now?' he said.

'She's working for the Glycero Ointment Company in Godalming.'

'Good God.'

'Why do you ask?'

'No reason.'

Tony moved round his desk and sat in his chair, as if he was now ready for official business.

'Sit down a moment, Reggie,' he said.

Reggie sat down.

'There's one thing I ought to tell you, Reggie. Perhaps I shouldn't.'

'Don't then.'

'No. I won't. It was the last night of our honeymoon.'

'I'm not sure I want to hear it.'

'No. We were having it off and it was making everything we'd done before look like a fashion show for Mothercare.'

'I'm sure I don't want to hear it.'

'And she moaned, "Oh Reggie, Reggie." Just that.'

There was a long silence.

'I can't think of anything to say,' said Reggie.

'I just thought I ought to tell you.'

'Thanks, Tony.'

'Just a piece of advice, Reggie, man to man. That one is very mixed up. But I mean mixed up. It could be very bad news.'

'Thank you, Tony,' said Reggie, standing up again.

'I'd give it a wide berth if I were you.'

They shook hands.

'Mind you, marrying it was the best thing I ever did,' said Tony. 'OK, it didn't work out, but it's made me grow up.'

As soon as he got back to the office, Reggie asked Miss Erith to get Joan.

'Mrs Webster on yellow,' said Miss Erith.

'Hello, Joan,' said Reggie.

'Hello, Reggie.'

'How are you?'

'Surviving.'

'I wondered if we could have lunch one day.'

'Lunch is difficult,' said Joan. 'Evenings are better. I could meet you one evening after work. There's a nice pub on the Hog's Back called the Dissipated Kipper.'

'Thursday next week?' said Reggie, not wanting to seem too keen.

'Why not? I must go now. Here comes my boss. I'll look forward to it, Reggie. Bye.'

Next he dialled Doc Morrissey, whose number he had been given by C.J., and asked him if he could call round at twelve on the following Tuesday. Doc Morrissey consulted his empty diary and said that he could.

There was a soft, uncertain knock on the door.

'Come in, David,' said Reggie.

David Harris-Jones tiptoed in cautiously.

'Sorry to barge in,' he said. 'I wondered if you'd like to check the memo I'm sending to Design about the harmless pills and powders and suppositories.'

Reggie looked it over briefly.

'Excellent,' he said. 'A minor masterpiece of succinct exposition. I've just seen your old sparring partner Tony Webster.'

'How is he?'

'Great.'

'Super. Still saying "great" all the time, is he?'

'Yes.'

'Super.'

'The older he gets, the younger he talks.'

'How are things at Sunshine Desserts?'

'Great.'

'Super. Prue and I are looking forward to this evening, Reggie.'

'Why? What are you doing?'

David Harris-Jones looked rather puzzled, then laughed half-heartedly.

Pools of sodium were reflected on the glistening pavements of the Poets' Estate as Reggie walked home. The rain that had swept dramatically in from the Atlantic now dripped lifelessly from the street lamps into the gutters.

He walked along Station Road, up the snicket, up Wordsworth Drive, turned right into Tennyson Avenue, then left into Coleridge Close. The curtains in the living-rooms of the spacious houses were closed upon scenes of domestic calm.

Reggie wondered if his curtains would be closed upon a scene of domestic calm when he informed Elizabeth that he was offering Joan the post of his secretary, instead of Miss Erith.

Perhaps he would say nothing, in case it never happened.

No, it would be even worse if he only broached the subject after he had seen Joan. He must raise it tonight.

The house was warm and cosy. The smokeless fuel glowed merrily in the grate.

'You haven't forgotten that Tom and Linda are coming to dinner?' said Elizabeth.

'Oh my God, I had.'

'And Jimmy.'

'Oh my God.'

'And Jimmy's new woman.'

'Oh my God.'

Jimmy, his divorce to Sheila still warm, had announced his engagement to a lady named Lettuce Horncastle.

'And the David Harris-Joneses.'

'Oh my God.'

'I am telling you that we are to spend the evening with several dearly-beloved members of our family, and all you can do is say "Oh my God".'

'I'm sorry, darling. But why on earth if it's a family do are we having the Harris-Jones's?'

'Because in your friendly sociable way you said: "We may as well get them all over together." '

'I'm not unsociable,' said Reggie, pouring himself a rather large whisky. 'I like people. I just don't like dinner parties. Ah, so that's why David Harris-Jones said he was looking forward to this evening? I thought it was a comment on his sex life.'

'He won't be having much of that. Prue's very pregnant. I told you all about it this morning, but you never listen to a word I say.'

Elizabeth had some final preparations to do so they went into the kitchen.

'Can I help?' said Reggie, eager to soften Elizabeth up for the conversation about Joan.

'You can prepare the fennel.'

'I don't know how to prepare fennel,' said Reggie.

'Well you can do the sprouts. You know how to do them.'

Reggie began to do the sprouts.

'I'm thinking of employing Joan Greengross,' he said.

'Oh?' said Elizabeth. 'What as?'

'My secretary.'

'Very nice for you.'

'Yes it would be. She's very efficient.'

'Oh good.'

'You aren't annoyed are you?' said Reggie, making unnecessarily savage cuts in a tiny Bedfordshire sprout.

'No. Why should I be?' said Elizabeth.

'Exactly,' said Reggie.

'I thought you had a secretary,' said Elizabeth.

'She's hopeless.'

'Not as much fun as Joan?'

'For God's sake,' said Reggie, hurling a handful of sprouts at the wall, where they bounced harmlessly against the 'Glory of the Lakes' calendar.

'I see now why you don't want me working there,' said Elizabeth. 'Now it's becoming clear.'

'This isn't the time to talk about it,' said Reggie, getting down on his hands and knees to retrieve the sprouts.

'How typical of a man,' said Elizabeth. 'You start the subject and then when I get upset, it's the wrong time to talk about it.'

'I'm sorry. I shouldn't have mentioned it,' said Reggie.

He got to his feet again and placed the sprouts back on the table.

'I want to come and work with you,' said Elizabeth.

'You can't be my secretary.'

'I don't want to be your secretary. I want to be your partner.'

'They'll be here soon, darling.'

'Let them come. I want an office of my own, a job of my own and a starting date.'

'Darling, they'll be here any minute.'

'Let them ring. There'll be no dinner tonight unless you agree.'

'That's an ultimatum.'

'Yes.'

'I won't negotiate under pressure.'

Elizabeth took off her 'Save The Children' apron.

'You can start the first Monday in January,' he said.

'Promise?'

'Promise.'

Elizabeth put on her 'Save The Children' apron.

'You'll be bored,' said Reggie. 'It's boring work.'

Elizabeth took the knife out of his hands.

'Let me do the sprouts,' she said. 'You'll take all night.'

Reggie opened the wine while Elizabeth did the sprouts.

'So when are you seeing Joan?' she inquired.

'Next Thursday at the Dissipated Kipper on the Hog's Back.'

'Why there? That's miles away.'

'She works round there.'

'On the Hog's Back?'

'She works in Godalming.'

'Oh. Godalming.'

'You say Godalming as if it has some special significance.'

'I don't,' said Elizabeth. 'What significance could Godalming possibly have?'

150

The doorbell rang. It was David Harris-Jones and his wife Prue, a pleasant young lady whose normally plump body was rendered huge by advanced pregnancy.

'I hope we aren't early, only we didn't want to be late,' said David.

'You're the first,' said Reggie. 'But somebody has to be first.'

'That's true,' said Prue.

'I must apologize for my wife's condition,' said David Harris-Jones.

'Well it is your fault,' said Prue.

'Drink?' said Reggie.

'Sherry, please. Super,' said David Harris-Jones. 'Oh. Sorry.'

'What for?' said Reggie.

'Prue has this idea that I keep saying super,' said David. 'She's trying to stop me.'

Reggie handed David and Prue their sherries.

'Super,' said David.

Next to arrive were Jimmy and his fiancée. She was a large woman of the kind euphemistically described as handsome. In the absence of anything else nice to say about it, people often said that her face showed sense of character. Reggie felt that Jimmy must have recruited her for military rather than sexual reasons. She would come in pretty handy driving a tank if the balloon ever did go up.

'This is Lettuce,' said Jimmy.

Drinks were poured. Introductions were effected. Congratulations were proffered with embarrassment and accepted coyly.

'New pictures,' said Jimmy, pointing to a selection of rather good abstracts. When Elizabeth's mother had died, she had left them her pictures and in order not to have to put them in the living-room Reggie had bought six paintings at the Climthorpe Craft Centre.

'Bit deep for me,' said Jimmy.

'Me too,' said Lettuce.

'I like them,' said Prue.

'How are things in your country retreat, Jimmy?' said Reggie.

'On course,' said Jimmy. 'On course.'

'What exactly do you do?' said David.

'Business,' said Jimmy. 'Import export, eh, Lettuce?'

'Very much so,' said Lettuce.

Elizabeth entered with bowls of Japanese cocktail delicacies. Further introductions were effected. Their drinks rested on coasters decorated with pictures of famous English inns.

'You were in the army, weren't you, Jimmy?' said David.

'Yes. Sacked. Too old. No hard feelings, though.'

'Hard feelings never won fair lady,' said Lettuce.

'And I have certainly done that,' said Jimmy.

'You certainly have,' said Reggie.

He topped up their glasses from the wide array of bottles on the sideboard.

'Tom and Linda are late as usual,' he said.

'Linda coming?' said Jimmy eagerly.

'Yes.'

'Niece,' said Jimmy to Lettuce. 'Don't know whether I've mentioned her in dispatches.'

'Once or twice,' said Lettuce.

'Favourite uncle, that sort of crack,' said Jimmy.

'How's Lofty?' said Elizabeth.

'Clive's in the pink,' said Jimmy.

Prue shifted her bulk uneasily in the largest of the armchairs.

'Are you comfy in that chair, Prue?' said Elizabeth.

'She's fine,' said David Harris-Jones. 'She doesn't want to be a nuisance, do you, Prue?'

'Actually I'd be much more comfortable in an upright chair,' said Prue.

'Sensible girl,' said Reggie, bringing forward a chair of exactly the kind indicated – viz. upright.

There was a pause.

'We ordered some garden recliners and a canopy on Saturday,' said David Harris-Jones.

'Canopies, can't beat them,' said Jimmy. 'Just the ticket out East.'

'I thought it was better to get the summer stuff in the winter when there's no rush,' said David.

'We'll need some garden furniture,' said Jimmy. 'Eh, Lettuce? We're both fresh air fanatics.'

'I've got four canvas chairs and a slatted teak table,' said Lettuce.

'Have you now?' said Jimmy.

'When are you going back to Cornwall?' said Elizabeth.

'First light,' said Jimmy. 'Crack of.'

'Which route do you take?' said David Harris-Jones.

'A.303,' said Jimmy. 'A.30 dead loss, motorway tedious.'

'I hate motorways,' said Elizabeth.

'Fond of the old A.303,' said Jimmy. 'Soft spot.'

'You're very quiet, Prue,' said Reggie. 'No thoughts about the old A.303?'

Prue smiled.

'I know David gets nervous and wishes I'd talk more and shine more,' said Prue.

'I don't,' said David Harris-Jones.

'You think people will think I'm dull,' said Prue. 'Probably they will. You see, Reggie, now that I've got the baby inside me, all growing and kicking and alive, well somehow I just can't be bothered to talk about things like garden furniture.'

'What a splendid young woman you've married, David,' said Reggie.

Linda arrived at last, but without Tom.

'Tom sends his apologies,' she said, accepting a drink and a handful of seaweed crunchies. 'He's suddenly come down with the most appalling cold.'

'Again?' said Elizabeth.

'He's having one of those winters,' said Linda. 'He's getting cold after cold.'

'That's the fourth cold he's had to my knowledge,' said Elizabeth, 'and it isn't even Christmas yet.'

'Winter colds are nasty,' said Lettuce. 'Sometimes they come back for a second bite.'

'Summer colds can be tricky customers,' said Jimmy. 'Persistent little pip-squeaks, summer colds.'

'There are an awful lot of awful colds around,' said David Harris-Jones. 'Especially in Surrey. Or so I heard.'

'I read that too,' said Lettuce. 'It said that the Bagshot district was practically awash.'

'Is it really? Amazing,' said Reggie. 'Any news of Woking?'

Elizabeth stood up hurriedly.

'Will you help me a moment, darling?' she said, striding to the door.

'Right,' said Reggie. 'Jimmy, give everyone a refill will you?'

'Message received,' said Jimmy. 'Drinks situation in control.'

'I had to get you out of there,' said Elizabeth, when they were in the kitchen. 'You looked as if you were ready to explode.'

'I'm sorry, darling, but it isn't exactly Café Royal stuff, is it? I mean I don't imagine Oscar Wilde said: "Hello, Bosie. What's the old A.282 like these days? Only I haven't seen it recently, because I've had this awful runny summer cold, I've been sneezing all over my new slatted garden furniture." '

Elizabeth peered into an orange casserole, and a succulent aroma of fowl and wine arose.

'Do you think Tom's all right?' she said.

'He's got a cold.'

'He's had several colds.'

'All right. He's had several colds.'

'It's not like him. He's not a cold person. He told me so himself.'

'I'm sure he did.'

She tasted the succulent dish, and it evidently pleased her, since she added no further seasoning.

'Do you think he's run down because things aren't "all right" between him and Linda?'

'What? Women and their imaginations – you're incredible. I distinctly heard Mrs Milford sneeze the other day. Is divorce pending, do you think?'

'Sarcasm is not a lovable trait, Reggie.'

'I'm sorry, darling. M'm, that smells good.'

Elizabeth laughed. He kissed her. They stood in front of the oven, and their tongues entered each other's mouths.

'Oops, sorry,' said Lettuce, turning scarlet. 'I'm looking for the powder-room.'

Reggie explained the way and Lettuce departed in some confusion.

'That'll give her something to think about while she clips her moustache,' said Reggie.

'Reggie!' said Elizabeth, and then she laughed. 'Poor Jimmy!' she said. 'Poor Jimmy and poor Linda. Do we ever like the people our loved ones love?'

Reggie behaved himself at dinner, and the wine and conversation flowed round the oval walnut table in the dignified, rarely used dining-room with its dark green striped wallpaper.

Tom arrived as they were finishing the kipper pâté.

'How did you get here?' said Linda.

'Taxi,' said Tom.

'How's your cold?' said Elizabeth.

Linda did a frantic sneezing and nose-blowing mime to Tom. He stared at her in astonishment.

'What cold?' he said. 'I haven't got a cold.'

'Linda said you had a frightful cold,' said Elizabeth.

'Several colds,' said Reggie.

'Of course I haven't got several colds,' said Tom.

'Tom!' said Linda.

'These are nice chairs,' said David Harris-Jones.

'Top-hole chairs,' said Jimmy.

'How could I have several colds?' said Tom.

'A-1 seating arrangements,' said Jimmy.

'One cold at a time,' said Reggie. 'You've been absent from our gatherings with a string of absolute snorters.'

'I haven't had a cold for six years,' said Tom.

'Tom!' said Linda.

'Have I said something wrong?' said Tom.

155

'Yes, Tom, you have,' hissed Linda. 'Those times you wouldn't come, I pretended you'd got colds.'

Elizabeth gave Tom some pâté. He sat between Prue and Lettuce and ate hungrily.

'If you said I'd got a throat it would have sounded more convincing,' he said with his mouth full. 'I do get the occasional throat. My throat's my Achilles heel. Some people are throat people. Other people are cold people. I'm a throat person.'

Linda burst into tears and rushed from the room. Jimmy hurried after her. He caught her up on the landing.

'Chin up,' he said, and kissed her.

'Not here,' she said, pushing him off. 'Not here.'

'Sorry. Out of bounds,' he said, handing her one of his demob handkerchiefs. 'Good blow.'

Linda blew her nose and returned to the dining-room. Lettuce gave Jimmy a cold look. Elizabeth brought in the casserole of pigeons in red wine and there were exaggerated cries of delight.

Tom patted Linda's hand across the table.

'Sitting at home, all alone, I thought what a fool I'd been,' he said.

'Every marriage, bad patches,' said Jimmy. 'Par for course. Bad patch in my marriage. Honeymoon to divorce.'

'That's all in the past,' boomed Lettuce.

'Thanks, Lettuce,' said Jimmy, stroking the rocky amplitude of her knees beneath the table. On its way back to his glass Jimmy's hand rested briefly on what he thought was Linda's thigh. Feeling his thigh being stroked, Tom gazed at Prue in some surprise.

'I'm sorry,' said Prue. 'I've gone a bit funny with food lately. I can't seem to eat birds.'

'She doesn't mind just sitting there and having nothing, though, do you?' said David Harris-Jones.

'There's one thing I would like, if you've got it,' said Prue. 'Bath Olivers and marmite.'

They demolished their pigeons and Prue demolished her Bath Olivers and marmite.

'Lettuce, Prue?' said Reggie, passing round the green salad.

'No thank you. It wouldn't really go,' said Prue.

'Lettuce, Lettuce?' said Reggie.

'Thank you,' said Lettuce.

Reggie caught Linda's eye.

Elizabeth asked Jimmy to help her clear up.

'Message received,' he said. 'Chin-wag time.'

In the kitchen Elizabeth said: 'I have to ask you. Will you give up your private army now you're engaged?'

' 'Fraid not, old girl,' said Jimmy. 'I've put Lettuce in picture. She approves. Grand girl, isn't she?'

'Yes.'

Jimmy picked up the large cut-glass bowl containing the lemon mousse.

'No oil-painting myself,' he said.

'It's been over two years,' said Elizabeth. 'Do you really think your army will ever be needed?'

'Hope not,' said Jimmy. 'Deterrent. Prevention better than cure.'

They all enjoyed the lemon mousse, except for Prue.

'It's the texture,' she said. 'I've suddenly gone all silly over textures.'

'You're a sensible girl not to be embarrassed,' said Elizabeth.

'Prue is a lovely girl,' said Reggie. 'She's not embarrassed. She doesn't talk about garden furniture. She's going to have a lovely baby.'

'I tell you what I'd really like,' said Prue. 'Some more Bath Olivers and marmite.'

They soon polished off the lemon mousse, and there was cheese to follow. Prue soon polished off the Bath Olivers and marmite, and there were Bath Olivers and marmite to follow.

'Last time I came to this house,' said David Harris-Jones, 'I got drunk. I got blotto. I got arse-holed.'

David Harris-Jones roared with laughter. Tom and Linda wanted to do the washing up. So did Jimmy and Lettuce.

'Let Tom and Linda do it,' said Reggie.

When they had left the room, Reggie said: 'They want to be alone for a few minutes to patch up their differences.'

David Harris-Jones fell asleep, and Prue's contractions began.

'I think I'm starting,' she said.

They woke David Harris-Jones up and told him the news. He fainted.

There was a loud crash of crockery from the kitchen, followed by the slamming of a door. Then the door slammed again, and a car drove off very fast.

David Harris-Jones began to come round, Prue had another contraction, and the doorbell rang.

It was Tom.

'Linda's driven off in the car,' he said.

Reggie took Prue, David and Tom in his car. He dropped David and Prue at the maternity home and took Tom to his home.

It was five past two when he got home.

'I don't dislike people,' he said. 'Just dinner parties.'

Doc Morrissey arrived promptly at twelve on the Tuesday. He sat down with alacrity and back-ache.

'What's the trouble?' said Reggie.

'No idea.'

'You ought to see an osteopath,' said Reggie, offering him a cigar.

'I shouldn't smoke,' said Doc Morrissey, accepting. 'I've got some kind of a breathing problem, don't know what it is.'

Reggie felt embarrassed in Doc Morrissey's presence. To the struggling medico, the three telephones, the cigars and the large desk must be vulgar signs of success and opulence.

'Well, how are things with you, Doc?' he asked with forced breeziness.

'I got dismissed from the British Medical Association.'

'Oh dear. What was it for?'

'Gross professional incompetence.'

'Oh dear.'

'I got these terrible stomach pains. I'd rushed a mutton vindaloo at lunch-time and I put it down to indigestion.'

'Treacherous chaps, mutton vindaloos.'

'Well exactly. My sentiments entirely. I paid a visit to this character, and lo and behold, he'd got the same pains as me. "Indigestion," I said, and I gave him the white pills. People like indigestion pills to be white, I find.'

'And it wasn't indigestion?'

'Acute appendicitis.'

'Oh dear.'

'I realized the truth when I collapsed at evening surgery and my partner diagnosed that *mine* was acute appendicitis.'

'Oh dear.'

Reggie leant forward persuasively.

'I've got a vacancy for a manager at my Climthorpe branch,' he said. 'How would you like it?'

Doc Morrissey stared at him in amazement.

'Me? You're offering me a job?'

'Yes.'

Doc Morrissey relit his cigar with trembling fingers.

'I think you'd be the ideal man for the job,' said Reggie.

'But I've never managed a shop in my life.'

'When you started out as a doctor, you'd never been a doctor.'

'No. And look what happened.'

'Healing was not your métier,' said Reggie.

'No.'

'You were a square peg in a round hole.'

'I felt that.'

Reggie held his lighter out and relit Doc Morrissey's cigar.

'I didn't get where I am today without knowing a square peg in a round hole when I . . . oh my God.'

'What?'

'I used C.J.'s phrase.'

Reggie was deeply shocked. Did it mean he was beginning to take his tycoonery seriously?

'Sorry. I'm a bit shocked,' he said.

'I'm not surprised. What a terrible thing to happen.'

'I didn't get where I am today by using C.J.'s phrases.'

'Absolutely not, Reggie.'

'Where were we, Doc?'

'I was being a square peg in a round hole.'

'Oh yes.'

Doc Morrissey abandoned the cigar. It had fractured and wasn't drawing.

'I'd like you to take the job, Doc.'

'I'd like to take it, Reggie.'

'Good. Let's go and have a spot of lunch.'

Reggie put an affectionate arm on Doc Morrissey's shoulder and steered him towards the door.

'I can't eat much,' said the stooping ex-diagnostician. 'My stomach's playing me up.'

'You really ought to see a doctor,' said Reggie.

'I don't trust them,' said Doc Morrissey. 'All they ever do

is give you two aspirins and tell you they've got it worse.'

The illuminated inn-sign of the Dissipated Kipper swung in the cold gusty wind high up on the Hog's Back in the Surrey hills. Motorists scurrying home at sixty-five miles an hour caught a brief glimpse of a dandyish smoked herring with a paunch and a monocle holding a glass of whisky in his hand while placing his bet at the roulette table.

Reggie swung carefully off the A.31 into the asphalted car park of the popular road house. His heart was beating fast as he stepped out of the night into the bright warmth of the bar.

Models of a Spitfire, a Mosquito and a Lancaster stood on the wide window-sills. Aeroplane propellers hung on both brick chimney pieces and a third concealed the florid wrought iron grille above the bar. A fourth smaller propeller adorned the upper lip of the beefy landlord.

'Pint of bitter, please,' said Reggie.

'Pint of bitter. Whacko,' rumbled mine enormous host.

'You're ex-RAF, are you?' said Reggie.

'Got it in one,' said the landlord. 'Have you heard the one about the Irish kamikazi pilot, flew twenty-seven successful missions? Did you hear about the Irish Bill Haley band, two o'clock, seventeen o'clock, nine o'clock rock?'

'Why is the pub called the Dissipated Kipper?' said Reggie, deliberately handing the landlord a ten pound note.

'Ah! Thereby hangs a tale. Thereby hangs a tale,' said the landlord, counting out Reggie's change. 'Nobody knows. All I know is, there's only one pub called the Dissipated Kipper, and this is it. Ask anyone from Dorking to Basingstoke where the Dissipated Kipper is, and they'll say: "That's Tiny Jefferson's place on the Hog's Back." '

Suddenly Joan was there beside him kissing him and all thoughts of Tiny Jefferson receded.

They sat in an alcove beside one of the brick chimney breasts. Joan winked shyly with her right eye and kissed him again.

'This is nice,' she said.

'Yes ... er ... yes it is.'

Reggie disengaged himself gently from the kiss.

'Joan, I ... er ... I have a proposition to make,' he said.

'That sounds promising,' she said.

'I'll give you fifty per cent more than you're getting at the moment,' he said.

There was a brief silence.

'What are we talking about?' she said.

'Money,' he said. 'I'm offering you a job.'

'Oh, I see.'

'Well what did you think ... oh, I see. No, Joan, I ... er ... I'm asking you to be my secretary.'

'Come on. Buy up or shove off, Farnham Rentals,' yelled Tiny Jefferson to a group of young men laughing pleasantly at the bar.

'How are things?' said Reggie.

'Pretty grim,' said Joan. 'My boss is a big man in ointment. I type letters about wonder cures for acne and blackheads.'

Reggie put a sympathetic hand on her knee.

'He's also the fly in the ointment,' said Joan. 'He's as randy as nobody's business.'

Reggie removed the sympathetic hand from her knee.

'The Tony business hit me hard,' she said. 'I don't seem to have much luck in marriage.'

'I'd like to wring his neck,' said Reggie.

'Join the queue.'

A large man with a ginger moustache, sitting in the alcove opposite, gave Reggie a smile of lecherous connivance.

'I want to make one thing clear,' said Reggie. 'Oh God, I sound pompous. My offer of a job is purely professional. Whatever happened before mustn't happen again.'

'Nothing happened before.'

'Whatever almost happened before mustn't even almost happen again.'

'I understand, Mr Perrin. You're important now. You've got too much to risk losing it by flirting with a bit of stuff at the office.'

'Well there's no more to be said then,' said Reggie.

'I'm sorry,' said Joan.

Reggie looked her straight in the eyes.

'I love Elizabeth,' he said. 'I can't imagine her going off to have assignations with people from Godalming, so I don't feel I should. If you think that my conditions will be too difficult . . .'

'You mean, if I feel incapable of being in close proximity to you without having irresistible sexual desires . . .'

Reggie laughed.

'Same again?' he said.

'My turn,' said Joan.

'No, no,' said Reggie. 'I asked you here.'

'I insist,' said Joan.

Reggie watched her as she walked to the bar.

She turned to smile at him and he looked away.

The man in the opposite alcove winked. Reggie thought about giving him a glacial stare, decided that would be intolerably priggish, and winked back.

When Joan returned, they sat in silence for some moments.

'Well?' said Reggie at length.

'I would have to make a condition as well,' said Joan.

'Fire away.'

'When I walked to the bar just then, I felt you looking at me.'

'I was.'

'No looks, Mr Perrin. If I am not to be allowed a personal relationship, you will give me no lecherous glances, no furtive looks when I cross my legs, no helping hand that strays slightly when I put on my coat, no meaningful remarks about how I spend my weekend, nothing whatever that could be regarded as in any way sexual.'

'I think that's fair,' said Reggie. 'But in that case I must make another condition. Phase Three of our Social Contract. If I'm not to look at you crossing your legs, you mustn't cross your legs. Nothing in any way provocative.'

'I suppose that's fair enough too,' said Joan.

'Do you think I ought to introduce the conditions into a written contract?' said Reggie. 'It might open a new chapter in industrial relations.'

163

'Won't it be a bit uncomfortable?' she said. 'Sitting there not touching each other and not looking at each other not crossing our legs.'

'It'll still be better than Miss Erith,' said Reggie.

'In that case I accept,' said Joan.

It was decided that she would start on the first Monday in February.

'How are your children?' he asked.

'What children? I haven't got any children.'

'What? But you always used to have three children.'

Joan blushed deeply and Reggie felt embarrassed for her.

'Wishful thinking,' she said.

He stroked her hand and explained about the lecherous man in the opposite alcove, and as they walked to their cars he patted her on the bottom and said 'Room 238' in a loud whisper. The man winked.

In the car park, while the sign of the Dissipated Kipper clanked in the rising gale, Reggie turned towards Joan.

'The conditions of employment are not yet binding,' he said.

Their lips met. They worked hungrily at each other's mouths.

A car swung into the car-park and they were flooded in the glare of its headlamps.

Then the lights were switched off, and their kiss ended.

'Try and have a good Christmas, Mrs Webster,' said Reggie.

On the Sunday before Christmas, news came at last of Mark's activities. A report in the *Observer* named him as one of the cast in a group of freelance theatrical mercenaries, dedicated to the incitement of revolutionary fervour through the unlikely medium of the plays of J. M. Barrie, rewritten by the legendary Idi 'Post-Imperialist Oppression' Okombe. Appearing with him were such shadowy figures of menace as Tariq Alhambra, known as the Red Gielgud, and lovely Belinda Longstone, the polystyrene heiress.

The news lent an unusual gravity to the seasonal toast of 'absent friends'.

Chapter 17

Swirling snow filled the world on the first Monday in January. Bewildered robins huddled in the nooks of apple trees, and the imprints of Elizabeth's Wellington boots on the white pavements of the Poets' Estate looked dainty beside the huge depressions left by Reggie.

It was the first time in more than twenty-five years of married life that they had set out for work together and their hands linked tenderly beneath their stout gloves. The trim gardens were transformed into white fantasies, and the names of the great poets were hidden beneath the snow.

On Climthorpe Station people stood five deep. No trains came. It was so quiet that you could have heard the shares of a pin company drop.

'Three inches of snow, and the nation grinds to a halt,' grumbled an investment consultant.

'I was in twenty-two inches of snow in Montreal, and my train was thirty seconds late,' countered a fabrics manufacturer.

'We had seven foot drifts in the suburbs of Helsinki,' put in a quantity surveyor. 'My train was one minute early.'

'I was standing by the St Lawrence river, waiting for a ferry,' said Reggie. 'There was a seventy mile an hour blizzard, four feet of level snow, and thick ice on the river. The ferry didn't come for three months.'

Elizabeth squeezed his arm.

They managed to force themselves on to the second train of the morning, and arrived at Waterloo at ten past eleven.

At twenty-five past eleven the joint managing directors of Perrin Products approached the main entrance of Head Office arm in arm. The sky was a dirty yellow and light snow was still falling.

They climbed the steps cautiously.

'You don't have to open the doors,' said Reggie. 'They slide automatically.'

'We *have* come up in the world,' said Elizabeth.

The doors jammed and they crashed into the glass. They were shaken but not injured.

Many people including Miss Erith had still not arrived. Mr Bulstrode didn't arrive at all. At two o'clock he decided to turn round and go home, and it was eight thirty-five before he managed it.

Reggie installed Elizabeth in her office, where she would oversee the creation of a European empire for Grot. There were three potted plants and pictures of Chartres, Speyer, Milan and Louvain cathedrals.

There was a hesitant knock on the door.

'It's your office,' said Reggie. 'It's for you to say: "Come in." '

'Come in,' said Elizabeth self-consciously.

It was David Harris-Jones.

'How's the baby boy?' said Elizabeth.

'Super,' said David. 'We're going to call him Reginald and we want you to be the godfather, Reggie.'

'Thank you,' said Reggie.

David Harris-Jones handed him a copy of the *Guardian*. It was open at page thirteen.

'Column three,' he said.

'Rumours of trouble at Sunshine Desserts, the London food manufacturers, were strongly denied last night by the Managing Director, Mr Charles Jefferson,' read Reggie in the financial news.

'Results at Bunshine Desserts have been disappointing for some time, but in recent weeks there have been rumours of a more disturbing kind, and there have been embarrassing delays in delicate merger negotiations with one of the convenience food giants.

'Shares have fallen steadily, closing on Friday at 57½p – 19p down in a month – and an interim divident declaration has been delayed.

'Mr Jefferson is something of a mystery man, cloaking his

166

personal life in obsessive secrecy. He is known to his employees simply as C.J., and is variously rumoured to hail from Riga, the Balkans and even America. He lives in a large house near Godalming, and his one known relaxation is fishing.

'In his statement Mr Jefferson said: "It has come to my notice that there are rumours of serious difficulties and irregularities at Sunshine Desserts. This is nonsense. We have had our troubles, but we will overcome them. O didn't get where I am today without learning how to overcome troubles.

' "I only wish these vile rumours could be printed, so that I could have an opportunity to sue these despicable sandal-mongers½ could have an opportunity to sue these despicable scandal-mongers.

' "It has been suggested that there is no smoke without a fire. I might reply that it is an ill wind that blows nobody any good."

'The exact meaning of Mr Jefferson's last remark is somewhat obscure, and it remains to be seen how his statement will be greeted by market sentiment, which is notoriously sceptical of protestations of innocence.'

'Very interesting,' said Reggie. 'So, his name's Charles Jefferson, is it?'

They went to the pub for lunch and everyone discussed how long it had taken them to get to work. One man had spoken on the telephone to a man whose brother worked with a man who had taken three hours to drive from North Ockendon to South Ockendon.

In the afternoon they set off for home. It was seven forty-five before they arrived.

It had not been a constructive first day for Elizabeth.

The cold snap passed. The trains returned to normal. Mr Bulstrode's pneumonia responded to treatment.

The shares of Sunshine Desserts slumped.

The first reactions to Grot's fifty per cent across the board price rises were favourable. Sales hardly dropped, and in some shops actually rose.

The shares of Perrin Products and of Grot rose.

The Honorary President of Climthorpe Albion Football Club, of the Southern League First Division South, collapsed at a health farm and died. Reggie was invited to take his place. He accepted with pleasure and took his seat in the directors' box in the rickety, green-painted, four hundred seater grand-stand. Also present were the Chairman of the Climthorpe Chamber of Commerce, and Reggie's bank manager, who intimated that he would feel happier with life at this moment in time if Reggie were to make more use of the bank's credit facilities.

A keen wind kept the crowd down to 327. Takings in the bar were twenty-eight pounds seventy-five pence.

Climthorpe beat Waterlooville 5–1, with goals from PUNT, FITTOCK, CLENCH (2) and RUTTER. They rose two places to fifteenth.

Truly it began to seem that Reginald Iolanthe Perrin had a magic touch. Many shrewd students of life were heard to aver that he was an all-round good egg.

Notices of dismissal were given to all Sunshine Desserts' employees, and the receiver was called in.

A scandal over illicit share dealings in Luxembourg, Guernsey and Rhodesia broke over the head of C.J. There were dark tales linking his name with the arrest of the master of a Swedish cargo vessel in Bilbao for gun-running, and the shooting in Chile of a Turk said to have been spying for the CIA in Poland.

C.J.'s brother, Mr Cedric 'Tiny' Jefferson, landlord of the Dissipated Kipper on the Hog's Back, spoke freely to thirsty pressmen about his brother. It seemed that C.J. had not been born in Riga, the Balkans or America. He was born and bred in Eltham, the son of a London Transport bus inspector, and had served in the Pay Corps during the latter stages of the Second World War. The brothers had drifted apart socially more than they had geographically, and Cedric 'Tiny' Jefferson had no idea if the rumours of scandal were true. But he had once met a foreigner with a duelling scar at C.J.'s house, so there might well be something in it. Had the thirsty pressmen heard the one about the Irish kamikazi pilot?

Climthorpe beat Trowbridge 2–1 away, with goals from MALLET and FITTOCK. Fittock became leading scorer for the season, with four goals.

Reggie and Elizabeth received an invitation to attend the wedding of James Gordonstoun Anderson and Lettuce Isobel Horncastle in the Church of St Peter at Bagwell Heath. They accepted.

Climthorpe beat Metropolitan Police 4–2, with goals by CLENCH, MALLET, FITTOCK and P. C. TREMLETT (own goal). The crowd was 426.

One evening, when the weather was dry with a moderate frost, and there was nothing much on television, there was a ring at Reggie's door.

A girl of about nineteen, shivering with cold and embarrassment, tried to smile at him and failed.

'Mr Perrin?' she said.

'Yes.'

'I work at your shop Grot. I'd like to talk to you.'

He invited her in. She refused a drink, saying she'd prefer coffee. Elizabeth went to get her one.

'Now then,' said Reggie, feeling suddenly rather old. 'What's all this about?'

She wasn't exactly pretty, but there was a certain rather delicate charm about her pinched features.

'It's Mr Morrison, the manager,' she said.

'You don't like Mr Morrissey?'

'He's all right. It's just that he . . .'

She hesitated.

'You can tell me,' he said. 'What's he done?'

She sat uncomfortably on the edge of her chair. There was a beauty mark on her left cheek, and a hole in her tights. Few of the Grot shops employed girls like this. Most of them employed dolly girls with voices like hysterical gravel. Reggie liked her.

'He hasn't done nothing really, not, you know, done.'

'Well what has he not done then?'

'He undresses us.'

'He takes your clothes off?'

'He sort of gives us these looks.'

'He undresses you in his mind?'

'Yeah. Me and Doreen.'

'And you don't like that?'

'Doreen doesn't mind. She'll give as good as she gets, that one.'

'But you're different?'

'Yeah. I know it's supposed to be permissive and that, but I'm not like that.'

Elizabeth entered with the coffee and sat beside the girl.

'Has he done anything else except look?' said Reggie.

'He sort of touches you, know what I mean? Not like touches you exactly, nothing you can put your finger on, he sort of brushes up against you, like it's an accident, only you know it isn't. Doreen says not to worry, they're all dirty old men at that age, but I don't like it. I know I shouldn't have come here, Doreen'll kill me if she finds out, but I like it there, I hated it at the shoe shop and the darts factory, I don't want to leave.'

She burnt her lips on the coffee, and her hands were chapped. Her inability to relax made Reggie tired.

'What do you want my husband to do?' said Elizabeth.

'I don't want to get Mr Morrison into trouble,' said the girl.

'You want me to stop him doing it, without telling him that I know he does. That won't be easy,' said Reggie.

The coffee was making the girl's nose run, and Elizabeth gave her a tissue.

'Does he do anything except give you looks and brush against you?' said Reggie.

'He makes remarks,' said the girl.

'What sort of remarks?'

'You know, remarks.'

'Suggestions?' suggested Elizabeth.

'Not so's you'd call them suggestions. Just remarks. I mean he's quite nice really.'

'And the running of the shop's all right?' said Reggie.

'I wouldn't like to run him down behind his back.'

'Of course not. So there's no problem apart from the looking and the touching and the remarks?'

'Oh no. I mean . . .'

'Yes?'

'There's the prices.'

'The prices?'

'He gives things away cheap to people he's sorry for.'

'What sort of people?'

'Kids. The old folk. Girls. Especially girls.'

The grandfather clock in the hall struck nine.

'So trade's good anyway?' said Reggie.

The girl seemed a little uneasy about answering.

'Put it this way,' she said at last. 'We're running out of things.'

'You shouldn't run out of things,' said Reggie. 'Why do you think you're running out of things?'

'It's not for me to say,' said the girl.

'Suppose I asked you directly why you think Mr Morrissey is running out of things.'

'He forgets to order them, if you ask me. I think he gets in a bit of a tiswas with the book side of things.'

She finished her coffee, sniffed as quietly as she could, and dabbed irresolutely at the end of her nose with the tissue.

'Thanks for the coffee,' she said.

'You're welcome,' said Elizabeth.

'Tell me,' said Reggie. 'Can you think of anything else Mr Morrissey does wrong apart from giving you looks and making remarks and brushing up against you and selling things cheap to kids, the old folk and girls, especially girls, and forgetting to make his orders and getting in a tiswas over the books?'

'No,' said the girl. 'And even if I could I wouldn't tell you. I wouldn't want to run him down behind his back.'

*

In the morning Reggie called in to see Doc Morrissey. The shop was in the High Street now, between the Leeds Permanent Building Society and the Uttoxeter Temporary Building Society. The single word *GROT* was painted in elegant gold, and the interior of the shop was decorated in green and gold.

Reggie could see that the shop was badly run. The window-display was uninspired, there were gaps on the shelves, and the items in the display-counters were haphazardly arranged.

The girl who had visited him blushed scarlet. The busty Doreen looked at her in surprise.

Doc Morrissey was reading the *Daily Mirror* in his office. He leapt to his feet when Reggie entered.

'I was just having a few moments to myself,' he said. 'We've been rushed off our feet all week.'

'Everything all right?' said Reggie.

'Splendid.'

'One or two lines seem a little non-existent.'

'Trade's so good. And I've got some stuff coming in the morning.'

'Good. Managing the books all right?'

'It's a doddle,' said Doc Morrissey, bringing an expansive hand down on a row of ledgers, from which a cloud of dust arose.

'No trouble with VAT?'

'VAT?'

'You're supposed to keep full VAT records.'

'Ah yes. I remember now.'

Reggie asked Doc Morrissey to come to the office on early closing day, and bring all the books with him.

As he was passing the War Memorial on his way to the station, a Grot van crawled by in the traffic. It was olive green and had on its side, in gold lettering: 'GROT – Never Knowingly Oversold.'

'Going to Climthorpe?' Reggie called out hopefully.

'No, squire. Uxbridge,' said the driver. 'No orders for Climthorpe.'

*

Miss Erith was working out her notice, and Reggie detected an icy hauteur beneath her habitual frigidity, as she said: 'Mr Fogden to see you, sir.'

Reggie re-read Owen Lewis's letter of recommendation.

'Dear Reggie,' it ran. 'I have a vague acquaintance called Fogden who invents things. He has a new line he thinks you may like. He's a founder member of the fruit-cake brigade and an absolute pain in the backside, uses my local when he's on parole from the loonie-bin. I happened to mention I knew you and he's been pestering me to put him in touch ever since. I'd be eternally grateful if you'd get him off my back.'

Reggie put the letter down and sent for Mr Fogden. There entered a small man with a bald head, a drooping moustache, a shiny suit, and a large, shabby portmanteau. He looked like a Hercule Poirot impressionist who had fallen on hard times.

'I've had a letter of recommendation from Mr Lewis,' said Reggie. 'He speaks of you in the warmest terms.'

'How gratifying,' said Mr Fogden. 'I always had the impression that he disliked me. Well, well. I shall go round to the hostelry that he frequents this very evening and purchase him a thankful libation.'

'Good idea,' said Reggie. 'He'll appreciate that. Now, what is your great idea?'

'Edible furniture.'

'I see.'

'I've had no joy at all at Waring and Gillow. Maples rebuffed me – I can use no other words – and for a store of style and initiative I felt that Heals treated me with short shrift.'

Reggie leant forward and favoured the little inventor with an incredulous gaze.

'Do you mean to say that you take your edible furniture seriously?' he said.

Mr Fogden looked affronted.

'But of course,' he said. 'It's cheap to make, comfortable to sit in and tasty to eat.'

'I see. Well why are you coming to me then?' said Reggie. 'My stores sell only useless objects.'

'You are my last hope,' said Mr Fogden. 'All other avenues are closed to me.'

'Well, what have you got to show me?'

'I have some samples in my portmanteau,' said Mr Fogden. 'They are miniatures to the scale of one in thirty.'

He opened the case with tremulous fingers. Reggie gazed at an array of minuscule chairs, tables and wardrobes.

'They look very nice,' he said. 'What exactly have you here?'

'Gingerbread chairs,' said Mr Fogden. 'Toffee tables. A marzipan pouffe. A G-plan macaroon. A steak chair . . .'

'A steak chair? Surely it'll go off, become a high chair?'

'They made the same cheap crack at Heals.'

'Do you really think, Mr Fogden, that people will want to eat stuff that has been sat upon by human bottoms?' said Reggie.

'Oh dear oh dear. Just what the man said at Waring and Gillow. Where is the spirit of innovation that made Britain great?'

Mr Fogden clipped his portmanteau shut.

'This nation is the graveyard of its own inventors,' he said. 'Boffin Island? More like Baffin Island, say I.'

And he set off towards the door.

'Wait a minute,' said Reggie. 'I'd like to try them.'

Mr Fogden re-opened his portmanteau, and Reggie nibbled at two chairs, bit firmly into a table and toyed with a chest of drawers.

Surely nobody would buy edible furniture that tasted horrid?

He hadn't taken Grot so seriously when he had founded it. Was he taking it so seriously now that there wasn't room to provide a little income for this harmless lunatic in his declining years?

'I'll put the idea up to the board,' he said.

Doc Morrissey sat in the easy chair by Reggie's desk, clutching his sparkling new briefcase so tightly that there were white patches on his knuckles.

'Are the shop girls all right?' said Reggie.

'Fine. Why?'

'Do you ever sort of look at them?'

'Do I ever sort of look at them? Well of course I look at them.'

'Do you ever make remarks?'

'Do I ever make remarks? Well, of course I make remarks.'

'Absolutely. Of course you do. Quite right too. Do you ever sort of brush up against them?'

'Do I ever sort of brush up against them?'

'Yes.'

'Somebody's been talking, haven't they?'

'No. No. I just thought: "I wonder if Doc Morrissey brushes up against people." It was a silly thought. I mean, why should you?'

'What are you talking about, Reggie?'

'What indeed? Idle chatter, Doc. Well, that's fine. Let's have a look at the books, then.'

Doc Morrissey opened his briefcase, then shut it again.

'I'm becoming a dirty old man,' he said. 'Give me one more chance, Reggie. I won't frighten the girls any more.'

'Can I be sure of that?' said Reggie.

Doc Morrissey sighed.

'Other species don't suffer like people,' he said. 'Lizards don't start to drink earlier and earlier in the day. Hartebeests don't become dirty old hartebeests. Orang-outangs don't dread redundancy. Llamas don't go through the change of life. Elderly chameleons don't fear old age and tell their bored infants: "Natural camouflage isn't what it was when I was a lad."'

'They all end in death,' said Reggie. 'And most of them are frightened every day of their life.'

'Yes.'

'And now I'm afraid I must look at the books.'

'Yes.'

Doc Morrissey opened his briefcase again, then closed it again.

'I don't seem to have got the hang of the books,' he said.

Reggie felt tempted to give him another chance. What did it matter?

Then he thought of the girls who worked at the Climthorpe branch, the staff that he had now built around him, their hopes and aspirations.

He thought of his new standing in Climthorpe, and how much it delighted and amused him.

'I'm afraid I've got to sack you, Doc,' he said.

'Oh. Oh, I see.'

'Business is business, Doc.'

'Quite.'

'Faint heart never won fair terms.'

'No. Well, thank you for giving me the chance, Reggie. I'm sorry I let you down.'

Doc Morrissey left, and Reggie sat deep in thought.

He had sacked a man for inefficiency. He had caught himself using C.J.'s phrases. He had been on the point of turning down Mr Fogden's edible furniture.

He didn't like it. He didn't like it a bit.

The weather improved. Climthorpe beat Tamworth 1–0 in the FA Trophy, thanks to a FITTOCK header.

Chapter 18

Joan started work on the first Monday in February. When Reggie arrived he found her already seated in her place in the outer office.

'Good morning, Mr Perrin,' she said.

'Good morning, Mrs Webster,' he said. 'Twenty-two minutes late. Obstacles on the line at Berrylands.'

It was almost like old times. He threw his umbrella at the hat-stand joyously, and watched it sail through the window, which was open for purposes of cleaning.

He picked up the yellow phone.

'Ah, Mrs Webster,' he said. 'Your ... er ... your first task. I wonder if you'd mind going out and round the back of the building and you'll find my umbrella stuck in a grating.'

'Certainly, Mr Perrin.'

When Joan returned, Reggie said, 'Ah, there you are!'

He must stop stating the obvious.

'Take a letter, please, Mrs Webster,' he said.

Joan sat in the dictation chair, began to cross her legs, remembered not to, and uncrossed them hastily.

They laughed nervously. The new relationship wasn't going to be easy.

'To C.J., Blancmange Cottage, Godalming. Dear C.J., I was deeply distressed to read of all the troubles that have assailed you so undeservingly.'

He noticed an ironic gleam in her eyes. It was unnerving.

'It must be very distressing to Mrs C.J. and you. Elizabeth and I send you our deepest sympathy. It is very sad when a firm of the reputation and quality of Sunshine Desserts runs into little difficulties such as ... er ... bankruptcy and liquidation, and even more distressing when it is associated with vile calumnies which I am certain have no basis whatsoever in reality.'

He smiled at Joan. Again, the irony flickered across her eyes, and he almost wished he was dictating to Miss Erith.

'I am about to enter upon an expansionist phase, in my little business, and will need to recruit extra staff. If you feel that it would be of interest to you to come and discuss the position, I would indeed be honoured.'

Elizabeth came into the office.

'Hello, darling,' he said.

'Hello, darling,' she said.

'This is my new secretary, Joan Webster, darling,' he said.

'Not exactly new, darling,' said Elizabeth.

'No, not exactly new, darling. My old secretary who has now become my new secretary.'

'We know each other,' said Joan. 'We worked together.'

'We're old friends,' said Elizabeth. 'Joan's been to our house.'

'Oh yes,' said Reggie. 'So she has.'

'But unfortunately I was away,' said Elizabeth.

'Yes, that *was* unfortunate,' said Reggie. 'That will be all, Mrs Webster.'

Joan closed the door behind her so softly that it was as if she was emphasizing how much she would have liked to slam it.

Reggie and Elizabeth exchanged the sort of meaningful looks in which each knows that the other is being meaningful but doesn't know what they are meaning.

'I thought you were rather bitchy then,' said Reggie.

'You're always surprised when you find that I'm human,' said Elizabeth. 'I'm sure Joan says bitchy things about me. Do you rebuke her?'

'I can't really. She's only my secretary. You're my wife.'

Elizabeth stood at the window and glared at the offices of Amalgamated Asbestos as if they were responsible for all the troubles in the world.

'I'm sorry,' she said at length. 'I was in the wrong. We mustn't let personal feelings interfere with our work.'

'Of course we mustn't.'

He went up to the window and kissed her.

'Personal feelings don't come into it,' he said, holding his hands lightly on her breasts.

'Business is business,' she said, running her hands gently round his backside.

'Someone from Amalgamated Asbestos will see us,' he said.

They waved to Amalgamated Asbestos. Nobody waved back.

When Elizabeth had gone, Reggie sat in his chair, had a quick swivel, and sent for Joan. He swivelled slowly round and round, not looking at her legs. She sat, pencil poised, not crossing her legs and not looking at Reggie.

'I'm sorry about my wife's remarks,' he said.

'I ignored them,' said Joan. 'We mustn't let personal feelings interfere with our work.'

'No. Quite. Ring Luxifoam Furniture of Market Harborough, would you, and try and get me a Flexisit Executive Chair for immediate delivery.'

'Certainly, Mr Perrin.'

'To Tony Webster. You have his address?'

'Of course I do.'

' "Dear Tony, I was sorry to hear the sad news about Sunshine Desserts. If you would care to join my modest little business ..." You've stopped, Mrs Webster.'

'I want to give in my notice, Mr Perrin.'

'You've only been here an hour and a half.'

'The situation is impossible. I'm not working here with him,' said Joan.

'We mustn't let personal feelings interfere with our work,' said Reggie.

Joan refused to reconsider her notice. She never crossed her long, lovely legs and Reggie never looked at her long, lovely legs.

C.J. wrote a guarded reply saying that he would be delighted to see Reggie and suggesting Tuesday, March the second, at three-thirty.

Reggie replied that Friday, February the twenty-sixth, at ten would suit him very well.

Tony Webster wrote a guarded reply saying that he would be in town on Friday, February the twenty-sixth, and any time that day would be great.

Reggie replied that it would be great if Tony could come and see him at three-thirty on Tuesday, March the second.

Despite the absence of leading scorer Fittock, Climthorpe Albion beat Wigan 3–2 away in the third round of the FA trophy, with CLENCH recording the first hat trick of his career.

Mr Bulstrode returned to work after his severe attack of pneumonia. He arrived two hours late due to snow.

In the West Country, severe floods caused water rationing.

The days grew longer, and the weather grew harder. The pond by the cricket ground was quite frozen over.

The day of Jimmy's wedlock approached apace. Elizabeth bought them a magnificent set of matching sheets, towels, pillow-cases, bath-mat and lavatory seat-cover.

The sales in Grot shops began to grow more quickly. The new gilt imprint was now being put on every single item.

Four new shop sites were found and approved. Each would be designed in a very fashionable style, emphasizing the exclusiveness of Grot as *the* place for rubbish.

Climthorpe defeated Ashford 2–0 to move into tenth place in Division One South of the Southern League. PUNT and RUTTER were the scorers. The crowd was 602. The Ashford manager complained that the match should have been called off due to frost on the pitch.

On the last day but one of the penultimate week of Joan's brief stay at Perrin Products, the Flexisit Executive Chair arrived.

The following day, prompt on the dot of ten, C.J. arrived.

Reggie felt a frisson as he picked up the red phone and heard Joan say: 'C.J. is here, Mr Perrin.'

'I shan't keep him a moment,' said Reggie.

He adjusted the position of the Flexisit chair, made sure that there were cigars in the box, tidied his hair, twiddled his thumbs, and sent for C.J.

Reggie had expected that C.J. would reveal some signs of

the disappointments and ordeals that he had been through, but there were none.

They shook hands firmly.

'Good to see you, C.J. Sorry to keep you waiting,' he said. 'Do sit down.'

He indicated the Flexisit chair. C.J. sat. The chair made a raspberry noise. Reggie laughed.

'I'm sorry,' he said. 'It's that damned new chair. Most embarrassing.'

'Yes,' said C.J.

'The perils of buying British,' said Reggie.

'Absolutely, Perrin,' said C.J.

'How are you?' said Reggie.

'Bearing up, Perrin,' said C.J.

'Cigar?' said Reggie, pushing the box to the end of the desk.

'Thank you.'

C.J. tried to reach the cigar without getting up from the chair, but the chair was too far away from the desk. He stood up, pulled the chair forward, took a cigar and sat down. The chair blew another raspberry.

'Well,' said Reggie. 'We meet in altered circumstances.'

'We do indeed,' said C.J.

'The slings and arrows of outrageous fortune, C.J.'

'Well put, Reggie.'

'The night is darkest before the dawn,' said Reggie.

'Precisely,' said C.J. 'I didn't get where you are today without knowing that the night is darkest before the dawn.'

C.J. knocked the ash off his cigar into a Grot ashtray.

'That's a Grot ashtray,' said Reggie. 'It's got holes in it.'

'So it has,' said C.J., lifting the ashtray off the arm of the chair and watching the ash descend towards the thick pile carpet.

'Not one of our best sellers,' said Reggie.

'You astound me,' said C.J.

Joan entered with a tray of coffee. She looked at the two men, Reggie behind the large desk, C.J. uneasy in the Flexisit chair.

'Thank you, Joan,' said C.J., accepting the proffered beverage. 'Enjoying working for Mr Perrin, again, are you?'

'I'm leaving next week, C.J.,' said Joan. 'We don't see eye to eye.'

'Ah! Very wise in that case,' said C.J. 'One can't put one's nose to the millstone if one doesn't see eye to eye.'

'One certainly can't,' said Reggie.

Joan closed the door gently behind her.

'I met your brother,' said Reggie.

'Ah!' said C.J. 'All men are brothers, but some are more brothers than others.'

'What are your work plans?' said Reggie.

'Nobody'll touch me with a barge-pole,' said C.J.

Reggie stirred his coffee slowly and deliberately – and unnecessarily, since he didn't take sugar.

'Do you think you could work happily with me as your boss?' he said.

C.J. drew thoughtfully on his cigar.

'I've always taken great pains not to talk in clichés,' he said.

'You certainly have, C.J.'

'Mrs C.J. and I have always avoided clichés like the plague.'

'Absolutely, C.J.'

'A cliché to me is like a red rag to a bull. However, it's the exception that proves the rule, as they say, and there is one cliché that fits my situation like a glove.'

'What's that, C.J.?'

'Necessity is the mother of intention.'

'Very apt, C.J.'

C.J. tipped his ash into a proper ashtray, sipped his coffee, and grimaced.

'What's your offer?' he said.

'The same in real terms as you gave me at Sunshine Desserts,' said Reggie.

'You strike a hard bargain, Perrin.'

'Yes. More coffee, C.J.?'

C.J.'s chair was now near enough to Reggie's desk to

enable him to hold his cup out without leaving the chair.

'I want you to work on our expansion into Europe,' said Reggie, as he poured the acrid liquid into C.J.'s cup. 'The opportunities are boundless.'

He almost felt sorry for C.J., but he fought against it. When had C.J. ever felt sorry for him?

'You would be a totally independent operator,' said Reggie. 'But you would be directly accountable to my Joint Managing Director, and you would work in close liaison with her.'

'Her, Reggie?'

'My wife.'

'Ah! Your wife. I see. I . . . er . . . I see. I'll take the job, Perrin.'

They shook hands, and Reggie sent for Elizabeth on red.

'You know Elizabeth, don't you?' he said.

'Yes, I . . . I know Elizabeth.'

'Of course you do. Well no doubt you'll get to know her a whole lot better now you're working together.'

'No doubt I will,' said C.J.

Elizabeth entered the office.

'C.J.!' she exclaimed.

'Hello, Elizabeth. Excuse me if I don't get up,' said C.J. 'My back's locked.'

He shook hands with Elizabeth and she sat in the chair next to him. It was not a Flexisit chair and it did not blow a raspberry.

'C.J. has agreed to join our little team, I'm delighted to say,' said Reggie.

'What?'

'You're surprised, eh?' said C.J.

'He'll look after our European efforts and he'll be directly responsible to you,' said Reggie.

'And you fixed all this up without consulting me?' said Elizabeth.

'Does the idea of working with me appal you, Mrs Perrin?' said C.J.

'Er, no, of course not.'

Elizabeth smiled weakly.

'Do you have something against C.J.?' said Reggie.

'Er . . . no . . . no. It's just that I like to be consulted,' said Elizabeth lamely. 'I don't like being presented with a fait accompli.'

'I hope I'm not a fait accompli worse than death,' said C.J., and he gave a sharp bark of mirthless laughter.

'I suggest that C.J. starts on Monday week,' said Reggie. 'That'll give us a chance to get an office ready.'

'Ah!' said C.J. 'An office!'

He glanced with approval at Reggie's large desk, elegant light fittings and large plate window, and gave a slight frown at the pictures by Drs Snurd, Underwood and Wren.

'I'm a bit of a stickler for offices,' he said. 'I didn't get where you are today without being a bit of a stickler for offices. What sort of thing did you have in mind?'

'Something very similar to what I had at Sunshine Desserts,' said Reggie. 'You always said how nice that was.'

'Ah. Yes. Quite. Good,' said C.J.

Reggie stood up. C.J. and Elizabeth followed suit.

'I thought your back was locked,' said Elizabeth.

'It's unlocked itself,' said C.J. 'Funny things, backs.'

C.J. and Elizabeth made the long walk towards the door side by side.

'One point, C.J.,' said Reggie.

'Yes?'

'Do you feel that you can take on a new and challenging job in a highly modern business concept with drive and enthusiasm?'

'I'm sure I can,' said C.J.

'Good,' said Reggie. 'I'm glad to hear it. We aren't one of those dreadful firms who think people are old-fashioned just because they're over fifty.'

Joan's voice was icy.

'Mr Webster is here,' she said.

'Send him in, Joan.'

Tony entered the office jauntily but not too jauntily. The

184

Flexisit chair had been returned to the makers on the grounds that it made an embarrassing noise, and he sat on a silent German model.

'Good to see you again, Tony,' said Reggie.

'Great,' said Tony.

'I was sorry to hear about Sunshine Desserts.'

'Yes. Dramatic happenings in jelly city.'

'Quite. Cigar?'

'Great.'

Tony took a large cigar and lit it with aplomb. Reggie ordered coffee.

'Great pad you have here,' said Tony, glancing appreciatively round Reggie's lush executive womb.

'Yes. What are you planning to do next, Tony?'

'I've a lot of offers. I don't know which to take up.'

'There's not much point in my offering you a job, then. Still, nice to see you.'

'Oh, sod it,' said Tony. 'This is cards-on-the-table-ville. Obviously in the long term, in the *long* term, Tony Webster's still the lad.'

'But in the short term?'

'Nobody'll touch me with the proverbial.'

'Tarred with the C.J. brush?'

'Well, I should have seen the crash coming. It doesn't reflect well on my vision.'

'No.'

'I've been a twat, Reggie. That bastard C.J. really stitched me up. It's taught me a lesson, though. I've grown up at last.'

Joan entered with the coffee. Tony sprang to his feet.

'I'll take it,' he said.

'I'll do it,' said Joan.

Tony sat down reluctantly. Joan served coffee in icy silence.

'Phew!' said Tony when Joan had gone. 'Ouch city. Icebergsville.'

'She's an attractive woman,' said Reggie.

'Oh, sure, it's got good form.'

'If you want to get anywhere with Joan,' said Reggie,

'may I suggest you trying saying "she's very attractive" rather than "it's got good form"?'

'Thank you, Professor Higgins. Any other advice?'

'Yes. Ask her out to lunch tomorrow.'

'No chance. But no chance. Is this why you've got me here, to bring us together again? I always thought you fancied her yourself.'

'I think that if you really want Joan, and if you show great patience, and eschew Helsinki ravers and their ilk, you could find yourself in Main Street, Reconciliationsville.'

Tony gawped, momentarily speechless.

'Now to business,' said Reggie. 'I can offer you a job here, but you will not have the same status as you had at Sunshine Desserts. You'll have to prove yourself anew.'

'I will, Reggie.'

'In that case, Tony, why don't you start next Monday?'

'Great.'

Reggie poured Tony a second cup of coffee.

'I gave another Sunshine Desserts man a job last week,' he said.

'Oh. Who?'

'That bastard C.J.'

'I should be more careful of my tongue, shouldn't I?'

Reggie picked up the red phone.

'Ask the Head of Expansion (UK) to come in, would you, please, Joan?' he said. 'Your new boss,' he explained to Tony.

Tony turned pale.

'It isn't C.J., is it?' he asked.

'Would I do a thing like that to you – make you work with C.J. again? Of course it isn't C.J.'

'Oh good.'

'It's David Harris-Jones.'

'What?'

'It's David Harris-Jones.'

'You mean I'm to be under David Harris-Jones?'

'Yes.'

'Bloody hell.'

186

'Yes.'

There was a soft knock on the door.

'Come,' said Reggie.

David Harris-Jones approached them like a grounded bat.

'Oh hello, Tony. Super to see you,' he said.

'Tony's going to join us, David,' said Reggie.

'Super.'

'He's going to be working under you, David. You're his new boss.'

David and Tony looked at each other in silence for some seconds. David seemed almost as thunderstruck as Tony.

'Great,' said David Harris-Jones at last.

'Super,' said Tony Webster.

Joan was late back from her lunch with Tony the following day.

'Ah, you're back,' said Reggie as she entered with her dictation pad.

'I'm sorry, Mr Perrin. I got held up,' she said.

'Nice lunch?'

'Yes.'

She began to cross her legs, remembered, and uncrossed them.

'Good. Good. To the Quicksek Employment Bureau. Dear Sirs, I am urgently looking for a high-class secretary . . . You aren't taking it down, Joan.'

'You haven't replaced me yet, then, Mr Perrin?'

'Not yet, Joan. I soon will, though, don't worry. To the Quicksek Employment Bureau. Dear Sirs, . . .'

'Would it be all right if I stayed on, Mr Perrin?'

It was in breach of their unwritten contract, but he gave her a kiss.

The weather turned cold again for the weekend. There was snow on many football grounds, and the Pools Panel was called in. There was snow at Hillingdon, causing the abandonment of the third round F A Trophy match between Hillingdon and Climthorpe. And there was snow at Bagwell Heath, but it wasn't the snow that caused the abandonment of the match between James Gordonstoun Anderson and Lettuce Isobel Horncastle.

Chapter 19

The organist gave a spirited rendition of old favourites, and the heating system accompanied him with a cacophony of squeaks and gurgles.

There was a large gathering in the spacious fifteenth-century church with its famous Gothic font cover.

On the left were the friends and family of the bride.

There were small men with skin like old brown shoes.

There were large, fierce women, their massive faces so dark beneath their huge hats that it almost looked as if they could do with a shave. Truth to tell, several of them could.

There was one beautiful young blonde and a very tall distinguished man in morning dress.

There were eight rather embarrassed Indians in flowing robes, and three physiotherapists with hacking coughs.

On the right were the friends and family of the groom.

There were Tom and Linda and their two children, Adam and Jocasta. Adam had started proper school and nose-picking.

There were some old army colleagues, including a white-haired old man in the uniform of a colonel in the Territorial Army. They had red noses indicative of liquid indulgence.

There were three rows of large men from the ranks of assorted families.

There were three rows of large men from the ranks of Jimmy's secret army. They looked like retired boxers, sacked policemen and failed security guards.

Reggie and Elizabeth were just about to take their places in the church when an ancient Land Rover drew up, squirting slush across the pavement to the very foot of the white-coated lych-gate.

Out stepped Clive 'Lofty' Anstruther. He sported a carnation in his trench coat.

'Hello there,' he called to Reggie in an urgent but low voice.

Reggie walked hurriedly over towards him.

'I've lost the groom,' said Clive 'Lofty' Anstruther.

'Lost the groom?' said Reggie. 'How can you lose the groom?'

'Pub down road, quick one, Dutch courage. Groom goes for piss. Excuse language. Doesn't return. I go look-see. Not pissing. Missing.'

'What are we to do?' said Elizabeth.

'He may have just wanted a bit of time to himself to collect his thoughts,' said Reggie.

'Vamoosed,' said Clive 'Lofty' Anstruther. 'Cold feet. Don't blame him.'

The vicar rode up on his bicycle and wobbled to a slippery halt in the slush.

'Good morning,' he said. 'I feared I was cutting it fine, but I see no sign of the happy couple.'

'You may not do,' said Reggie. 'We appear to have lost the groom.'

'Lost the groom?' said the vicar. 'How can you lose the groom?'

'Stop off, pub, quick fortifier,' said Clive 'Lofty' Anstruther. 'Groom goes for a . . .'

'Groom goes to smallest room,' said Reggie hastily. 'Doesn't return. Best man worried. Best man goes to smallest room. No groom.'

'I see,' said the vicar. 'Well, maybe he just wanted a few minutes to himself. Believe me, in the nervous excitement of one's wedding day, anything can happen. Even I, so calm when officiating, felt decidedly queasy when I was on the receiving end. I expect he'll draw up any moment in a taxi.'

'He's vamoosed,' said Clive 'Lofty' Anstruther. 'He's gone AWOL.'

'He's a military man,' said Reggie.

'Ah!' said the vicar, as if that explained everything.

The vicar looked up and down the road.

'Still no sign of the lovely bride either,' he said.

'Without wishing to strike an uncharitable note on such a potentially auspicious occasion,' said Reggie, 'I think it is germane to the issue that the bride cannot by any stretch of the imagination be described as lovely.'

'Reggie!' said Elizabeth. 'What an awful thing to say!'

'Bloody true, though,' said Clive 'Lofty' Anstruther. 'She's as ugly as sin.'

'Sin is not ugly, because it is redeemable,' said the vicar. He glanced at his watch. 'What is the groom like? Is he also – excuse my bluntness – an horrendous specimen?'

'I'm his sister,' said Elizabeth.

'Dear lady, forgive me,' said the vicar.

'That's all right,' said Elizabeth. 'He isn't horrendous, but he's no oil-painting.'

'Perhaps the bride won't turn up either,' said the vicar.

'He's vamoosed,' repeated Clive 'Lofty' Anstruther. 'He's deserted in the face of the enemy.'

'And here comes the enemy now,' said Reggie.

A beribboned Rolls-Royce drove slowly round the edge of the churchyard, past the great yew.

'Oh dear, oh dear,' said the vicar, and he rushed up the snowy path and round the side of the church.

'You've still got your bicycle clips on,' called Reggie, but he was too late.

The driver of the Rolls-Royce braked. The car slid remorselessly onwards across the treacherous slush. It struck the vicar's bicycle a glancing blow before running gently into the back of the Land Rover.

'Bloody hell,' said Clive 'Lofty' Anstruther.

The driver descended from the car and examined the damage. Clive 'Lofty' Anstruther hurried over to remonstrate with him and examine the rear of the Land Rover.

The radiant bride descended slowly from the car. Nothing, it seemed, could spoil the greatest day of her life. Her incredulous father stepped out behind her, and two tiny bridesmaids in shocking pink held her proud white train clear of the slush.

Reggie stepped forward to speak, but his hesitant 'er . . .

excuse me' was tossed into the sky by the mocking wind of March.

The bride slid remorselessly past him, as unstoppable in her white tulle as a great tanker gliding down the slipway into the smooth waters of a Japanese inlet.

The procession swept into the church, and moved slowly up the aisle, while Reggie and Elizabeth crept round the side-aisle to their seats.

The organist, who had been approaching the end of his repertoire, struck up 'Here Comes the Bride' with joyous relief. The happy music swelled and burst upon bearded lady, bewildered Indian, bewhiskered colonel and bored right-wing fanatic alike. The right-wing fanatics gazed at Lettuce in open-mouthed astonishment.

Her father stepped back to stand alongside Clive 'Lofty' Anstruther, and the hapless cleric stood irresolute in his bicycle clips, as the bride turned a face stiff with exultation towards the empty space where the groom should have stood. The organist came to the end of the tune, and the church was filled with a dreadful silence, broken only by the coughing of the three physiotherapists.

The radiance on the bride's face turned to puzzlement. The vicar cleared his throat. The organist began 'Here Comes the Bride' at the beginning again.

Once more the resonant notes of the organ died slowly, like the last rumblings of celestial catarrh. There was a deep, damp, vaulted silence.

'We are gathered here today,' said the vicar, 'to witness the ceremony of Holy Matrimony, to join together two happy and radiant souls, one of whom we see here today. Alas, the efforts of the other to be present at the greatest day of his life seem to have met with some misfortune, some setback which is doubtless not unconnected with the inclement road conditions which are affecting Bagwell Heath and its environs, not to mention large areas of the Northern Hemisphere.'

The vicar glanced at his watch. It was the largest congregation he had had for years, and he wasn't going to let it go without a fight.

'Let us pray,' he said.

The congregation knelt.

'Almighty God,' improvised the vicar, 'Who hast delivered many travellers safely to their havens through danger and peril, storm and avalanche, flood and snow-drift, fog and typhoon, landslide and water-spout, grant, we beseech Thee, that Thy blessed subject James Gordonstoun Anderson, may be safely delivered to this place of worship through the perils of the March snow and the dangers of the new experimental one-way traffic system in Upper Bagwell, with its linked traffic lights and mini-roundabouts, that he may be truly and gratefully and joyously united in Holy Matrimony, through Jesus Christ our Lord, Amen.'

The congregation sat. The vicar, still ignorant of the partial destruction of his bicycle, walked as slowly as he dared into the pulpit, coughed as often as he dared, fixed the congregation with a fierce glare for as long as he dared, and finally, when he could delay no longer, spoke.

'What is Holy Matrimony?' he said. 'It is the union of two souls, is it not?'

The eight Indians, who had been looking somewhat puzzled, nodded.

'It is a solemn sacrament, which should not be entered upon lightly.'

'If at all?' whispered Reggie.

'S'ssh,' whispered Elizabeth.

'Vicar man's got a big nose,' said Adam.

Reggie thought about his infrequent visits to church. They seemed doomed to irregularity. On the last occasion he had attended his own memorial service, having no right to be there. Now Jimmy was not attending his own wedding, having every right, nay, obligation to be present. Reggie reflected on the many-layered ironies of life, while the vicar talked on, in the desperate hope that the groom would find unsuspected reserves of courage, and would finally arrive.

'Marriage is essentially a partnership,' he was saying, 'a matter of give and take.'

'Give up, vicar,' said Lettuce, in a loud, firm, resolute voice. 'The bastard isn't coming.'

Only on the exposed banks were there still traces of snow in the headlights. Relentless rain swept across the roads, filling the West Country rivers, turning Exe and Lyn and Dart into torrents, swelling Taw and Torridge and Tamar into muddy flood. On the darkened motorways the juggernauts sent jets of water streaming over Reggie's car, and on the good old A.303 the leak in the side window of Clive 'Lofty' Anstruther's Land Rover was worse than ever.

Where would Jimmy make for but back to earth, back to Trepanning House, in the County of Cornwall?

It had been decided that Reggie and Linda would stay at the Fishermen's Arms, Clive 'Lofty' Anstruther would keep vigil at Trepanning House, Elizabeth would wait at home, and Tom would look after Adam and Jocasta.

Tom had wanted to go in place of Linda, but she had insisted.

'Jimmy'll need cheering up, Tom,' she had said.

'Linda's right, Tom,' Reggie had said. 'Jimmy'll need cheering up. You'd better not come.'

As they drove over Bodmin Moor, where the remains of deep drifts were turning dull and grey in the rain, it was comforting to know that they had booked rooms in the hospitable old stone inn.

The road dropped steadily off the moor towards the anonymous, eponymous town. They were heading now for the ancient battered coasts where even a gorse bush was a minor miracle. The grey villages were silent and deserted in the cruel rain.

The last bell rang just as they drew up outside the Fishermen's Arms.

They drank beer and whisky chasers.

'We've seen nowt of him,' said Danny Arkwright. 'Nowt of him nor t'long bugger.'

'Well he'll have had to hitch-hike,' said Linda. 'Clive's got their car.'

'I made sure he were wed by now,' said the landlord. 'Hey, Annie!' he shouted.

The former canteen operative joined them.

'T'feller from Trepanning House what's getting married today, he never turned up.'

'Ee,' said the landlady. 'Who'd have thowt it?'

'I would for one,' said the landlord. 'She come down here back end, stayed like. I've seen better faces on pit ponies. Mind you, she'd come in handy pulling a truck of coal, I grant you that.'

'She wasn't that bad,' said the landlady.

'She was t'roughest I've seen for a long while. I'd rather marry Keith Kettleborough,' said the landlord.

Time passed. The lights were dimmed, and the dying firelight flickered faintly on the ceiling. Linda caught Mr and Mrs Arkwright giving her strange looks, and she felt certain that they recalled her evening in the bar with Jimmy.

Mrs Arkwright insisted on giving them ham and eggs, which proved highly palatable.

When Mr Arkwright opened the door to the back yard, a gusty wind blew in and rattled the sign over the bar which announced: 'Danny and Annie welcome you.'

At three in the morning, while they were discussing football coverage on television, they heard a Deep Sea Aggregates lorry thundering down the darkened road.

'Which is the best football commentator, John Motson or Tony Gubba?' asked Mr Arkwright.

'There's a lorry,' said Reggie. 'It's stopping.'

'I reckon it's six of one and half a dozen of the other,' said the landlord.

'It's stopped,' said Linda.

'*Sheffield Star* "Green Un" could see them both off. Fred Walters, John Piper,' said the landlord.

'He's coming this way,' said Reggie.

'He'll not listen,' said the landlady. 'Not while he's talking about his famous "Green Un". First time we went to London, he said, "Hey up, our Annie. They've got a 'Pink Un' here," and he bought two copies of the *Financial Times*.'

There was a knock on the bar door.

'It's him,' said Reggie.

The landlord unbolted the door, and Jimmy staggered in. He was wearing full morning dress with a wilting carnation.

'Sorry,' said Jimmy. 'Saw light on. Out on my feet. Got such a thing as a bed?'

'Friends of yours here,' said Mr Arkwright.

Jimmy kissed Linda and shook hands warmly with Reggie.

'Drinks all round,' he said. 'What are you doing here?'

'You may have forgotten,' said Reggie. 'But we went to your wedding today.'

'Haven't forgotten,' said Jimmy. 'How did it go off?'

'It didn't go off,' said Reggie.

'You did,' said Linda.

'Yes.'

Jimmy took a swig of whisky and sighed.

'Poor Lettuce,' he said. 'Couldn't face it. Coward. Bad business. Drummed out of regiment. Conduct prejudicial. How did she take it?'

'Very bravely,' said Linda.

'It was her finest hour,' said Reggie.

'Nice filly,' said Jimmy. 'Salt of earth. Not on, though. Poor cow. Nasty business, was it?'

Reggie told the tale of Jimmy's wedding.

'Oh God,' said Jimmy. 'Consolation. She's better off without me. Dictum. Never marry sort of chap doesn't turn up at own wedding.'

The weather relented; Climthorpe Albion began to catch up on their backlog of postponed games and stretched their unbeaten run to twelve matches; Jimmy returned to his bachelor ways; Lettuce found that she could bear the absence of Jimmy better than the kind sympathy of her friends; the Harris-Jones's lived in peaceful harmony and listened to their baby boy's lungs developing healthily; President Amin led the applause for *The Admirable Crichton*, that classic play about the overthrow of imperialist authority, and C.J. and Tony Webster took up their position at Perrin Products.

'Let's have lunch,' said C.J., putting his head round her office door on his second day.

It was the moment that Elizabeth had dreaded.

'Certainly,' she said. 'Provided Reggie doesn't mind.'

'Why should he?' said C.J.

'No reason,' said Elizabeth. 'But you know how unpredictable he is.'

'It's only a business lunch,' said C.J., 'for you to report on your feasibility studies into the viability of the European side of our operations.'

'Were you wanting to have lunch today, darling?' she asked Reggie.

'Not especially,' he said, without even looking up from his desk.

'Oh,' she said. 'Only I thought maybe you wanted to discuss my ideas for children's toys.'

Realizing that whatever elaborate train sets you give young children they prefer to play with battered old biscuit tins, Elizabeth had suggested that they sell battered old biscuit tins at slightly less than the price of train sets.

'We can do that tomorrow,' said Reggie. 'Why?'

'Well C.J. wants me to go out to lunch with him, and I thought you might not want me to.'

Reggie looked up at last, to gaze at her in surprise.

'Well of course I want you to,' he said. 'You're his boss.'

C.J. leant round the huge candle that dominated their little table in the crowded trattoria.

'It's wonderful to be with you again, Elizabeth,' he said.

'It's nice to work with you, C.J.'

'Call me Bunny.'

'You said I shouldn't call you that at work,' said Elizabeth. 'This is supposed to be a business lunch.'

The waiter set the whitebait down in front of Elizabeth with a big smile.

'No, I'm the whitebait,' said C.J.

The waiter whipped the whitebait away and set the pâté in front of Elizabeth.

'No, I'm avocado,' she said.

'So sorry,' said the waiter. 'All today is cock-up. Molto cock-up. We not can get staff.'

As soon as the waiter had gone, C.J. peered round the candle again.

'Will you ever call me Bunny again?' he said.

'Possibly,' said Elizabeth.

'In Godalming? There's been quite a build-up of papers to sort.'

'I can't come to Godalming. Your wife's there.'

'She's going to Luxembourg to see her relatives.'

The waiter brought Elizabeth her lasagne.

'No, I'm avocado,' she said.

'Bloody kitchens,' said the waiter. 'Nobody speaka da English.'

He whipped the lasagne away angrily.

'Reggie's so jealous,' said Elizabeth.

'Please promise to come to Godalming,' said C.J.

'I think the most feasible cities for our European spearhead are Paris, Brussels, Amsterdam . . .'

'Amsterdam in the spring,' said C.J. 'We could go to Amsterdam together.'

'I can't see Reggie letting us go to Amsterdam together,' said Elizabeth, as the waiter presented her with a steaming plate of mussels.

'I think C.J.'s going to suggest that I go on a European tour with him,' said Elizabeth as they walked to Waterloo that evening.

'What an excellent idea,' said Reggie.

Chapter 20

April produced magical days, treacherous days, stormy days, but no boring days.

Climthorpe Albion lost two league games on the trot but reached Wembley in the F A Trophy, where their opponents would be Stafford Rangers.

C.J. settled in at Perrin Products and Tony Webster learnt to say 'great' and sound as if he meant it when David Harris-Jones came up with another of his super ideas.

Sales and production boomed. Newspapers wrote articles about Grot. A plum site at Brent Cross was purchased, another in Leeds shopping precinct.

In Cornwall, the private army was in a state of full readiness waiting for the day when the balloon went up.

April produced magical days, treacherous days, stormy days, but the balloon did not go up.

Reggie's joke had prospered beyond belief. Never had he dreamt, when Grot was a faint sparkle in his bloodshot eye, that he would own his own factory and forty-six shops, be chairman of Climthorpe Albion Football Club, be wined and dined on the Poets' Estate, have C.J. working under him and be able to put Tony Webster under David Harris-Jones.

Why then was he restless? Why did he feel tempted towards old and familiar paths, to be outrageously rude to people he loved, to call his deceased mother-in-law a wart-hog, to say 'waste-paper basket' instead of 'annual report'?

Had his joke lost its savour on the bedpost overnight?

April produced magical days, treacherous days, stormy days, but no boring days.

Yet Reginald Iolanthe Perrin was becoming bored.

Ponsonby sat peacefully on Reggie's lap. He was an old cat now.

They had the house to themselves. Elizabeth had gone to dinner at Tom and Linda's. Reggie had refused to go.

It was half past seven on an April Saturday evening. They sat by the french windows looking out over a garden exultant with spring.

'Is this the result of my great bid for freedom, Ponsonby?' said Reggie.

Ponsonby miaowed enigmatically.

'Every day I get up, dress, go downstairs, have breakfast, walk down Coleridge Close, turn right into Tennyson Avenue, then left into Wordsworth Drive, go down the snicket into Station Road, catch the train, arrive at Waterloo twenty-two minutes late, walk to Perrin Products, dictate letters, send memos, make decisions, hold conferences, have lunch, hold conferences, make decisions, send memos, dictate letters, leave Perrin Products, walk to Waterloo, catch the train, arrive at Climthorpe twenty-two minutes late, walk along Station Road, up the snicket, up Wordsworth Drive, turn right into Tennyson Avenue, then left into Coleridge Close, enter the house I left that morning, have supper, go up the stairs I came down that morning, take off the clothes I put on that morning, put on the pyjamas I took off that morning, clean the teeth I cleaned that morning, and get into the bed I left that morning. Is that success, Ponsonby?'

Ponsonby miaowed, reserving judgement.

'Oh, some days I make love and some days I do not. Some days we go out and some days we do not. Some days we have visitors and some days we do not. These differences seem to me like ripples on the Sargasso Sea. They barely stir the weed.'

A small charm of goldfinches twittered across the garden in the clear, cool evening. Ponsonby stiffened, decided that the game wasn't worth the candle, there were plenty more where those came from, and relaxed. Reggie patted his head in sympathetic understanding.

'There's magic out there,' said Reggie. 'Nature's annual magic. A cycle of infinite subtlety and variety, performed in an exquisite rhythm so slow that the human eye can never see it change. No maintenance engineer has ever seen the leaves of a tree turn golden and russet in October. No dental mechanic has ever witnessed the moment when the soft furry green of budding spring settles gently on the trees. No man has ever heard the first cry of the cuckoo. Only other cuckoos hear that.

'And while this infinitely patient and wonderful cycle is being carried out in perfect stealth by billions of inter-dependent creatures and plants, we have gone through our crass and pedestrian cycle three hundred and sixty-five times. How about that, Ponsonby?'

Ponsonby made no reply.

'Supposing we had an annual cycle as well, Ponsonby? Supposing we got up on February the sixteenth, had break-fast from the twentieth to the twenty-fourth, spent the twenty-fifth on the lavatory, worked from March the first to August the eleventh, with Wimbledon fortnight for lunch, were invited to the Smythe-Emberrys for cocktails from August the fourteenth to the twenty-seventh, spent Sep-tember having dinner, and went to bed on November the third. We could put on our trousers so slowly that the eye could not detect the movement. We would be freed entirely from the need to rush around at speed, killing everything in our path. We would be freed from all the tentacles of routine. We could aspire to being as subtle as the colouring of the leaves on the trees.'

They considered the prospect in silence for several minutes. Reggie felt a sense of utter peace, alone with his cat in the eye of the storm of life.

'And Tony Webster would be able to achieve his ambition of making love eighty-two times in one night,' he said.

When Elizabeth got home at half past eleven, Reggie still hadn't eaten his supper.

'What's all the hurry?' he said.

C.J. wanted to leave for their European tour on April the twenty-fifth.

'I'm afraid I won't be able to come,' said Elizabeth. 'Reggie and I have got to go to the FA Trophy Cup Final on April the twenty-eighth.'

'We'll postpone the tour,' said C.J. 'We'll go on May the second. I didn't get where I am today without going on May the second.'

'I don't want to go to Europe with C.J.,' said Elizabeth over supper.

'Why not?' said Reggie.

'I don't like him,' said Elizabeth.

'Well of course you don't,' said Reggie. 'Is that all?'

'I don't want to travel round Europe with a man I don't like.'

'I don't expect he likes you either,' he said. 'I expect he's dreading the prospect just as much as you are. That isn't the point. It's business.'

Reggie and Elizabeth had lunch with the Climthorpe team at their secret hide-out. Then they drove in the team coach to Wembley.

A part of Reggie felt loftily uninvolved. Another part felt sick with nerves.

'What does it matter, darling, in the scheme of things, whether Climthorpe beat Stafford Rangers or whether Stafford Rangers beat Climthorpe?' he said as they crawled past the shoppers of Ealing. 'On limestone hills that have been there for millions of years joyous little lambs will still be born to mothers whose joy has been dulled by their knowledge of the brevity of life. In the stews of Calcutta and the shanty towns of Guatemala the hungry and the maimed will remain hungry and maimed. Sad-faced workers in brown overalls will ride squat, ugly bicycles from dreary regimented homes to dreary regimented factories in dull suburbs from Omsk to Bratislava. None of them will ever know whether Climthorpe Albion beat Stafford Rangers, or whether Stafford Rangers beat Climthorpe Albion.'

'Don't let the team hear you talking like that,' said Elizabeth.

'I'm glad Clench has recovered from his hamstring injury,' said Reggie.

They entered the stadium. The 24,218 crowd looked dwarfed in the vast concrete saucer. Reggie nodded to the Milfords, the Peter Cartwrights, his bank manager, the cashier with the perpetual cold at Cash and Carry, the landlord of the Ode and Sonnet, the Chief Education Officer, the man who ran the bookstall at Climthorpe Station, the woman who ran the man who ran the bookstall at Climthorpe Station, the big couple from Sketchley's, and the fireman whose wife had run off with the man from the betting shop. All favoured him with smiles – joy unalloyed at the sight of this symbol of Climthorpe's success, the amazing Reginald Iolanthe Perrin. Reggie felt a rising panic, disbelief, anger, twisted tripes of inappropriate emotion.

He stopped to chat with Mr Pelham.

'Never a day passes,' said that worthy, 'but what I think: "Mr Perrin swilled out my porkers." '

'A lot of swill's flowed under the sty since then,' said Reggie.

'You're not wrong,' said Mr Pelham. 'Think we'll win?'

'Of course,' said Reggie.

'I wouldn't bother,' said Mr Pelham. 'Football, I can take it or leave it, let's face it, it's only a game, grown men kicking a ball about, but it's my boy, lives for it.'

'The trouble-maker?'

'Turned over a new leaf, Mr Perrin.'

'Gratifying news indeed, Mr Pelham.'

More smiles, more hellos, big cry of 'We are the champions' from the Climthorpe fans.

'And how's your lovely daughter?' said Reggie.

Mr Pelham's face darkened.

'We don't talk of her,' he said. 'Women! Present company excepted, of course.'

Arrival of Mr Pelham's nice boy with a souvenir programme. Introduction of that Mr Perrin I was telling you about. Farewells. Cry from Mr Pelham, over heads of crowd: 'Pigs aren't what they used to be. We miss you, Mr Perrin.'

Much-missed lucky mascot and friend of the porker Reginald Iolanthe Perrin borne seat-wards on a crowd of expectation. Suddenly, Linda beaming. Tom, smiling rather shyly. Adam and Jocasta, excited.

'What a surprise,' said Reggie.

'Can't let our Climthorpe down,' said Linda.

Happy family heart atom pulsating with anticipation, bleeding heart exploding atom without Mark suddenly so sorely missed this day.

Raucous cries, foul oaths, rattles, foul oaths, flat beer in plastic glasses, rhythmic swaying of many scarves, rosettes, foul oaths.

'They'll learn the words sooner or later anyway,' from Tom. 'We don't believe in protecting them.'

Take them Gorbals-wards, Tom. Take them Scotland Road-wards. Take them to deprived sores of inner cities, urban pustules. Take them to Soweto.

Or live in the Thames Valley, thank your lucky stars and shut up.

Climthorpe fans hurtling past – good to see the enthusiasm.

Stafford fans hurtling past – bloody yobbos.

Needless division! Heedless attrition!

Glad Clench fit though.

Waving and smiling even while thinking, living on three levels – conscious, sub-conscious and self-conscious. Amazing machine man, comic and cosmic.

Climthorpe inspecting pitch, dwarfed, awful semi-sharp suits.

Stafford inspecting pitch, huge, quarried from Northern rock, Climthorpe no chance, raucous cheers. Awful semi-sharp suits.

Words heard from afar in this small-time big-time hothouse of confusion. Tom saying, far away in distant reality, 'This is the one where they don't pick the ball up, isn't it?' Boring pose of ignorance. Smile smile. Conceal inner confusion almost. Don't let Climthorpe down, mighty man mascot. Tom again, 'I'm not a football person.' Nor am I,

Tom. What am I, Tom? 'Stafford crap.' This from Adam, aged five. Life goes on.

A drink with the directors. Hold on, Reggie. Do not slide down philosophical banisters. Elizabeth looking worried sensing inner turmoil.

'I'm glad Clench's hamstring's cleared up,' said surface Reggie.

'Never doubted it would,' said surface the Manager of the Climthorpe Branch of the Abbey National Building Society – God bless mammon and all who sleep with her. 'Not with your luck, Reggie.'

So – teams on pitch, take your seats, check on potted biographies in programme – it wasn't just Climthorpe that was threatened when Dangle's appalling back pass led to Stafford's first goal. It was the power of Reggie Perrin's influence over events.

Should I pray to God, thought Reggie as a brilliant move made it 2–0 to Stafford in the seventeenth minute. How can I pray to God? I believe that life is a matter of chance. Dame Fortune is a perverse and wilful hag.

Or do I?

Is there – good pass – any such thing as – oh, well saved – Free Will?

Should I, rather than praying to a possibly hypothetical God, cry out, 'Climthorpe, Climthorpe, CLIMTHORPE, Climthorpe!' to a definitely non-hypothetical Climthorpe. Unless we're all solipsists – well we can't all be solipsists – if I'm a solipsist none of them exist – and it makes no difference – you're rubbish, Fittock, whether you exist or not.

3–0 to Stafford? No. A good save from veteran custodian, Ted Rowntree.

Free will – true or false? Ted Rowntree's save inevitable, no credit to him? Applause of crowd philosophically naïve?

Another wave of Stafford shirts. Rowntree out of position. Dangle makes amends with goal-line clearance.

Turning point?

A shot from Clench. Weak, and straight at the keeper, but at least it was a shot.

Turning point?

Green and white joy. FITTOCK from sixteen yards. 1–2. Good old Fittock.

Half-time. Everybody drained.

Outplayed. Lucky. But only one down.

As the second half began Reggie felt that no result would please him.

If they lost, he would be sad.

If they drew, it would be boring.

If they won, it would seem to be an affirmation of his unwanted influence.

Climthorpe getting on top slowly. Suddenly, two goals in a minute. PUNT, after fine work by Clench. Then tit for tat, CLENCH, put through by Punt. 68 minutes. 3–2. Uproar. Goodbye, existentialism. Farewell, logical positivism. Hello, football. Stafford in tatters. Should be four. Could be five. Might be six. It isn't.

Stafford come back. 83rd minute. Great goal. 3–3. Nobody deserves to lose. Great players or fate's playthings?

88th minute, six man move, Climthorpe inspired, FITTOCK scores. 4–3.

We can never know whether it is possible for things to be other than they are – and it makes no difference.

We can never know whether we are part of an ordered pattern or whether we are tumbleweed tossed by fate – and it makes no difference.

Mr Tefloe (Redditch) is adding on too much time for injury – and it could make a hell of a difference.

The final whistle. Joy unconfined. Reggie's excitement deep and primeval. Happy faces. Tom beaming. Elizabeth laughing. Linda laughing. Even Mr Pelham looking pleased.

Shyly, feeling surplus to requirements, visiting the rowdy changing room, sweat, buttocks, bollocks, carbolic and champagne. Smile please.

Dinner at the Climthorpe Park Hotel. Holding on. Hanging tight. Drinking. Eating. Smiling. Laughing. Speeches. Reggie speaks. Audience laughs. Everything for the best in the best of all possible Climthorpes. Clench does a drunken dance and his hamstring goes.

'Well done, Reggie,' says the Chairman of the Climthorpe Chamber of Commerce.

It is time, thinks Reggie, for the bubble to burst.

April produced magical days, treacherous days, stormy days, but the bubble did not burst.

Chapter 21

Reggie carried Elizabeth's suitcases and she carried her hand-luggage. The concrete walls of the short-term car park at London Airport were daubed with welcoming messages like 'Wogs out' and 'Chelsea Shed'.

C.J was waiting. He had already booked in his luggage. He hadn't got where he was today without having already booked in his luggage.

Elizabeth went to the bookstall to find something for the plane. She didn't want to have to talk to C.J.

Reggie and C.J. guarded the luggage. Above their heads the indicator board rattled with information about delays. Facing them, on a circular display rostrum, was a scarlet fork-lift truck.

'I want to ask you to promise me something,' said Reggie.

'Ask away,' said C.J. 'If you don't ask, you don't get.'

'Very true,' said Reggie. 'Elizabeth seems rather nervous about this trip. Will you look after her, cherish her, pay her as much attention as you can?'

'I'll try,' said C.J.

They boarded at Gate Fourteen, and Reggie watched the Boeing 727 take off for Amsterdam.

It was Monday evening. They would be away four nights.

Tuesday

'I am extremely sorry to hear that your supplies of edible furniture have not arrived. This is due to non-arrival of supplies,' dictated Reggie.

He had spent the evening feeling vaguely lonely in the saloon bar of the Ode and Sonnet, and he had not slept well. Now he felt crumpled.

'Surely that's obvious, Mr Perrin?' said Joan.

'What's obvious?'

'That the supplies haven't arrived due to non-arrival of supplies.'

'Exactly. It's obvious. It's repetitive. It's self-explanatory. It's tautologous. It's saying the same thing twice in different ways. Shall we continue?'

As he dictated he paced restlessly round his executive cage.

'I am however astounded to hear that you have not received our new range of dentures for pets, which are proving so popular with bloody idiots who put little dog dentures in glasses of water beside kennels and even budgie dentures beside their silly little pets' cages. I can only assume that the delivery of this range is having teething troubles. You aren't taking it down, Joan.'

'No, Mr Perrin.'

'I know what you're thinking. His wife's away for one day and already he starts going berserk.'

'You're getting fed up again, aren't you?' said Joan.

Reggie flung himself into his swivel chair, and leant forward across his huge desk.

'Success is a trap,' he said.

'Like failure,' said Joan.

'Don't worry,' he said. 'I won't go berserk like I did before.'

'You couldn't,' said Joan. 'You've got too many people dependent on you.'

'Absolutely. I couldn't. I don't want to. Cross your legs.'

'We have an agreement, Mr Perrin.'

'Agreements are made to be broken. Please, Joan. Just this once.'

'Well, all right.'

Joan crossed her legs, revealing a shapely knee and the beginnings of a widening thigh.

'Thank you.'

They went to the pub for lunch. They stood in a crowded corner, drinks lodged perilously on a narrow shelf, meagre portions of cottage pie in hand, elbows jostled by the Amalgamated Asbestos crowd.

'How are things going with Tony?' said Reggie.

'They aren't,' said Joan. 'He's still frightened of being tied down.'

'You need to make him jealous,' said Reggie. 'Make him think of you as highly desirable and sexy – which of course you are.'

'You mean go out with someone else?'

'Yes.' Beer down crutch, bloody Asbestos apes. 'Yes. We must find you some suitable man, somebody who wouldn't go too far, of course. A married man would be ideal, wife away, loyal but lonely. A simple innocent dinner in some safe place. A few words in the right direction. Jealousy in the male breast. Bob's your uncle.'

'I know a nice little Armenian restaurant in Godalming,' said Joan.

'Very apt,' said Reggie. 'Very safe. Godalming is not an erogenous zone.'

Darkness had fallen over canals and ornately gabled houses, over hurdy-gurdies and city gates with swollen brick bellies, over huge pylons, vast docks and great motorway complexes.

Darkness had fallen over the breasts of fat black prostitutes hanging pendulously over window-sills in the red light district of Amsterdam, and over the dead tasteful open-plan living-rooms of Philips executives in the electric light district of Eindhoven.

Darkness had fallen over diamond smugglers, Lutheran vergers, barmen in homosexual clubs, and Indonesian waiters with teeth like smoke-stained Mah Jongg tiles.

Darkness had fallen over the Amsterdam Crest Motel.

'I have a confession to make,' he said. 'I think it may come as rather a shock.'

'Confess away,' she said.

'When I invited you to Godalming, those papers that required sorting were a ruse. I had unsorted them deliberately.'

They were sitting over a nightcap in the Tulip Bar. The lights were shaped like tulips, and there were tulips on every table.

The background music was 'Windmills of my Mind'.
'Why don't you say anything?' he said.
'I can't think what to say,' she said.

They had toured the city, deciding on the sort of area and property which might be suitable for Grot, and met several estate agents. They had lunched and dined with business colleagues. It had been a good day.

Now the tide of life had receded and they were grounded in the muddy reaches of evening.

'Another apricot brandy?' he said.
'No, thank you.'
'Sit with me while I have another parfait d'amour.'
'For a few minutes.'

Darkness had fallen over Guildford and Haslemere and the broken sandstone country of the Surrey hills.

Darkness had fallen over the Godalming Armenian Restaurant.

He drove her home. The moon began to rise, and he felt romantic stirrings.

'Shall I tell Tony we've been out together or will you?' she said.

Wednesday
On his way to the station, Reggie thought of Elizabeth and C.J.

Perhaps C.J. would be a different kettle of fish on the continent. On the dreariest of cross-channel ferries Reggie had seen the staidest of men begin to kick over the traces before the ship had even cleared Dover jetty. And Amsterdam was a far cry from Godalming.

Godalming! A horrible certainty gripped Reggie as the train lurched across the points outside Raynes Park.

He looked out dismally through windows encrusted with grime.

He was suffering from a fate worse than death. He was being cuckolded by C.J.

No! It was impossible! It was against nature.

Yet the images persisted.

Who could have told, seeing the successful businessman gazing out at Clapham Junction Station, that he was seeing C.J. and Elizabeth, dancing cheek to cheek, transferring a tulip from one mouth to the other, in a windmill transformed into an elegant night-club?

He called in on Tony's office shortly after ten and said, 'Just popped in to see if you want the heating back on.'

The heating had automatically gone off on the last day of April, and the weather had promptly turned bitterly cold.

'I wouldn't mind,' said Tony.

'Good. Good.'

Suddenly Reggie doubled up and clutched his stomach in agony.

'Ouch! O'oooh!' he groaned.

'Are you all right?' said Tony, vaguely alarmed.

'Indigestion,' said Reggie. 'It must be those pike balls I had with Joan in the Armenian restaurant in Godalming.'

'Really?'

Reggie's simulated attack passed, and he stood upright again.

'Yes,' he said. 'Yes, I ... er ... I took Joan out. Yes.'

'Great,' said Tony.

'Well, Joan,' he said. 'I told Tony.'

'What did he say?'

'Great.'

'Just great?'

'Yes.'

'Wonderful.'

'Armenian restaurants in Godalming are too public,' said Reggie. 'We ought to go somewhere private.'

'Such as?'

'Come home to dinner tonight, Joan. All strictly above board. We are adults, after all.'

Reggie led Joan through the quiet streets of the Poets'

Estate, where never an inquisitive face is seen, although they are there all right.

He poured them a drink and found some beef bourguignon in the deep freeze. He put the oven on at a low heat and opened a bottle of claret.

'I bet Tony's eating his heart out at this moment,' he said. 'Imagining all sorts of dreadful goings on.'

'Not knowing what respectable, controlled adults we are.'

'Speak for yourself,' said Joan, and she kissed him on the lips.

'Don't,' said Reggie.

She lay back on the settee and kicked her shoes off.

'Remember the last time I was here?' she said.

Reggie smiled.

'I'm hardly likely to forget it,' he said. 'It's not every day a beautiful girl comes to my house and I take her upstairs to bed and half my family comes round and she has to crawl out through the garden.'

He flung open the french windows and breathed in the cool, unsullied air of early May. Everywhere there were birds singing.

Ponsonby came in from the garden, saw that Reggie had company, and left in a huff.

'Ponsonby's jealous, anyway,' he said.

'You were relieved when all those people came round,' said Joan, lying back still further and raising her knees so that her dress slid up her legs.

'I wasn't,' said Reggie. 'I most certainly was not.'

'You were worried that you wouldn't be able to go through with it.'

'Don't be ridiculous,' said Reggie. 'Of course I wasn't.'

'If I said to you now "Come upstairs", you'd be terrified.'

'Of course I wouldn't. How can you say a thing like that? I'd be up those stairs before you could say "I'm all right, Jack Robinson".'

Joan got up off the settee and walked slowly towards him.

'Come on then,' she said.

'Don't be silly.'

'You said you'd be up there like a shot.'

'Ah! Yes! That was a hypothetical example. There's Elizabeth and there's Tony and . . . er . . . ooh!'

Further words were impossible. Joan kissed him gently, slowly on the mouth. He had a vision of Elizabeth kissing C.J. gently, slowly on the mouth in an attic behind an ornate gable in the Grand Place in Brussels.

'Come on then,' he said.

They went slowly up the stairs, kissing as they did so.

They entered the spare bedroom. Reggie turned the picture of the Queen to the wall.

'Sorry, your Majesty,' he said.

They kissed again.

'No buttons on this dress,' said Reggie.

'No.'

'Just a zip. Easier to undo really.'

'Much easier.'

'Much improved lately, British zips. They went through a sticky patch, but . . . er . . .'

They heard a car pull to a halt.

They froze.

'It can't be here,' said Reggie. 'Lightning never strikes twice in the same . . .'

'Hello!' cried Linda cheerfully.

'Hells bells. I left the french windows open,' whispered Reggie.

'Just coming,' he called out.

'Stay here,' he whispered to Joan. 'I'll get rid of them.'

He dressed hurriedly, examined himself for traces of lipstick and disorder, and hastened downstairs.

Tom and Linda stood in the living-room, smiling.

'Hello! What a surprise,' he said. 'I was just changing out of my office clobber.'

'But you're still in your office clobber,' said Tom.

'I mean I was just going to change out of it,' said Reggie. 'Then you came, just as I was starting, and I thought, "Quicker not to change out of it really." Like a quick drink before you go?'

'Yes. Thanks,' said Tom.

'We've got a baby-sitter,' said Linda. 'And we thought we'd see if you felt like coming out to dinner. We rang before we set off, but you weren't in.'

Tom had a dry sherry and Linda plumped for a Cinzano bianco.

'We're going to this marvellous new Armenian restaurant in Godalming,' said Linda. 'We've booked provisionally for three.'

'It's marvellous, according to the Smythe-Emberry's,' said Tom.

'I'm sure it is,' said Reggie. 'I'm sure it's the best Armenian restaurant in Godalming, but I happen to dislike Armenian food.'

'When have you ever had Armenian food, dad?' said Linda.

'Yesterday.'

'Yesterday? Where?'

Oh God. Here we go.

'At the Armenian restaurant in Climthorpe.'

'I didn't know there was an Armenian restaurant in Climthorpe,' said Linda.

'It opened last week,' said Reggie.

'We must try it,' said Tom.

'Let's go tonight,' said Linda. 'Godalming's* an awful long way.'

'You've booked there,' said Reggie.

'We can cancel,' said Linda.

'It's full tonight,' said Reggie.

'How do you know?' said Linda.

'I tried to book,' said Reggie.

'But I thought you didn't like Armenian food,' said Tom.

Oh God.

'Not for me. Someone else asked me to book,' said Reggie.

'We'll go next week when mum's back,' said Linda.

* Note: It is believed that this book mentions Godalming more than any other book ever written, including *A Social, Artistic and Economic History of Godalming* by E. Phipps-Blythburgh. Ed.

'It's closing down on Saturday,' said Reggie.

'Closing already? Why?' said Linda.

'It's a flop,' said Reggie.

'But you said it was full tonight,' said Tom.

Oh God.

'They've got a party of Armenian nuns tonight,' said Reggie.

'Where on earth are they from?' said Linda.

'Armenia,' said Reggie.

'All the way from Armenia to eat in a bad restaurant in Climthorpe?' said Tom.

Reggie topped up their glasses like an automaton, glancing involuntarily at the ceiling as he did so.

'They're from the Armenian monastery at Uxbridge,' he said.

'I didn't know there was an Armenian monastery at Uxbridge,' said Tom.

Oh God.

'It's just opened,' said Reggie.

'I'd have thought they'd be guaranteed a steady trade, then,' said Linda.

'The nuns have to take a vow only to eat in a restaurant once a year,' said Reggie.

'I'm sure the Armenian restaurant in Godalming is a very different kettle of pike balls,' said Tom.

'Pike balls?' said Linda.

'It's a joke,' said Tom.

'Oh,' said Linda and Reggie.

'You keep telling me to make jokes,' said Tom. 'And when I do, look what happens. I'm just not a joke person.'

'I didn't get it,' said Linda.

'The normal phrase is a kettle of fish,' said Tom, 'but a speciality of the Armenian restaurant in Godalming is pike balls. It's a fish dish, so instead of saying "a kettle of fish" I said "a kettle of pike balls".'

'Brilliant,' said Reggie. 'You should send it to Morecambe and Wise. It'll come in handy if they ever do an Armenian evening.'

'Why should Morecambe and Wise do an Armenian evening?' said Tom.

'It was a joke,' said Reggie.

'Do come with us, dad,' said Linda.

'I've got some food on anyway,' said Reggie.

'I don't believe you,' said Linda. 'You're making excuses. Deep down you're anti-social.'

'Go and look for yourself if you like,' said Reggie.

And Linda did just that.

Reggie walked to the french windows. A mistle-thrush was leading the evening chorus. The sudden absence of human sounds was blissful. Soon they would go, and he would make love to Joan.

'Another quick sherry before you go?' he heard himself saying, much to his dismay.

'I wouldn't say no,' said Tom.

Give Tom credit for one thing. When he said he wouldn't say no, he didn't.

Linda returned from the kitchen.

'There's enough for an army,' she said.

'I'm very hungry,' he said.

'Why don't we stay and help you eat it?' she said.

'Because you've booked into an Armenian restaurant,' said Reggie.

'I don't think I'd like Armenian food anyway,' said Linda.

'But what about the recommendation of the Smyth-Emberrys?' said Reggie.

'They've got no palate,' said Tom.

'Don't you want us to stay, dad?' said Linda. 'Do you have other plans or something?'

'I'd love you to stay,' said Reggie. 'I'll just change out of all this office clobber.'

And so he walked sadly up the stairs, along the corridor, opened with trepidation the door of the spare room, and smiled queasily at Joan.

'Bit of a problem,' he said. 'They're staying to dinner.'

'Oh God.'

'You ... er ... you know the way out, I think. Down the drain-pipe and ... er ... oh God.'

When he went downstairs again Tom said, 'But you're still in your office clobber.'

'Oh yes,' he said. 'I forgot what I went upstairs for.'

'I don't like Brussels,' said C.J. 'One ornate square, sprouts, and a little boy who widdles. It isn't enough.'

They were having a nightcap in the British bar of the Brussels Dragonara. There were large photographs of the Tower of London, Hampton Court, Dovedale, Ullswater and the Middlesbrough Dragonara.

They had enjoyed a constructive day. In the morning they had sorted out the property situation in Rotterdam, and after lunch on a TEE train they had done the same thing with regard to Brussels.

'Didn't you like me a little in Godalming?' said C.J. 'I had a feeling that you liked me a little in Godalming.'

'Yes, I liked you a little in Godalming.'

'Surely, if you liked me a little in Godalming, you could like me a lot in Brussels?'

'It isn't a question of geography,' said Elizabeth. 'I was upset then. I had been through bewildering experiences.'

'Now *I* have been through bewildering experiences,' said C.J.

'Mutatis mutandis,' said Elizabeth.

'I can't speak French,' said C.J. 'All I know is business.'

'A far cry from Renaissance man,' said Elizabeth.

'Pardon?'

'Nothing.'

'Have another peach brandy?'

'No, thank you.'

'Stay with me while I have another tia maria.'

'Just for a few minutes.'

She couldn't bear to see him like this. It was as if she had caught Krupp taking a teddy bear to bed.

Thursday

The Bavarian evening was in full swing. The grotesque fat

218

man in shorts and braces twirled the pig-tailed maiden round and round. Her traditional skirt swirled and revealed naked thighs above her white socks. The audience banged their beer mugs, and roared.

The couple turned to face the audience, and Reggie saw that they were C.J. and Elizabeth.

They began to undress. The audience howled with pleasure, and Reggie woke up.

He went straight to Tony's drab little office and said 'Ah, Tony! Just the man I wanted to see.'

'I guessed I was when I saw you come into my office,' said Tony.

'Quite. Stupid thing to say, really. Tony, I'd like you to tour all Grot shops, incognito, no great hurry, and just check on how they're being run, quality of displays, assistants, etcetera. Full expenses, of course.'

'Great.'

'Seeing much of Joan these days?'

'I've been a bit tied up lately,' said Tony.

'She was round my house last night,' said Reggie. 'Very pleasant.'

'Great.'

'Morning, Joan,' he said, as he passed through the outer office. 'Twenty-two minutes late. A badger ate a junction box at New Malden.'

'You don't believe those excuses, do you, Mr Perrin?' said Joan coldly.

'Of course not,' said Reggie. 'But I admire their creative powers, even if a touch of desperation has crept in of late. Come through a moment, would you?'

He entered his office, threw his umbrella towards the hat-stand, missed, straightened one of Dr Wren's horrific sketches of Ramsey, Isle of Man, and sat at his desk.

Joan sat opposite him, pad poised, legs aggressively un-crossed, and wearing her longest skirt.

'First of all,' said Reggie. 'Deepest apologies for last night.'

Joan made no reply.

'It really wasn't my fault, you know.'

Joan remained silent.

The red phone rang. Joan answered it.

'New York on red, Mr Perrin,' she said, handing Reggie the receiver.

'Hello,' he said. 'Mr Perrin has been admitted to an isolation hospital. He has a rare variant of green-monkey fever, known as mauve-baboon fever. Ring back in six months. Goodbye.'

He put the phone down.

'You see how important you are to me,' he said.

'I'm sorry,' said Joan. 'I know it wasn't your fault really, but it's a bit humiliating sliding down married men's drainpipes.'

'It wasn't in vain,' said Reggie. 'I spoke to Tony, and there were definite signs of jealousy.'

'Really? What did he say?'

'It wasn't so much what he said exactly.'

'What did he say, Mr Perrin?'

'Great.'

'Just "great"?'

'It was the way he said it. The signs are there, but we're doing it all wrong. The male possessive instinct is very bound up with territory. Suppose I come to your place tonight? That'll hook him.'

The white walls of Joan's little bedroom in her flat in Kingston-on-Thames were covered in Spanish mats, with orange the predominant colour. A soft dusk was beginning to fall as Reggie and Joan found coitus uninterruptus at last.

They lay side by side in the narrow bed, happy, incredulous.

Then the doorbell rang. Four short staccato rings.

'Oh my God,' said Joan. 'That's Tony's ring. He always rings like that.'

She ran naked out of the room and rushed along the corridor to the window above the door.

'I'll be down in a minute,' she called out of the window. 'I've just had a bath.'

She returned more slowly to the bedroom. Reggie looked at her questioningly from the bed.

'There's a very solid drain-pipe,' she said. 'It shouldn't be too difficult.'

'I know I'm not particularly human,' said C.J. 'My worst enemies couldn't accuse me of being particularly human. But I can change.'

'No,' said Elizabeth.

'You can take the leopard to the water, and he'll change his spots,' said C.J.

'No,' said Elizabeth.

They were enjoying an early nightcap on the Rhine Terrace of the Holiday Inn, Düsseldorf. Great caravans of barges slid slowly up the broad brown river in the last of a lingering dusk.

Elizabeth yawned. All this travel was proving tiring.

'Bored?' said C.J.

'No.'

'I know I'm boring.'

'No.'

A young page in a blue jacket with gold buttons was searching vainly for a Mr Antinori of Poggibonsi. He had concealed his acne spots beneath white powder.

'Elizabeth?' said C.J. in a husky whisper.

'No,' said Elizabeth.

'You don't know what I'm going to say,' said C.J.

'No,' said Elizabeth.

'I was only going to say that I love you,' said C.J.

'No,' said Elizabeth.

Friday

'Twenty-two minutes la . . .'

'Thank you,' said Joan, kissing him excitedly on the mouth. 'Thank you, you darling man.'

'What is all this?'

'It worked,' said Joan. 'It worked.'

'Well of course it . . . what worked?'

'Your plan. Tony's moving back in with me tomorrow.'

'Oh. Good. Good. Wonderful.'

'I let him see you as you slid down the drain-pipe.'

'Wonderful.'

'Thank you.'

'It's our last night,' said C.J.

'Yes,' said Elizabeth.

'Tomorrow night you will be in Reggie's arms, and I'll be at home too.'

'Yes.'

They were having a nightcap in the Tongan bar at the Paris Post House. Pictures of the burly Tongan rulers adorned the walls, and the ashtrays were in the shape of the island.

'Soon Mrs C.J. goes to Luxembourg. Would it be wrong of me to hope that some minor complaint will again keep her recuperating in that lovely land? A mild but persistent attack of yellow jaundice, perhaps.'

'Yes,' said Elizabeth. 'It would be very wrong.'

Her constant rebuffs, gentle and inevitable as they were, were beginning to make Elizabeth feel mean. She closed her eyes and fought off this dangerous feeling. She conjured up a picture of Reggie alone with Ponsonby in the quiet Climthorpe night, steadfast in his love and affection for his unworthy wife who hadn't even had the wit to take Grot seriously when he had first presented the idea to her.

She longed, with all her being, for the moment when she and C.J. would drive away from London Airport in separate cars.

'Penny for them,' said C.J.

'What? Oh, I was just thinking what a romantic place Paris was,' she said, getting up to go to bed.

C.J. sighed.

'Yes,' he said. 'I suppose it was.'

Saturday

'So you had a nice time with C.J., did you?' said Reggie.

'Not bad,' said Elizabeth. 'Quite nice, considering.'

'Quite,' said Reggie. 'You got on all right together, then?'

'Not too badly, considering.'

They were sitting in the living-room, having a pot of tea. It was four o'clock on a grey, cold Saturday.

'How did *you* get on?' said Elizabeth.

'Oh not too bad,' said Reggie. 'Not too bad, considering.'

'You weren't too bored and lonely, then?'

'No, I . . . I wasn't too bored and lonely. I found one or two things to do.'

'Oh good.'

Elizabeth lifted the tea cosy, which had purple lupins embroidered on it, and poured them a second cup.

'One isolated lapse isn't the end of the world,' said Reggie. 'I mean, what is unfaithfulness and adultery compared to terrorism and gun-running and drug rings and bank raids and imprisonment without trial and mass torture and genocide and kidnapping and corruption and massacre?'

Elizabeth's hand shook as she poured Reggie his cup of tea.

'What are you trying to tell me?' she said.

'I'm trying to tell you, darling, that if anything occurred between you and C.J. that shouldn't have occurred, I forgive you.'

'Anything occurred between me and C.J.! Of course it didn't.'

'No, of course it didn't. I wasn't for a moment suggesting that it had. I was just saying that *if* it had, *if* it had, I'd forgive you. No, of course it didn't. How could it, with C.J.? The mind boggles.'

A plane roared overhead, carrying, as it chanced, forty-six members of the Grenoble Philatelic Society, on their annual trip to buy cheap sweaters at Marks and Spencers.

'Did you really think I was having an affair with C.J.?'

'No. No. Darling, how could you think I could think such

a thing? No, I just formed the idea, probably quite wrongly, that it was C.J. you were seeing in Godalming.'

'It was.'

'Ah!'

'But nothing happened. Nothing could ever happen between me and C.J.'

'Why didn't you tell me it was C.J.?'

'I thought you'd be cross.'

'I would have been.'

An unnatural darkness had descended from a constipated sky, and the electric fire glowed brightly.

'I thought for a minute you were going to tell me *you* had had an affair,' said Elizabeth.

'Me!' said Reggie. 'Me! No! How could you think a thing like that?'

'I didn't, till you mentioned the subject.'

'If I had had an affair – I haven't, but if I had – would you forgive me?'

'I'd try to. I might find it difficult.'

Reggie put his arm round Elizabeth.

'I'm glad you're back,' he said.

'From now on we must do everything together,' he said. 'Everything.'

It pains me, faithful reader, to admit that from then on they did not do everything together. That very evening Reggie did something on his own. He opened his heart to Ponsonby.

Elizabeth, being much fatigued after her travels, had retired early to bed. It was ten o'clock on a chill May night. Ponsonby was purring on Reggie's lap. A glass of whisky stood on the smallest table in the nest.

'You are Watson to my Sherlock Holmes,' Reggie told Ponsonby. 'Hercule Poirot had his Hastings, Raffles his Bunny. I have my Pussy. These side-kicks of literature performed valuable functions, Ponsonby. They did. They were emotional hot water bottles, confidantes, sounding-boards, call them what you will.'

Ponsonby called them nothing.

'And they provided useful information for the reader. They were a convenient literary device. Since I'm not a fictional character I don't need a literary device. But I do need a confidante. You are a perfect confidante, since you don't understand a blind word I say.'

Ponsonby looked up at Reggie with earnest eyes.

'You do try to understand, don't you? Do you ever feel a sense of humiliation as the words wash over you, utterly beyond your well-meaning grasp?'

Ponsonby miaowed.

'I am trapped in a success story that I never expected, Ponsonby. I have got to escape from it.

'I have created a monster called Grot. I have got to destroy that monster.

'I could sell it, Ponsonby, but I prefer not to do that. I would rather destroy it myself – I who created it. That would be much more pleasing.

'I want to destroy it secretly, so that nobody will ever know that it was deliberate. I want to destroy it from within, slowly, so that those with the sense to see what is happening can leave of their own free will, in good time. I have responsibilities to them, you see.'

Ponsonby miaowed. It seemed that he saw.

'How am I going to do it, I hear you ask. Well, it's very simple. I am going to employ in key roles people who are utterly unfitted for those roles, people uniquely qualified to destroy my empire. What do you think of that as a wheeze?'

Ponsonby acquiesced silently.

'Oh good. I'm glad you agree,' said Reggie.

Chapter 22

'I didn't think I'd see the inside of this office again,' said Doc Morrissey.

'How are things?' said Reggie.

'Very promising,' said Doc Morrissey. 'There are gleams on the horizon. There are fingers in pies. There are irons in fires. These things take time.'

'How would you like a job with me, Doc?'

Doc Morrissey's jaw dropped in astonishment.

'But you sacked me?'

'This would be a completely different job, Doc. Cigar?'

'Doctor's warned me off them. Thanks.'

Doc Morrissey leant forward to light his cigar, and there was an ominous cracking of bone.

'What's it to be this time, Reggie? Assistant boilerman?' he said.

'No. Head of Forward Planning.'

'Head of Forward Planning?'

'I believe that your talents do not lie with the specific. Whatever you do – diagnosis of ailments, running a shop, maintaining a boiler – will be a fiasco.'

'Thank you, Reggie.'

'You're a visionary.'

'I am?'

'Come to the window.'

They stood at the window and looked across at the lighted windows of Amalgamated Asbestos.

'Look at that rabbit warren. Look at all that amazingly tedious routine.'

'I can see it, Reggie. Awful.'

'You can cut a swathe through all that, Doc. I believe that in your mind, so bogged down in the mundane details of day-to-day existence, I am buying a superb machine for the creation of over-all strategy.'

'Good God.'

'Are you happy as an estate agent?' said Reggie.

'Happiness doesn't really come into it,' said Tom.

They were sitting on the terrace of a Thames-side hotel. It was the first really warm day, and swans were picking their stately way among the oil-drums and plastic bags at the side of the river.

'The epitome of England,' said Reggie.

The Spanish waiter brought them vast menus with shiny black covers.

'I'm not a mid-week lunch person,' said Tom. '95p for smoked mackerel. What a mark-up.'

'Outrageous,' said Reggie.

'What a stupid way to write the menu,' said Tom. '*Le bœuf rôti avec le pudding de Yorkshire*. It's ridiculous.'

'Ludicrous.'

Tom ordered smoked mackerel and *le bœuf rôti avec le pudding de Yorkshire*.

'Do you feel you have a vocation for property?' said Reggie.

'Oh no. I just am an estate agent, that's all.'

'You must have become one at some stage,' said Reggie. 'I mean when you were born the nurse didn't tell your proud father: "It's an estate agent." '

The terrace faced a small island, where the white pillars and porticoes of an abandoned pre-war night-club could still be faintly seen among the vegetation.

'Do you mean to remain an estate agent until you retire?' said Reggie.

'That's a question,' said Tom. 'That really is a question.'

'Supposing you answer it, since you've identified it so accurately,' said Reggie.

'Sometimes I look at that board "Norris, Wattenburg and Patterson", and I think: "You're a man of substance, Tom Patterson." '

'It provides reassuring evidence that you exist?'

A pleasure steamer ploughed demurely upstream. Reggie waved. One boy waved back.

'Then I think: "Norris is as thick as two short planks. Wattenburg's going ga-ga. Why am I third on the list? Is there no justice?"'

'No.'

'I think you could say that Linda and I are serious-minded people, Reggie.'

'I think I could, yes.'

'We think about world problems, Reggie. We care. We exercise our vote.'

'You make it sound like a dog,' said Reggie.

'It might as well be, for all the good it's done,' said Tom. 'We might as well have universal Jack Russells instead of suffrage. I've voted six times – twice labour, twice liberal, and twice conservative. What a contribution I've made to democracy.'

The Spanish waiter informed them that their table was ready.

'What I'm trying to say is this,' said Tom. 'I believe in social justice and equality, and I don't think I do want to be an estate agent all my life.'

'Splendid,' said Reggie. 'Come and work for me.'

Tom was speechless for almost a minute.

'You're offering me a job? What as?'

'Head of Publicity.'

Walking back from Climthorpe station the following evening, his legs leaden in the early heat-wave, Reggie saw a man with a pink face weaving gently along the pavement.

'Thirsty weather,' he said.

'You're right there,' said the man in a Limerick accent.

'I'll be half an hour, darling,' Reggie told Elizabeth. 'I've just got some business to do.'

Elizabeth's eyes indicated the tipsy Irishman questioningly. Reggie nodded. Elizabeth looked annoyed and surprised as she trudged home alone through the soupy evening air.

'How about a drink?' said Reggie.

'In the Station Hotel?' said the Irishman. 'I never use that house myself, sir.'

'Routine made Jack a dull boy.'

'I'll drink to that.'

Over their pints of vinegary bitter in the cavernous public bar of the Station Hotel, which had an unusable dartboard with seats and a table beneath it, and two boring pictures of the outside of the pub in thick snow, Reggie talked to his new acquaintance.

His name was Seamus Finnegan, and he had not worked that day, due to an urgent appointment at Kempton Park.

'My system failed me,' he said.

'What is your system?' said Reggie.

'I always back the grey. If there isn't a grey, I back the sheepskin noseband. That's about the size of it, sir.'

Reggie smiled. This man promised to be ideal.

'Where do you work?' he inquired.

'I'm working on the new Climthorpe Slip Relief Feeder Road, sir. We're held up at the moment till they move the pigs out of the piggery.'

'Pelham's Piggery?'

'That's the one, sir. I talked to your man last week. He's taking it very hard, sir. The piggery, I wouldn't give it house room, but it was in the blood of the man, you see.'

'Then why did he sell?'

'They found irregularities, sir. They threatened to close it on health grounds – that was about the size of it.'

They sat with their backs to the dartboard, and their pints were nearly drained. Seamus Finnegan's eyes were clouded with drink.

The seats were upholstered in red leather which had cracked and burst.

'Have you ever worked in management?' said Reggie.

'No, sir. My genius for management remains a secret between me and my Maker.'

'Do you have any experience of administration?'

'No, sir. That's one fellow I've never met.'

'I run a firm called Perrin Products. We have some shops

called Grot. I would like you to be my Admin Officer.'

'Would you be having a bit of fun, sir, with a simple Irishman from the bogs?'

'I'm offering you the job.'

'Jesus Christ! I'd better bloody take it, then, before you change your mind.'

Later that evening Reggie telephoned Mr Pelham.

'Ridiculous, isn't it?' said Mr Pelham. 'Cutting out food for roads. I thought they were trying to make this country self-deficient.'

'Can I do anything?' said Reggie.

'The boy got up a petition, Reg. Two hundred and thirty-seven names.'

'Did you send it in?'

'Yes. They laughed at me. The boy meant well.'

'I don't understand.'

'He filled it out a bit. He couldn't get many real people. I haven't many friends.'

'Filled it out a bit?'

'Oliver Cromwell, Louis Pasteur, that sort of thing. There were only twenty-nine real names on the list – and seven of them were my boy.'

'I'm terribly sorry,' said Reggie.

'Don't you lose any sleep, old son. There may be another world, I don't know, but we're on our own in this one.'

'I wondered if you'd like a job.'

'What? In a factory? No fear.'

'You'd be a director.'

'Much appreciated, old son, but it's not for me. Sleep well.'

And there was a click as Mr Pelham rang off.

Letters to Cornwall elicited no reply. Telephone calls to Trepanning House met with no response. All of which was very inconvenient, when Reggie wished to offer Jimmy a job.

And so, on the first day of June, Reggie and Elizabeth drove down to Cornwall.

'I can't understand why you're offering all these people these jobs,' said Elizabeth, as they skirted the magnificent country of Dartmoor.

'Conscience,' said Reggie.

'You can't run a business on conscience,' said Elizabeth, 'but I love you for it.'

As they crossed the border into Cornwall, Elizabeth said: 'I can't see Jimmy giving up his private army.'

'You can only ask,' said Reggie.

They stopped off at the Fishermen's Arms, to secure their accommodation.

'It's not your usual room,' said the landlord. 'We've got a party of French cyclists. They don't seem to hit it off with our crisps.'

'Have you seen my brother?' said Elizabeth, as Reggie bought them drinks.

'I said to this French chappie, I said: "We've not got plain. We've only got smoky bacon or salt and vinegar." He said *"merde." "Merde,"* he said! Who won the war, that's what I want to know?'

'We did,' said Reggie.

'Thank you,' said the landlord.

'With the French on our side,' said Reggie.

'Oh aye, they were on our side, I grant you that, but that doesn't give them the right to be rude to my crisps.'

'Yes, but have you seen my brother?' said Elizabeth.

'You've heard, then,' said the landlord.

Elizabeth went pale.

'Heard what?' she said.

'The tall bugger. He's shoved off wi' t'bloody lot.'

'Oh my God.'

'What exactly's happened?' said Reggie.

'All I know is this,' said the landlord, ringing the final bell and putting cloths over the pumps. 'It were Tuesday night. No, I tell a lie. Monday.'

'Tuesday,' said the landlady, still flushed from cooking the lunches. 'I didn't get back while Tuesday.'

'Tuesday. I were right first time,' said the landlord.

'Yes, but what happened?' said Reggie.

'They were in here, your brother and tall bugger, and they were shifting some. I said to Annie, "Annie," I said, "them two are supping some lotion tonight." It were right odd. "It's a rum do, our Annie," I said. "Tall one's pretending to drink a lot and t'other one's shifting them like buggery. Tall one's usually t'biggest drinker, tha knows." Oh aye. Definitely. We notice these things, tha knows, being in t'trade. We're trained to it.'

'Yes, but what happened?'

'T'other one, not your one, he says can they stay, be accommodated like, because they've had too much to drink, which I don't reckon he had had, t'other one, not your one, he had had too much.'

'Yes, but what happened?'

'He's hopeless,' said the landlady. 'If it were left to him to tell the tale you'd be here till Christmas. You'd be here till Doomsday.'

'You tell it, then, Annie,' said the landlord, and he came round the bar to collect the empties.

'I will,' said the landlady. 'I will and all. Well, we had two rooms, one single, one double adjoining, which we wouldn't have had, 'cos it's an early season this year, only I'd been back home, my mother's been none too clever, and me dad, he's come over all unnecessary, so we'd run the accommodation side of it down – the hotel side, like – he can't cope on his own, it worries him.'

'Yes, but what happened?'

'I'm telling you. In t'morning, tall one had gone.'

'Buggered off,' said the landlord, dumping a leaning tower of pint glasses on the bar.

'Aye. Gone. There was no sight nor sign of him. And when your brother got back to t'farm, whole lot had gone, money and that and I don't know what else.'

Reggie and Elizabeth set off urgently for Trepanning House.

Jimmy made sure that every window was sealed, that the

cracks round every outside door were filled with old news-paper. He even ripped up the book of the flags of the nations given to him at school by Patrick Williamson.

He had been round to all the men personally, to explain the fiasco. They had all seemed strangely resigned to it, as if they had always known that it was only a dream.

He realized now that there were no other cells, there was no famous person behind the scenes, the balloon never could have gone up.

He switched all the gas appliances full on. The gas began to fill the dank air in the old Cornish farmhouse.

Clive would be caught, of course. He might get away with the money, but he'd never be able to sell the weapons safely.

The farmers who had occupied this dreary house had gone, after a lifetime striking bargains with an impoverished land. Vets who had come here at five in the morning to tend dying cows were themselves dead now. Nettles lapped round their neglected graves, and the cows had no monuments.

Sheila was gone, the army was gone, the private army was gone, Linda was untouchable.

He lay with his head in the oven, to speed the end. Vaguely he registered the distant ringing and knocking.

The wind was thick with the whisperings of the tor-mented souls of the old tin workers as Reggie knocked and rang to no avail.

Then they noticed that the door was sealed up.

Reggie broke a window with a large stone, reached in and opened it. He climbed in and let Elizabeth in through the front door.

Soon they had all the appliances switched off and Jimmy out in the mild night air.

He didn't seem too ill.

'Too soon,' said Jimmy. 'Wanted to die. Damned slow, this high speed gas.'

Reggie laughed.

'What's so funny?' said Elizabeth indignantly, and even Jimmy looked hurt.

'North Sea Gas isn't poisonous,' said Reggie.

Back at the Fishermen's Arms they had ham and eggs and discussed the dastardly qualities of Clive 'Lofty' Anstruther.

'No more a colonel than that pepper pot,' said Jimmy. 'Bogus. Should have seen through him. I'm an idiot. Whole life caput, plug-hole.'

Reggie offered him the job of Head of Creative Thinking.

Chapter 23

A lovely summer enveloped the land, and still the bubble did not burst.

Turnover and sales continued to rise. New lines were introduced, including fattening foods for masochists on diets, and a second silent LP. This was advertised on TV as: 'More Laryngitis, featuring the silence of Max Bygraves, Des O'Connor, the Bay City Rollers, the Sex Pistols and Rolf Harris.' It sold millions.

Tom and Linda booked a holiday in Brittany; Tony Webster and Joan resumed cohabitation; Climthorpe signed two new players; Reggie and Elizabeth had good weather for their holiday on Elba; swifts screeched happily in soft blue skies; skylarks sang exultantly above ripening corn; Mrs C.J. tripped getting off the coach on a mystery tour to Namur, and broke her other leg; and in *Peter Pan*, that moving tale of a revolutionary leader whose ruthless courage earns him the gift of perpetual youth, the lovely Belinda Longstone, the polystyrene heiress, demonstrated a heroic abnegation of the looks given her by fortune, when she chose the role of the crocodile in preference to Wendy.

Reggie was not unduly upset that the bubble did not burst. He was content to wait until the new arrivals had settled in.

Not everybody approved the new appointments, especially that of Seamus Finnegan as Admin Officer. 'I didn't get where I am today by having Irish labourers promoted over my head,' was one anonymous comment. But, bearing in mind Reggie's new reputation as a genius, everybody was happy to give them a chance.

One morning Reggie visited the new arrivals in their identical offices on the third floor. Each office had a green carpet, a teak veneer desk, expandable grey wall filing units, two cacti, three chairs, and an inspiring view over a heavily-pitted open-air National Car Park.

Tom's desk was covered in pieces of paper on which he had written various slogans and hand-outs. On the floor around the dark green waste-paper basket were many crumpled up pieces of badly aimed waste paper.

'How's it going?' said Reggie.

'I'm not really a slogan person,' said Tom.

'Nonsense. Read me some.'

On the filing units, Tom had placed photos of Linda and the children.

'Perrin Products are very good, because they are very bad,' he read.

'Excellent,' said Reggie. 'The essential paradox in a nutshell.'

'Go to Grot shops and get an eyeful
Of Perrin Products with a wide range of goods that are really pretty awful.'

'Very good.'

'It doesn't rhyme properly.'

'It almost rhymes, Tom.'

'I have the feeling my stuff isn't snappy enough.'

'It's exactly what I'm paying you for, Tom.'

Jimmy was staring blankly at a blank piece of paper. There were two neat piles of paper on his desk, and six sharpened pencils of equal length. He had added no decoration to the office.

'How's it coming along, Jimmy?' Reggie asked.

'Mustn't grumble. Learning the ropes.'

'Any ideas?'

'Not yet. Fly in the ointment.'

'Keep up the good work, Jimmy.'

Doc Morrissey had drawn pictures of naked girls on all the pieces of paper on his desk.

236

'Well, how's advanced planning coming along?' said Reggie.

'I did have one idea,' said Doc Morrissey.

'What's that?'

'January sales.'

'Yes. A nice idea, but something similar has been done before.'

'In September.'

'I see. Yes.'

'With ... er ... I don't know whether I'm on the right lines, Reggie, but I have tried to understand your ... er ... philosophy ... with the prices of everything going up instead of down.'

'I see.'

'I just thought it would be different.'

'It is. It is. I wish I'd thought of it myself.'

To Reggie's surprise the walls of Seamus Finnegan's office were covered in neat graphs and well-ordered lists. Three photographs of Arkle provided a more human touch.

'How's it going, Seamus?' said Reggie.

'Slowly, sir. It's a new field for me and thoroughness, he's the man for me, he's the fellow.'

'Quite. What are all these graphs and things?'

'Well, sir, I find there has been a considerable dis-improvement in organization of late. We are running, at a rough calculation, at only 63 per cent of internal capacity. Production methods leave much to be desired and delivery to the shops is a horse of a similar complexion.'

Seamus had his window wide open and warm sunshine was flooding in.

'You seem to be doing pretty well.'

'If I may say so, sir, without courting immodesty, I am in the way of being a bit of an organizational genius. You may recall my mentioning the fact.'

'I certainly do, yes.'

'It is a quality that I have not had much opportunity to develop in a world that had me marked up for an ignorant

237

Irish git from the land of the bogs and the little people.'

'A mistake I certainly didn't make.'

'You most assuredly did not, sir. May I ask how exactly you spotted my qualities for the job?'

'Instinct, Seamus. Call it instinct.'

Towards the end of July, Reggie called a planning meeting in Conference Room B. Reggie sat at one end of the oblong table and Elizabeth at the other. Seated on one side of the table were C.J., David Harris-Jones, Tom, and Seamus Finnegan. Seated on the other side were Tony Webster, Doc Morrissey and Jimmy. Beside Jimmy, on the floor, was his old tuck box. It was ten-thirty on a shirt-sleeve morning. In front of each person was a blotter and a glass.

Under each person's armpits were two spreading patches of damp.

Three carafes of water stood in the middle of the table.

Reggie began with a general homily on the success of the firm, and asked Elizabeth to chair the meeting.

Elizabeth explained that she would call everyone in turn to report on their progress. She would start with the Co-ordinator for European Expansion.

C.J. – for it was he – explained that they had secured shop sites in Amsterdam, Düsseldorf and Paris, and were in the middle of negotiations in Rotterdam, Cologne and Brussels. They were examining the possibility of opening a Eurogrot factory in Luxembourg, with a fleet of Grotmaster lorries, but these developments would not occur until they had at least a dozen European outlets. It was no use putting the cart before the horse. He gave the meeting to understand that neither he nor his betrothed had ever put the cart before the horse. If they had, he intimated, it might have been a case of the tail wagging the dog.

David Harris-Jones, the Head of Expansion (UK), explained that the British end of the operation now extended to sixty-one shops, with five more in the pipeline. The possibility of a separate Scottish enterprise, with exactly the same range but everything tartan, was being considered. He recommended that a committee of inquiry should be established to study its feasibility. David Harris-Jones summed up the UK prospects in one well-chosen word: super.

Tony Webster, Deputy Head of Expansion (UK), reported on the achievements of individual shops and the lessons that could be learnt from them in the siting and design of future shops. David Harris-Jones had described the prospects as Super. Tony Webster would go further. They were Great.

Seamus Finnegan, Admin Officer, outlined the organizational changes that were needed. Streamlining, Mr Finnegan suggested, was the man who would lead them on their way. Close behind would be those two splendid fellows, centralization and rationalization. Everyone was impressed. The appointment of the greying son of Erin was regarded as Reggie's master stroke, and Reggie hid his chagrin with difficulty.

Joan brought in coffee and a selection of biscuits, including rich tea, rich osborne and garibaldi.

'You can see how prosperous we are,' said Reggie, 'from our wide range of pumice stones.'

'Pumice stones?' said C.J.

'When I say pumice stones, I mean biscuits,' said Reggie. 'What does it matter what we call things?'

Elizabeth, C.J., David and Tony avoided each other's eyes in embarrassment.

Reggie held a garibaldi aloft.

'Garibaldi was a great man,' he said. 'He made the biscuits run on time.'

Doc Morrissey, Head of Forward Planning, explained his idea for the September sales, and also suggested the creation of Grot trading stamps, enabling the holder to collect a range of even more useless items from Grot redemption centres. The less stamps you had, the more you would collect.

Tom, Head of Publicity, gave some of his ideas for adverts, slogans and publicity hand-outs. There is not space to reveal them all in this modest tome, but perhaps his best effort was the slogan:

> 'Grot's the ideal place for gifts,
> Because it's all on one floor so there aren't any lifts.'

Jimmy, Head of Creative Thinking, spoke last. The leathery ex-soldier stood rigid from a mixture of habit, sciatica and embarrassment.

'Not come up with much,' he said. 'New business, feeling my way, walk before you can fly.'

'Come come,' said Reggie. 'I know you've got one or two exhibits in that Pandora's box of yours.'

Jimmy's weatherbeaten face flushed like an Arctic dawn.

'Couple of things here,' he said, and he lifted from his tuck box a very complicated, messily constructed machine – a mass of wheels, pulleys and chains, like a cross between the insides of a clock, a pit-head wheel, a mangle, a big dipper and a praying mantis. He placed it on the table and began to turn a handle. The machine clanked, clattered, rotated, slid, rose and fell.

Everybody watched in rapt silence.

'It's great,' pronounced Tony Webster.

'Super,' affirmed David Harris-Jones.

'It makes Heath Robinson look like Le Corbusier,' said Seamus Finnegan. 'It is a nag of distinct possibilities.'

'What is it?' said C.J.

That was the only snag. Jimmy had no idea what it was.

'It isn't anything,' he said.

'Brilliant,' said Tony Webster. 'Completely useless.'

'I didn't get where I am today without knowing a completely useless machine when I see one,' said C.J.

'It should be possible to refine it until all its functions cancel out all its other functions,' said Seamus Finnegan.

'Well done, Jimmy,' said Elizabeth.

'Another idea here,' said Jimmy, emboldened by his success.

He produced a squat, mis-shapen object like an upside-down kiln covered in huge warts.

This was greeted with less than widespread enthusiasm. The reluctance of the British public to buy upside-down kilns covered in huge warts is a sine qua non in trading circles.

Reggie permitted himself a smile. This was more like it.

'What is it?' said Doc Morrissey hoarsely.

Jimmy's courage, so potent during tactical exercises on Lüneburg Heath, failed him now.

'Guess,' he said lamely.

'I didn't get where I am today by guessing what upside-down kilns covered in huge warts are,' said C.J.

'You have to guess,' said Jimmy stubbornly, hoping that someone would hit upon a suggestion less foolish than his own.

'Oh, I see,' said David Harris-Jones. 'We call it the "Guess What It's For". A sort of extension of our game with no rules. Hours of fun for all the family.'

'Not a bad idea,' said Tom.

'A gelding of an intriguing hue,' said Seamus Finnegan.

'Well done,' said Elizabeth.

Jimmy shuddered. Elizabeth's phrase had reminded him of Clive 'Lofty' Anstruther, and the glory that might have been.

Failure is a perverse mistress. Fear her, and she is in your bed before you can say redundancy. Court her, and she hides coyly behind life's haystacks.

So it was with Reggie. The greater efforts he made to fail, the greater his success became.

Summer ripened into autumn, and the success of Perrin Products and of Grot continued unabated.

Seamus Finnegan's reorganizations were already paying dividends. The first European shops were opened, and business was brisk. Tom's adverts became a minor cult. In a medium where slick rubs shoulders with smooth, his clumsy efforts caused laughter and admiration. After he had been dubbed the McGonagall of Admass, there was no looking back. And Jimmy's useless machine and his Guess What It's

For proved highly promising sellers. A leading colour supplement reflected – in black and white – upon the relationship between art and commerce. Commerce, it suggested, habitually paddled in the waters where art had bathed. If it found the water not to be too cold, it ventured further in. Thus it should not be surprising to anybody that, two decades after the heyday of Theatre of the Absurd, we should find ourselves with Commerce of the Absurd.

The cruet sets with no holes in them were displayed at the Design Centre.

Other shops copied Grot, but they had not the same aura of exclusivity.

Perhaps the greatest success of all was Doc Morrissey's idea for January sales in September. Messages like 'Great January Sale – four months early', 'Giant Rubbish Sale', 'Huge Increases', '50 per cent on everything' received saturation coverage on television and radio.

Outside the Grot shop in Oxford Street, Europe's premier shopping blot, people began to queue two days before the sales.

ITN reporter Fergus Clitheroe interviewed the front runners.

'Where are you from?' he asked a heavily bearded giant.

'Tennant Creek in the Northern Territory of Australia,' replied the hirsute man-mountain. 'Do you want a tube of Fosters?'

'But if you waited a fortnight, you could get all the stuff you wanted for fifty per cent less.'

'Wouldn't be interviewed on television, would I? Do you want a tube of Fosters?'

Two schoolboys explained that they were playing truant from school and if they bought Christmas presents in the sale people would know that they loved them because they'd spent so much. A cockney lady said, 'It's a sale, innit? That's good enough for me,' and a dark sallow melancholy Welshman said, 'Queueing's in my blood, see. My mam missed the whole of the 1936 Derby. She was queueing for the ladies, see. Minding her P's and Q's, you might say. The war was

242

the time, you queued to join queues then. Nowadays it's just the Bolshoi and the sales. People are friendly in queues, see. Like the old days. Can't get the queueing in Lampeter, see. Under-population, that's the bugbear.'

And of course, when the triumphant September sales ended, and all the prices were reduced by fifty per cent again, there were further queues from bargain hunters. Doc Morrissey had invented the fifty week a year sales.

Clearly, more desperate measures were needed from Reggie, if Grot were ever to be destroyed.

A golden opportunity for self-destruction soon presented itself.

Chapter 24

On Monday, October the fourth, as Reggie was getting out of bed, Simon Watkins, MP for Climthorpe, collapsed and died after an all night sitting in the House of Commons.

The weather was cloudy but dry. Breakfast was perfect. Ponsonby was listless. The newspapers were gloomy. Reggie's motions were adequate.

One of the less gloomy newspaper articles was in the *Guardian*. It was an in-depth interview with Reggie Perrin.

'I'll show them,' thought Reggie, as he read of his success. 'I'll give them "middle-aged fairy story".'

Climthorpe Albion lay at the top of the Southern League First Division South, having beaten Dorchester 4–1, with goals by FITTOCK, CLENCH (2, 1 pen) and new signing BLOUNT. It seemed that Reggie's powers as a fairy godfather were not yet waning.

The post brought a letter from Mark. It said: 'Dear Mater and Pater, I still love you. One day you will understand. Your affectionate son, Mahmood Abdullah. PS Love to Ponsonby.'

It also brought two invitations. He was asked to address the Climthorpe Ladies Circle on 'Women in a Man's World' and to discuss the proposition that 'The Profit Motive is a Dirty Word' with the Climthorpe Manor Hill Boys School Debating Society.

That morning Perrin Products announced record profits, and Reggie dictated a letter to the Climthorpe Manor Hill Boys School Debating Society, saying: 'I do not wish to discuss your illiterate proposition, but I am prepared to debate the subject: "The Profit Motive is Three Dirty Words."'

In the afternoon he was approached by representatives of all three television channels, *Guardian* readers to a man, and asked to give an exclusive interview.

What an opportunity!

What a showcase!

He accepted all three invitations.

On Tuesday evening he appeared on BBC1's magazine programme *Pillock Talk*. The eponymous interviewer was Colin Pillock.

They sat in elegant armchairs with a circular table behind them.

Colin Pillock introduced Reggie as the man behind the High Street miracle.

'Less than three years ago,' he said, 'Reginald Perrin opened a shop called Grot in the dreary London suburb of Climthorpe. In its window was a sign saying: "All the articles sold in this shop are useless." Now Reginald Perrin has more than sixty shops and is well on his way to becoming a millionaire.'

Reggie raised his eyebrows and smiled pleasantly. Upstairs, in the control box, Elizabeth was astounded by his self-confidence.

Colin Pillock described some of the objects sold in Grot shops. A faint ridicule could be detected beneath his surface sarcasm.

Then he turned to Reggie.

'Reginald Perrin?' he said. 'Are you a con man?'

Reggie paused, thinking out his reply, determined not to be thrown out of his stride by this interviewer's inhumanity to man.

'I announce clearly that every item is useless,' he said. 'Con men don't usually wear sandwich-boards that say: "Watch out. I am a con man." No, I think I'm one of the few shopkeepers who isn't a con man.'

'But you sell people stuff that is useless. Doesn't that worry you?'

'Thousands of people sell stuff that's useless. I'm the only one who admits it.'

'In other words, Mr Perrin, you have hit upon a gimmick that enables you to sell worthless items at high prices, without anybody being able to do anything about it?'

245

'Those certainly are other words.'

'What words would you use, Mr Perrin?'

'I am providing a valuable social service.'

Colin Pillock smiled his 'ho ho ho, viewers, we've got another one here and you're all going to be on my side, aren't you, because I'm the champion of your rights' smile.

'Come, come, Mr Perrin. You're not trying to tell us that you provide a social service, are you?'

'I'm not trying to tell you that. I'm succeeding in telling you that.'

Colin Pillock smiled his 'give a man enough rope' smile.

'All right then,' he said. 'In what way are you providing this social service?'

'Have you half an hour? Then I'll begin. People like to buy our stuff for many different reasons — As a joke for instance.'

'A rather expensive joke.'

'Jokes are splendid things. Why should they be cheap? And people buy my things as presents. A lot of people are very self-conscious about giving presents. They fear that their presents will seem ridiculous. No such fear about my goods. Everybody will know the presents are ridiculous and were meant to be ridiculous.'

'But surely people often buy your products for themselves?'

'Of course.'

'Why?'

'Perhaps you ought to ask them.'

'I'm asking you.'

'Well, Mr Pillock, maybe they like to have useless objects lying around. It shows they can afford to spend quite large sums of money on useless things.'

'Quite large sums of money!' repeated Colin Pillock gloatingly. 'Would you agree, then, that your prices are high?'

'That isn't the word I'd use,' said Reggie.

'What word would you use, Mr Perrin?'

'Exorbitant.'

Colin Pillock was actually speechless for several seconds.

In the control box, the director had a feeling – part horror, part utter delight – that he would never speak again.

But he did.

'Are you seriously suggesting that people like throwing money away?' he said.

'Of course. People certainly love spending money. It's one of the few enjoyable things you can do with it. Have you ever been to a race meeting, Mr Pillock?'

'Yes.'

'Have you noticed many people racked with greed as they try to get their grubby little fingers on their ill-earned lucre? Oh, some, of course, but I notice far more people flinging money around recklessly, cheerfully admitting how much they've lost. It shows what men of the world they are, what good chaps. There's no point in having money to burn if nobody comes to the fire. Would you say that most restaurants in this country, if not all, are bad?'

'Yes.'

'When people go out to dinner, are they more likely to go to a cheap restaurant or an expensive one?'

'An expensive one.'

'Well there you are then. The point is to show that you can afford it. "One pound eighty for that," people say when they buy my things. "What a liberty. It's only two bits of paper. I could have made it myself for 5p." It gives them a wonderful feeling of superiority over the makers. Wouldn't you say that was performing a social service?'

Colin Pillock couldn't remember when he had last been asked five questions without getting a single one in himself.

He ought to fight back, but he just didn't feel up to it. It was the end of a long series, and his holidays were coming up.

'Reginald Perrin, thank you. And now a man who farms worms. Yes, worms,' he said.

On Wednesday it was the turn of ITV. Reggie met the producer of *The World Tomorrow Today* in the hospitality

247

room, where enough drink is dispensed to make the inter-
viewees indiscreet without being indecent.

The producer seeemed narked.

'You didn't tell us Pillock was doing you,' he said.

'You didn't ask.'

'It's spiked our guns.'

'Use different guns.'

'We'll have to put you back to the end. We may not even
get to you if Ethiopia over-runs.'

'Wonderful.'

But Ethiopia did not over-run, and they did get to him.

The interviewer was Sheridan Trethowan. They sat in
elegant armchairs, with a glass table between them.

Sheridan Trethowan gave a brief resumé of Reggie's
achievements. He took great care not to sound scornful or
patronizing. He didn't want to fall into the Pillock trap.

'Tell me, Mr Perrin, how did you get the idea for all this
in the first place?' he said.

'It's not really such an extraordinary idea,' said Reggie.
'Most of our economy is based on built-in obsolescence. I
just build it a bit further in. The things are obsolete before
you even buy them. I haven't gone as far as I'd like to.
Ideally I'd like to sell things that fall to pieces before they
even leave the shop. What a gift to capitalism that would be.
"Oh, it's fallen to pieces. I'll have another one." "Certainly,
sir." "Oh, that's fallen to pieces too. I'll have another one." '

'Did you really expect that you would be as successful as
you have been?'

'Good Lord, no. I only started it all as a joke.'

'A joke?'

'Yes.'

'But you are on record as saying that you perform a social
service.'

'Yes. I thought that was the sort of thing they like to hear
on the BBC, so I said that on *Pillock Talk*, which you asked
me not to mention. Incidentally, your drinks are better than
theirs.'

'But do you believe that you perform a social service?'

248

'No.'

'But you said you did.'

'I'm a liar. A congenial liar.'

'Don't you mean a congenital liar?'

'No. I'm in a very good mood.'

Sheridan Trethowan looked as if he was about to be sick. Those with colour sets rushed to adjust them.

'Social service schmocial schmervice,' said Reggie. 'I'd given a quarter of a century to puddings. I'd ended up working on a pig farm. I wanted a bit of fun. I thought I'd go down with flying colours, cock one last snook.'

'Instead of which you've been a great success?'

'Terrible, isn't it?'

'You don't welcome your success.'

'Of course not. Frightful bore.'

Reggie smiled angelically.

'Very briefly, because we don't have much time . . .,' said Sheridan Trethowan, thinking privately: 'Thank God.'

'That's your fault,' interrupted Reggie. 'You shouldn't have squeezed me in at the end of the programme because you were narked with me for talking to the BBC.'

'Very briefly, Mr Perrin, where do you go from here?'

'Home. You should have cut that item about the re-organization of local government. Boring boring. Yawn yawn.'

'Reginald Perrin, thank you.'

Nobody seemed very upset that Reggie had so blatantly contradicted himself. In fact they all said that they would watch him on *Money-Go-Round* on BBC 2.

The producer of *Money-go-Round* seemed a little narked.

'You didn't tell us you were going on BBC 1 and ITV,' he said, in the hospitality room.

'You might not have wanted me on your programme if I had,' said Reggie with a sweet smile, accepting the proffered glass of whisky.

'Anyway,' said the producer, 'I don't go for the recriminations bit. Besides, your appearances have sparked off some interest.'

'Oh good,' said Reggie. 'I'm trying to make things interesting for you by saying different things on each programme. I thought tonight I'd talk about the philosophical questions posed by my shops.'

'I'm afraid that won't be quite relevant,' said the producer. 'You're part of a series about British businessmen moving into Europe. Last week we did a featurette about how our washing up liquids are cleaning up in the Iberian peninsula.'

'Oh, I see,' said Reggie. 'I see. Is the programme live?'

'Yes. We still go for the live bit here. It keeps us all on our toes, keeps us up to the minute news-wise.'

'Good,' said Reggie. 'Good.'

The interviewer was Peregrine Trembleby. They sat in elegant chairs at either side of a glass table.

'Britain in Europe,' said Peregrine Trembleby, following a montage of introductory shots of the continent in question. 'Tonight we meet Reginald Perrin, one of the most fascinating men on the British shop scene. High Street prankster or social visionary? Well, Europe is soon going to have a chance to make its own mind up, because Mr Perrin's rapid-growth brain child, the rubbish chain Grot, is really beginning to move into the *Hauptstrasses* and *grandes rues*. Which countries are you aiming to infiltrate, Mr Perrin?'

'Well, Peregrine, I'd like to talk if I may, briefly, about the philosophical basis of my commercial enterprise. I confess to being worried that there are innate and inevitable paradoxes inherent in the concept behind Grot.'

'And you feel that this is relevant to what you may find in Europe?'

'No.'

'But it's the European side of the venture that we are interested in tonight.'

'Ah!'

Peregrine Trembleby smiled. His smile had charmed Vietnamese generals, British politicians, French financiers and even Norman Mailer. He saw no reason why it shouldn't charm Reginald Perrin.

'Let's leave individual countries for a while,' he said, 'and talk about Europe in general. How do you expect the average man in the rue and the Strasse to react to your shops?'

'I state that everything in our shops is useless,' said Reggie. 'Yet people buy them. Either they buy them because they can find a use for them, in which case they are ipso facto not useless, or they buy them because they like useless things. Are they therefore no longer useless? Isn't to be liked to be of use?'

'Mr Perrin, I do wish to discuss your ventures with particular regard to Europe. Have you had any marketing surveys made on the Continent?'

'I'm glad you asked me that,' said Reggie.

He paused. Peregrine Trembleby gave a little half smile. His little half smile had charmed half the little Vietnamese generals he had interviewed. He hoped desperately that it would half charm Reginald Perrin.

'Let's posit a man who makes an entirely pointless speech,' said Reggie. 'He is told: "I thought your speech was pointless." He replied: "That was the point. I wished to prove that one can make a completely pointless speech." Was his speech pointless or did it in fact have a point? I'm no philosopher. I just toss these things into the cauldron of speculation.'

A thin film of sweat was breaking out on Peregrine Trembleby's domed brow.

'Mr Perrin, I am talking about Britain in Europe,' he said.

'I'm frightfully sorry, Trembleby old man,' said Reggie. 'None of your questions has yet fired me with enthusiasm. Try again, though. We may get the European kite into the air yet.'

'Have you learnt anything from the highly successful experiences of firms like Marks and Spencer in Europe?'

'Take a cruet set with no holes. We say: "The purpose of a cruet set is for condiments to emerge when it is tilted, the better to season our food. We tilt this cruet set, but it has no holes in it. Therefore no condiments emerge. It is useless." '

251

'Mr Perrin, please . . .'

'It is useless *as a cruet set*. But maybe it is decorative. Maybe it is prettier than a cruet set with holes. Maybe it amuses people. What merry laughter will ring round the family table as short-sighted Uncle George endeavours to season his soup!'

'I don't want to talk about cruet sets.'

'But I do. Because a pretty little proposition now awaits us. We posit an object which is useful *as a cruet set with no holes*. We may then say of all other cruet sets: "What a useless cruet set with no holes. It's got holes. See, the salt and pepper are trickling out. What kind of a cruet set with no holes is that?" '

'Mr Perrin!'

'Perhaps my quest for true uselessness is useless,' said Reggie. 'Perhaps the pursuit of uselessness is the only truly useless thing.'

'Reginald Perrin, thank you,' said Peregrine Trembleby.

The reaction to Reggie's television appearances appalled him. People shook him by the hand and said it was about time those TV interviewers were taken down a peg or two.

At Perrin Products several people thought it was all a splendid publicity gimmick.

Early on Friday evening, trudging home wearily through the Poets' Estate, Reggie suggested to Elizabeth that they stop for a quick one at the Ode and Sonnet.

The Ode and Sonnet was mock-Tudor outside and reproduction furniture inside. They were hailed by several members of the early evening Climthorpe crowd who were discussing the death of their MP.

'I wonder who we'll get to replace him,' pondered the Branch Manager of a finance company.

'The usual bag of dum-dums, I expect,' put in a history master noted for his cynicism towards anyone born after 1850.

'I had a lot of time for Simon Watkins,' admitted the managing director of a clock factory.

'He wasn't a Winston Churchill,' opined a solicitor. 'He wasn't an Aneurin Bevan. He wasn't even a Barbara Castle. But he was a good constituency man.'

'When he first got in everybody thought he was a dum-dum,' recalled Reggie.

'That's politics,' declared the history master.

'Why don't you stand, Reggie? You've got the gift of the gab,' suggested an ear, nose and throat specialist.

'What would he stand as?' posed Elizabeth.

'Independent. We need a bit less of the party line in this country,' averred a systems analyst. 'We need a few individuals.'

'Stand as the party of the individual,' agreed the branch manager of the finance company. 'Give them all a run for their money.'

'Why not?' said Reggie.

Chapter 25

Reggie decided that if he was to have any chance of destroying his empire he must sack the four men whom he had appointed in order to destroy it.

He arranged to see them all in his office at hourly intervals, on Monday, October the eighteenth.

Tom came first. He sat down, glanced with ill-concealed distaste at the paintings by Drs Snurd, Underwood and Wren, and waited confidently, ignorant of the storm that Reggie was intending to break over his head.

'Well, Tom,' said Reggie. 'You're having quite a success.'

'I'm amazed,' said Tom. 'I had no idea I was a publicity person.'

'Nor did I,' said Reggie. 'Yes, you've done very well. It's a pity you aren't happy.'

'I am happy, Reggie.'

'You're a man of conscience, Tom, a man of integrity. You're miserable in your work.'

'I'm not.'

'I assure you that you are, Tom.'

'I've never been happier in my life, Reggie. Linda and I – we always tried to conceal it from you, but we went through some bad times. We're happy now, Reggie.'

'This happiness is a cloak, Tom, with which you hide your misery.'

'I've never heard such nonsense,' said Tom.

'I'll give you a golden handshake.'

Tom stared at him in astonishment.

'I don't want a golden handshake,' he said. 'I don't want anything for nothing. I'm just not an anything for nothing person. I want to work here, Reggie. Anyone could have done my job at the estate agent's, but I doubt if there's a single person in the whole world who could do my job here quite like I do it.'

'No,' said Reggie. 'I doubt if there is.'

He would sack the other three, but he couldn't sack Tom, for Linda's sake.

Jimmy came next. The grey on the unfrocked warrior's hair was spreading steadily, but his back was still ram-rod straight.

'Well, Jimmy,' said Reggie. 'Still hankering after the smell of cordite and the rumble of distant guns?'

'Fighting days over,' said Jimmy. 'Learnt my lesson. Lüneburg Heath, tactical exercise, captured Fidel Castro single-handed. Not really Fidel Castro of course. Second Lieutenant Jelly. Represented Fidel Castro. Proud moment, though. Never thought I'd be as happy. Am.'

'I see.'

'Clive Anstruther, thing of past. Wound healed. No bitterness. May he rot in hell. I've a new life here, Reggie. Alongside you. Alongside big sister.'

He couldn't sack Jimmy, for Elizabeth's sake.

He would sack the other two, but he couldn't sack members of his own family.

With Doc Morrissey he tried a different tack.

'I've got the Doc's report, Doc,' he said.

'Yes?'

Reggie had persuaded Doc Morrissey to undergo a medical examination.

'It doesn't mean a lot to me,' said Reggie. 'You were a doctor. You'll understand it.'

'Yes,' said Doc Morrissey without conviction.

'You have advanced carconic deficiency of the third testricle and incipient nephritic collapse. Your hydrophylogy is weak and there's faint pullulation of the sphynctular crunges.'

'I see,' said Doc Morrissey, shifting nervously in his chair.

'As I understand it, these symptoms are not necessarily

grave individually, but the combination is pretty serious. But you don't need me to tell you that.'

'Well, I'm a bit vague about some of these terms,' said Doc Morrissey. 'There are a whole lot of new parts of the body since I was at medical school. It ... er ... it doesn't sound good.'

'No.'

Doc Morrissey stood up. Suddenly he looked old. If Reggie hadn't known that there was no such thing, he would have thought the ex-medico was suffering from incipient nephritic collapse.

And Reggie realized how much he liked his old friend, how deep was the bond formed by their changing fortunes.

'I made all that up,' he said wearily.

'What?'

'You're in excellent health for your age. All that stuff about testricles was balls.'

Doc Morrissey sat down again. He gave a sigh of relief and mystification.

'I didn't want to tell you this,' said Reggie. 'I employed you because I thought you'd be a failure.'

'I see.'

'Do you? I wanted to destroy all this. You've let me down, all of you. You've been successful.'

Doc Morrissey grinned ruefully.

'I surprised myself,' he said.

'I can't sack you,' said Reggie. 'Have a cigar?'

Doc Morrissey took the ritual cigar. His hands were shaking.

'I seem to have a natural talent for overall strategy,' he said. 'You were right, whether you meant to be or not.'

'I'll give you a ten per cent rise,' said Reggie, 'if you'll try not to be quite so brilliant in future.'

'It'll be difficult,' said Doc Morrissey, 'but I'll try.'

He would sack Seamus Finnegan, but he couldn't sack old friends.

There was a gleam of sharp intelligence in Seamus Finnegan's eyes. Reggie would have noticed it when they first met if it hadn't been dulled by drink.

'What do you think of my pictures?' said Reggie, noting the Limerick wizard's glance.

'Novices,' said Seamus Finnegan. 'They will fall at the first fence.'

'How are the reorganizations coming along?' said Reggie.

'Very well, sir. A little too well for you, I think.'

'What can you mean by that?'

'Well, sir, I think when you employed me and some of the other eejits you were thinking you would bring the company to its knees.'

'Why on earth should I want to do a ridiculous thing like that?' said Reggie.

He knew then that he would never sack anybody.

The employment of C.J. had also turned out to be a mistake. Not only was he running the European side of things too efficiently, but he was mooning over Elizabeth. It had become so obvious of late that even the tea-lady had noticed.

A mention of this might perhaps persuade C.J. to leave.

'Come,' said C.J. with a residue of his erstwhile hauteur.

Reggie entered.

'Ah, Reggie. Welcome to my modest den.'

Reggie sat in the chair provided. C.J.'s office was a drab symphony of window, filing cabinet and dingy brown paint, much like Reggie's office of yore.

'You're in love with my wife,' said Reggie.

'What?' said C.J., turning pale.

'Will you go to the trade fair on the ninth?'

'Oh . . . er . . . yes. For one moment I . . . what trade fair?'

Reggie met C.J.'s eyes and smiled pleasantly.

'You gaze at her like a love-lorn moose,' he said.

'I . . . er . . . I'm sorry,' croaked C.J.

'Milan,' said Reggie. 'I think it's about time we tried to break into the Italian market. Turin, Milan, Florence, Rome.'

'I don't see why not,' said C.J. 'Certainly in the north.'

'If you find the situation embarrassing and want to leave, I shall understand,' said Reggie.

'Yes, I . . . I . . . yes. I'll bear that in mind,' said C.J.

'Good. Well, perhaps you'd like to go on a four day Italian recce, then.'

'I'm sorry Reggie,' said C.J. with difficulty. 'Nothing like that has ever happened to me before, and it won't happen again. I didn't get where . . .'

'. . . you are today . . .'

'. . . by being in love with . . .'

'. . . my wife.'

'Perish the thought, Reggie.'

'Goodbye, C.J.'

Mr Milford had set up a committee to organize Reggie's election campaign. Bar takings at the golf club were down two point three per cent.

Reggie would make his first election speech on Saturday. Encouraging support had been promised. The venue was the Methodist Hall in Westbury Park Road. There was no hall on the Poets' Estate. It had never occurred to anyone that the inhabitants could possibly want to meet each other.

A loudspeaker was being fitted on to Mr Pelham's car, and Reggie would tour the shopping areas on Saturday.

Leaflets and posters were the responsibility of Climthorpe Football Club through their usual printers, G. F. Fry (Printers) of Hanwell.

FITTOCK, CLENCH (2) and PUNT had all promised votes.

Reggie had seen the photographs of the Conservative, Labour and Liberal candidates. All three looked like dumdums.

Even so, it was a surprise, on opening the *Evening Standard* on Thursday, October the twenty-first, to read the results of the first opinion poll.

Thirty-four per cent said they would support Reggie.

'My God,' he said, as they turned out of Wordsworth

Drive into Tennyson Avenue. 'I'm going to get into Parliament now.'

Elizabeth squeezed his arm.

'I'm so proud of you,' she said.

Chapter 26

Friday, October the twenty-second dawned bright but windy. Breakfast was perfect. Ponsonby was listless. The newspapers were gloomy. Reggie's motions were adequate.

The post brought nine invitations. They were flooding in, following his TV appearances and the announcement that he would stand as the Individual Party candidate for the Parliamentary constituency of Climthorpe.

He was asked to appear on the panel of the Climthorpe Rotary Club's Charity 'Just a Minute' evening. He was implored to talk to the Hemel Hempstead Flat Earth Circle on 'Dissent in the Age of Conformity', at a reception to mark the launching of their first and last single: 'It's Love that Makes the World go Flat.'

It was even proposed that he should deliver the L. de Garde Peach Memorial Lecture in Chipping Campden Corn Exchange.

Reggie and Elizabeth set off for work together as usual.

Reggie was feeling a turmoil of claustrophobia and frustration. He had grown to hate going to Perrin Products as much as he had grown to hate going to Sunshine Desserts. He must destroy his reputation soon. He would make great efforts today. Yes, today he would really go to town.

Elizabeth was thinking that they had better prune the rose bushes before the election campaign really got going.

Neither of them knew that they were taking their walk for the last time.

They turned right into Tennyson Avenue for the last time, then left into Wordsworth Drive, and down the snicket into Station Road.

They stood by the door marked 'Isolation Telephone' for the last time, and reached Waterloo twenty-two minutes late for the last time. The loudspeaker announcement blamed an escaped cheetah at Chessington North. If they had thought, they might have known that this excuse could never be topped.

Reggie asked Joan into his office, missed the hat-stand with his umbrella for the last time, and smiled at Joan across his desk.

'How are things going with Tony?' he said.

'Very well.'

'Good. I'm glad.'

He went over to her and kissed her hard and full on the mouth. He flinched, expecting a slap across the cheek that never came.'

'Thank you, Mr Perrin,' she said.

'You don't mind?' he said.

'Why should I mind?' she said. 'I find you attractive.'

'Ah! Take a letter, Joan. To the Manager, Grot, Shrewsbury. Dear Sir, it has come to my notice that you are serving Welsh people in your shop. I did not think it necessary to mention this. I want no Welsh people served from now on.'

Joan took the letter down without protest.

'You find that letter perfectly all right, do you, Joan?' he said.

'I'm learning to have faith in your judgement,' said Joan. 'Besides, I understand how you feel. I once had a horrid evening with a boy from Clun.'

At twelve o'clock he interviewed a Mr Herbert who had applied for the post of manager of Grot's Retford branch.

Mr Herbert was anxious, naturally nervous. He had receding black hair, with heavy dandruff.

They shook hands.

'Have to get rid of that dandruff,' said Reggie.

'Yes, of course,' said Mr Herbert, sitting uncomfortably.

'There's a chap in Switzerland, clears dandruff in a fortnight. Painful course. Starvation and electrolodes. But I will not have dandruff in this firm.'

'I understand,' said Mr Herbert.

'Where would the Metal Box Company be now if they

hadn't come down so heavily on athlete's foot? And your socks are dreadful. Have you no taste?'

'They were a present from an aunt.'

'Aunts are one thing, commerce is another.'

'I realize that,' said Mr Herbert.

'You don't mind my talking to you like this?'

'You've a right to.'

He couldn't go through with it. He couldn't go on insulting this harmless little man. It was the wrong way to go about it altogether.

'I'm sorry,' he said. 'I really am truly sorry.'

Mr Herbert almost looked disappointed, as if Reggie's giant status as the eccentric boss of Grot, the man you were proud to love to hate to work for, was melting away before his eyes.

'Do take the job,' said Reggie.

He walked over and patted Mr Herbert's shoulder.

'Let's go and have lunch,' he said.

Mr Herbert stood up obediently.

'You're a very nice, personable, good-looking, attractive man,' said Reggie. 'You'll be a credit to Retford.'

Mr Herbert was by now looking thoroughly alarmed, and he looked even more alarmed when Reggie put a friendly arm round him and steered him towards the door.

'I like your socks,' said Reggie. 'I really do. And a touch of dandruff can do wonders to brighten up a lifeless jacket.'

Mr Herbert fled.

The incident gave Reggie an idea. He would start making homosexual advances. He asked Joan to send for the manager of the Oxford Street branch.

At half past four he saw Mr Lisburn, the manager of the Oxford Street branch.

Reggie felt nervous. Anxious though he was to shock, he was going to find this interview difficult.

Mr Lisburn entered somewhat fearfully. He was a small man with a pointed beard, a stiff little walk and a tight bottom.

'Drink?' said Reggie.

'Gin and bitter lemon's my tipple,' said Mr Lisburn, with a faint trace of cockney beneath elocution lessons.

Reggie poured him a gin and bitter lemon. To do less, under the circumstances, would have been churlish.

'I expect you wonder why I've asked you here,' said Reggie.

'Well, yes, Mr Perrin, I do.'

'Call me Reggie, please.'

Reggie's voice was coming out in a strained croak. He wanted to give up but fought against it. Somewhere, somehow, the seeds of his destruction must be sown.

'It's Percy, isn't it?'

'Yes, Reggie.'

Reggie sat on the top of his desk, looking down at Mr Lisburn and swinging his legs.

'These are the 1970s,' said Reggie, and Mr Lisburn did not demur. 'Social taboos are breaking down. Certain practices, once considered horrifying, are practically *de rigueur* in certain circles.'

He forced himself to go on. Fury, allegations, scandal – they beckoned like the sweet handmaidens of Araby.

'I'm married,' said Reggie, 'but I have certain inclinations. Do I make myelf clear?'

The astonished Mr Lisburn nodded, then took a large swig of his gin and bitter lemon.

'Oh good. Good,' said Reggie. 'I fight against it. God knows, I fight against it. But it's no good. It's too strong for me. If only . . . if only I hadn't gone to a public school. But there it is, I did, and there's nothing that can be done about it. Do you understand?'

'Oh yes,' said Mr Lisburn.

'Every now and then it just . . . well, anyway, I was wondering if we could . . . er . . . as it were . . . perhaps we could go to a hotel or somewhere some time and . . . er . . . as it were . . . together.'

'Sure. Suits me fine. I'm free every evening next week.'

'Ah! Ah! Yes. Next week is a little difficult. I'm all

tied up,' said Reggie, and immediately wished he hadn't.

'I'm free Sunday,' said Percy Lisburn.

'Ah!' Reggie stood up. 'Sundays are slightly difficult.'

'The week after next, then,' said Mr Lisburn.

'Yes. Absolutely. Let's hope so.'

'I can't get over it, Mr Perrin. I'd never have dreamt you were like that.'

'No, nor would I. Well, better run along now, Percy.'

Reggie held out his hand, then hastily withdrew it.

Mr Lisburn walked stiffly towards the door. Then he turned.

'I've got a friend, lays on business orgies, if you're interested,' he said.

'Ah, that is interesting,' said Reggie.

'Luxury flats. Films. People of any sex, creed or colour. Cabaret. Yacht. All very discreet. No risk of scandal.'

'Excellent. Excellent. We must go into that. Goodbye, Percy.'

'Bye bye then, Reggie. Or is it just *au revoir*?'

No it bloody isn't.

'Yes,' said Reggie. '*Au revoir*, I should say.'

'Thanks for el liquido refreshmento. See you the week after next, I hope,' said Percy Lisburn, blowing Reggie a faint kiss.

'Yes ... er ... we'll keep our legs ... er ... our *fingers* crossed.'

When Percy Lisburn had gone, Reggie was sick into his window-box.

C.J. and Elizabeth were having dinner with some French estate agents, so Reggie walked home alone. His heart was heavy.

He put on shorts, cricket boots, and one of Elizabeth's blouses, and managed to create for himself a passable pair of breasts.

He felt a certain anticipation as he entered the saloon bar of the Ode and Sonnet in his grotesque garb. He could just imagine the outrage.

A roar of laughter greeted his appearance. Drinks were pressed upon him, the solicitor revealed a highly creditable wolf whistle, and the managing director of the clock factory said: 'I get it. Individual party. Individually dressed. Good gimmick, Reggie.'

Reggie downed an embarrassed pint and walked sadly home.

There had been showers during the day but the evening had cleared again.

Dusk was approaching.

Reggie changed out of his absurd outfit and put a portion of frozen chicken casserole in the oven.

Then he poured himself a gin and tonic, and sat in his favourite armchair, with Ponsonby on his lap.

'Well, Ponsonby,' he said, stroking the gently purring cat. 'What do I do next? How do I destroy this empire I don't want?'

Ponsonby put forward no theories.

'Exactly. You don't know. Nor do I. The invitations are pouring in, Ponsonby. Everybody wants me to talk to them, waiting for me to be unpredictable. And when I am they'll say: "There he goes. He's being unpredictable. I thought he would. Oh, good, he's saying something completely unexpected. I expected he would." '

Ponsonby purred faintly.

'Nothing I do can shock anyone any more, Ponsonby. What a fate.

'So what of the future, Ponsonby? Am I to go on from success to success? Grot will sweep the Continent. I'll get the OBE. We'll win the Queen's award for industry. I'll get into Parliament. I'll be asked to appear on *Any Questions*. Climthorpe will be elected to the football league. Local streets will be renamed Reginald Road and Perrin Parade.'

Ponsonby gave a miaow so faint it was impossible to tell whether the prospect delighted or appalled him.

'A new stand will be built at the Woggle Road end of the football ground. It'll be named the Perrin stand. The walls of the Reginald Perrin Leisure Centre will be disfigured with

265

the simple message: "Perrin Shed." I'll be made Poet Laureate. On the birth of Prince Charles's first son I shall write:

> The bells ring out with pride and joy
> Our prince has given us a boy.

'I shall become richer and richer, lonelier and lonelier, madder and madder. I shall believe that everybody is after my money. I shall refuse to walk on the floor, for fear of contamination. And, unlike Howard Hughes, who seemed strangely trusting in this respect, I shan't be prepared to walk on lavatory paper, because that will be equally contaminated. I shall die, tense, emaciated, rich, alone. There will be a furore over my will. What do you think of all that as a prospect, Ponsonby?'

Ponsonby thought nothing of all that, because Ponsonby was dead. He had died an old cat's death, gently upon a sea of words.

Reggie cried.

Chapter 27

Saturday, October the twenty-third. A perilously bright morning.

They buried Ponsonby beyond the lupins. Nothing sickly and sentimental. A shallow depression, and stuck in the ground a gardener's label. It said, simply: 'Ponsonby.'

Reggie glanced at Elizabeth. He had talked to her till three in the morning. She had agreed, in the end to everything that he said.

'Are you still sure?' he said. 'Are you absolutely sure?'

'I'm sure,' she said.

All day, while Elizabeth made preparations, Reggie campaigned. He spoke, loud and confident, to the shoppers of Climthorpe.

At eight o'clock he entered the Methodist Hall in Westbury Park Road, to make his inaugural speech as the Individual Party Candidate for Climthorpe.

The hall was crowded. There wasn't a spare seat.

Every single person in the hall wore a large rosette in the middle of which was Reggie's smiling face. It was distinctly unnerving – all those smiling Reggies grinning up at him.

The chairman was Peter Cartwright, self-styled agent of Reggie Perrin. He spoke in hesitant but fulsome praise. His voice seemed very far away.

Reggie looked out at the sea of faces. He noticed Tom and Linda, Doc Morrissey, David Harris-Jones and Prue, Tony Webster and Joan, Mr Pelham and his Kevin, Seamus Finnegan, the Milfords, Jimmy, and the whole of the Climthorpe Football Team, who had consolidated their lead at the top of the Southern League First Division South, by beating Salisbury 2–0, with goals by that shrewd duo of voters, FITTOCK and CLENCH.

It was Reggie's turn to speak at last. He stepped forward.

There was a prolonged, thunderous ovation, dying electrically into expectation.

'I understand,' he began 'that there are six hundred and forty-one more people here tonight than at the Liberal meeting yesterday. I would like to thank all six hundred and forty-two of you for coming.'

A thunderous wall of laughter struck him. It went on and on and on. Political laughter has nothing to do with humour. It is an expression of mass solidarity, of reassurance – an affirmation that the bandwagon is rolling and the audience has chosen the right side. People laughing at political meetings always look round to show everybody else that they are laughing.

At last the laughter died down. CLENCH had laughed so much that he had aggravated his old hamstring injury.

Reggie took off his jacket.

My message is simple,' he said. 'Some might call it stark.'

He took off his tie.

'I am a simple soul,' he said. 'I only want to get things in proportion.'

He took off his shirt. There was a buzz of conversation, as he stood there, naked from the waist up, in front of all his supporters. He waited, calmly, until there was silence again.

'Do I need to list the inhumanities that man has committed to man?' he said, bending down to remove his shoes.

When he had taken his shoes and socks off, he stood upright again and waited once more for silence.

'I intend to stand before you stark bollock naked,' he said. 'Do you think that an unsuitable thing to do? If so, you may withdraw your support from my campaign. If the sight of a human body outrages you, and the dreadful cruelty of the world does not, I don't want your support. And now I'll shut up, because I hate being pompous.'

To mounting uproar in the hall, mixed with giggling and laughter, and to mounting indecision on the platform, Reggie took off his trousers and underpants.

He stood and faced the audience, white and vulnerable,

hairy and veiny, thin and paunchy by turns, a man in middle age.

He stared at the audience with a fixed gaze, and raised his right hand in an appeal for silence.

Slowly the hubbub died down. Total silence fell on the Methodist Hall.

'Are there any questions?' he said.

The lane dipped towards the sea. The headlights picked out the fiery splendours of late autumn.

They passed through a little village of chalets, bungalows and cottages. Many were shuttered for the winter.

Reggie pulled up in the Municipal Car Park. The attendant's hut was closed for the winter, and the telescope was locked.

The night air was cool, with a sharp breeze from the east. Reggie removed their suitcases from the boot.

In the suitcases were the spare clothes and disguises that Elizabeth had bought on Saturday.

There were also eleven hundred pounds that Reggie had stored in the loft during the last two prosperous years.

Had he always suspected that one day it would come to this?

The wind was making the shutters on the beach café bang.

'I wonder where the stock goes in the winter,' said Reggie. 'Is it all still there, gathering dust and damp behind those shutters – the tin buckets, cheap wooden spades, brightly coloured balls of every size, frisbees, hoops, beach shoes, dark glasses, sun-hats, insect repellents and sun-tan oils?'

Elizabeth remained silent, deep within her fears.

They went down the steps past the lifebelt, and out on to the shingle.

It was hard walking on the shingle. Reggie wanted to carry Elizabeth's case, but she refused.

'Whatever we do from now on, we're equal partners,' she said. 'I think I deserve that. After all, I have married you twice.'

Soon they were under the huge sandy cliffs to the west of

269

the village. There was no light except for the regular beam of a lighthouse away to the east.

Then the clouds were swept away and the moon shone brightly on their half-naked bodies dwarfed beneath the cliffs.

They put their new clothes on. They felt strange and prickly and damp. They adjusted each other's wigs. It was nice to have Elizabeth there this time, to fix his beard.

They left some money and documents in their old clothes, and on top of the clothes they pinned their suicide note. It spoke of intolerable pressures and the disgrace of the political meeting.

Reggie looked down at his pile of old clothes. 'Goodbye, Reggie's clothes,' he said. 'Goodbye, old Reggie.'

'Goodbye, Elizabeth's clothes,' said Elizabeth uncertainly. 'Goodbye, old Elizabeth.'

A gust of wind brought a hint of rain, then the wind dropped and the sky cleared once again.

They walked back to the end of the cliffs and struggled off the beach on to the cliff path.

They set off along the path towards the west. Behind them the eastern sky began to pale.

Reggie squeezed Elizabeth's hand.

'We'll see them some time, somehow,' he said. 'Tom, Linda, the children, Jimmy. Even Mark. We'll find a way.'

The path climbed steeply. Every few minutes they paused to get their breath back and transfer their cases from one hand to the other.

'We need a name,' said Reggie.

'Mr and Mrs Cliff,' said Elizabeth.

'Mr and Mrs Sunrise,' said Reggie.

'Mr and Mrs Oliver Cromwell,' said Elizabeth.

'Mr and Mrs Nathaniel Gutbucket,' said Reggie.

'Names don't matter,' said Elizabeth.

'That's why they're so difficult to choose,' said Reggie.

A glorious sunrise sparkled in the east, and sent traces of glowing light across the sea far below them. It was a magnificent morning for starting a new life.

The path wound up through gorse and scrub. The black-berries were finished.

Far below them a lone cormorant sped low over the waves.

They skirted a pit, roped off for fear of falls.

'If we find a suitable name in that pit, we'll be happy ever after,' said Reggie.

'I'm frightened,' said Elizabeth.

They gazed down into the pit.

'Mr and Mrs Tin-Can,' said Elizabeth.

'Mr and Mrs Dead-Thrush,' said Reggie.

'Mr and Mrs Morning-Dew,' said Elizabeth.

'Mr and Mrs Rabbit-Droppings,' said Reggie.

'Mr and Mrs Gossamer,' said Elizabeth.

They walked on up the path and came to a little open space where a seat had been provided by a benevolent council.

'Shall we rest a moment, Mrs Gossamer?' he said.

'Why not, Mr Gossamer?' said she.

They sat and rested, watching the day gather strength. Far away to sea a little coaster was making too much smoke.

Beside them was a telescope, which the council's tele-scope locker-up had forgotten to lock for the winter, and behind them a hedge marked the edge of a field of rape.

From the hedge there slowly emerged an old tramp, dressed in filthy rags, his face smeared in grime.

The tramp shambled towards them.

'10p for a cup of tea, guv'nor,' he said.

Reggie fished out a 10p piece. There was something vaguely familiar about the tramp which he couldn't place.

'I didn't get where I am today without asking for 10p for a cup of tea,' said the tramp.

He pointed towards the beach, indicated the telescope with his eyes and set off slowly on his shambling way.

Elizabeth handed Reggie a 10p piece. He inserted it in the slot and looked down at the beach through the telescope.

Already, there were thirty-nine sets of clothes side by side on Chesil Bank.